PRAISE FOR *Once Removed*

"Colette Sartor's stories shimmer with a radiant, unsettling light. She strips away the veils that we hide behind and exposes our deepest fears and desires, revealing who we inescapably are. The stories are laced with dark humor and raw, earned emotion, and they proceed from page to page with a beautiful urgency. Her prose sings and her wounded characters linger in readers' memories like people you've known, people you could have been had luck gone the other way. This is trenchant, gorgeous fiction, the voice of a writer you'll follow anywhere, everywhere."
　　—Bret Anthony Johnston, author of *Remember Me Like This*

"*Once Removed* is that rare book that succeeds on both micro and macro levels; the stories focus on the specific intimacy of individual lives yet also participate in the larger project of a whole world made of these stories—dependent on them, in fact, supported and enlarged and sustained by them. Sartor's women suffer the internal and external scarring of the dangerous terrain they navigate: love, family, self, community. They ask uncomfortable questions, both of themselves and of the reader; it's hugely satisfying to reach the end of the book and feel the resonant strength of the answers it proposes."
　　—Antonya Nelson, author of *Bound*

ONCE REMOVED

FLANNERY
O'CONNOR
AWARD
FOR
SHORT
FICTION

Once Removed STORIES

Colette Sartor

The University of Georgia Press ❀ Athens

The following stories were originally published in
slightly altered form: "Bandit" in *Colorado Review*
and *Redux*; "Daredevil" in *Kenyon Review Online*,
The Drum, and *2013 Press 53 Open Awards Anthology*;
"Extra Precautions" as "A Walk in the Park" in *Fugue*;
"Lamb" in *Prairie Schooner* and *Law and Disorder:*
Stories of Conflict and Crime; "F-Man" in *Carve*
Magazine; "Jump" as "Nothing Ventured" in *Five*
Chapters; "Once Removed" in *Printers Row Journal*;
"Elephant Teeth" in *Crab Orchard Review*; and
"La Cuesta Encantada" in *Carve Magazine*.

Published by the University of Georgia Press
Athens, Georgia 30602
www.ugapress.org
© 2019 by Colette Sartor
All rights reserved
Designed by Erin Kirk New
Set in Minion Pro
Printed and bound by Thomson-Shore, Inc.
The paper in this book meets the guidelines for
permanence and durability of the Committee on
Production Guidelines for Book Longevity of the
Council on Library Resources.

Most University of Georgia Press titles are
available from popular e-book vendors.

Printed in the United States of America

23 22 21 20 19 P 5 4 3 2 1

Library of Congress Cataloging-in-Publication Data

Names: Sartor, Colette, author.
Title: Once removed and other stories / Colette Sartor.
Description: Athens : The University of Georgia Press, 2019. |
Series: Flannery O'Connor Award for Short Fiction
Identifiers: LCCN 2018057933| ISBN 9780820355696 (pbk. : alk.
paper) | ISBN 9780820355689 (ebook)
Classification: LCC PS3619.A753 A6 2019| DDC 813/.6—dc23
LC record available at https://lccn.loc.gov/2018057933

To my son, Luke,

who helped me become an adult,

and to my husband, Bob,

who taught me how to trust.

Contents

Bandit

After Hannah finished scraping the decorative border from the nursery walls, she placed an ad in the university housing office. Summer break had just started, but within days someone called. Rune was her name. "Like the fortune-telling alphabet," the girl said, her voice throaty and low. Hannah imagined thick black bangs veiling the girl's eyes, a mouth tense with secret sorrow.

In person, there was nothing mysterious about her. She came to see the newly painted room when their quiet Cambridge neighborhood was shimmering with midday heat. Clive was at a lunch meeting. Hannah kept glancing over her shoulder as she led Rune upstairs. The girl's petite frame made Hannah more aware of her own body, still unwieldy with baby weight. Tucked under the girl's arm was an orange motorcycle helmet. Her short hair was spiky, inky roots giving way to shades of red. Henna tattoos snaked from beneath her jacket and encircled her slender fingers in ornate flourishes. She was remarkably chatty, hurling questions at Hannah in a breathy contralto. How long was the walk to campus, to the nearest bank and grocery store? Could she have overnight guests? And could she pay half the rent on the first and half on the fifteenth, just until school started and her financial aid kicked in? Hannah's head started to pound.

When they reached the room, the girl strode past her, craning her neck at the crown molding. "Female students only," Hannah had been careful to note in the ad. No dirty boxers piled everywhere, and a female tenant felt less intimidating. At the last minute she'd dragged in a wing chair from Clive's office to angle by the window. A perfect study spot. Any college girl would love it.

"I guess this'll work," Rune said, tossing her helmet on the chair. She sat on the bed and bounced, as if testing the springs, then gazed at the wedding ring quilt, her lips curled in a half-smirk. Hannah pictured the quilt stuffed in the closet, replaced by a threadbare coverlet that smelled faintly tangy and unwashed.

Rune flopped back. "Stars and moons would be nice up there. Bishop and I had them. They glowed in the dark. We made up constellations. Cat eyes in the north, a witch's wand in the south." She rested her cheek on the quilt and stared at Hannah.

"Who's Bishop?"

"My fiancé. Ex-fiancé." There was the slightest hitch in her voice. She brushed her arms up and down, as if making angel's wings in the snow. "He got the apartment. I got the scooter. He doesn't know it yet."

Downstairs, the front door opened. Clive's footsteps thumped up the stairs.

"Come meet Rune," Hannah called and stepped into the hallway.

He stopped on the landing. "Who?"

"Our new tenant." Like that, she'd committed herself. She hadn't meant to and wouldn't have if not for Clive's knee-jerk frown. She itched to give him a little shove.

"Professor Jacobs, hi." Rune stood in the doorway, her fists balled in her jacket pockets. "I didn't know you lived here."

"Have we met?" he said in his lecture voice. He smiled politely.

"I was in your urban myths class last fall."

Hannah watched his expression glaze. Students passed through so quickly, he often complained, that he'd stopped trying to remember their names.

"I'm sorry," he said. "You don't look familiar."

Rune waved her hand dismissively. Her tattooed fingers flickered through the air like butterflies. "I sat way in back."

He peered into the room. "Is that my chair?"

"I left the other one," Hannah said. Clive stared at her until she looked away.

"I guess we'll be seeing more of each other," he said to Rune and marched down the hall. His study door clicked shut, an unfriendly, obstinate sound.

꽃

Later that evening he leaned against the doorjamb between their bedroom and the master bathroom while Hannah brushed her teeth. From the television in the bedroom she could hear a program blaring about a teen rescued in March from her family's handyman, who'd kept her captive for months. Hannah had been following the story, aching when the parents pled on the news for their daughter's safe return.

Behind her, Clive said through a mouthful of something, "Did you check her credit or ask for references? Something's not right about her."

She stared at his reflection. He clutched a candy bag to his gut. His face had a ruddy tinge. She spit out her toothpaste.

"For God's sake, she's a college student. One of *your* students."

"So she says. What do we know about her, really? She could steal us blind or shoot us in our sleep. I can't believe you didn't think about that."

He sounded like his old self, vehement, impassioned, as if a circumscribed sliver had been dislodged, one that she had been yearning to butt up against. This was a man who could fend off regret, calm the memories that still ambushed her. She had been in the home stretch, then suddenly the emergency C-section. A morphine drip had burned in her arm; restraints had cut into her wrists. So briefly hers, the boy and the girl, with tiny, bluish nails and fluttering chests.

In the bathroom mirror she could see the bedroom TV flickering with images, first a sweet-faced blond girl, then the wild-haired, unwashed handyman turned kidnapper. These true-crime shows, reporting the darkest events: day workers abducting little girls, children poisoning parents to collect on insurance policies. Husbands and wives drifting apart, unable to grasp the parameters of each other's grief, the private rules of the other's recovery. They needed this tattooed girl. Already she was getting them talking again.

"Clive, don't you see—"

"Why would you take such a huge risk?"

"I'm trying to put us back on track."

Instantly his expression went blank. "Right," he said. "Business as usual."

He turned away, shoveling more candy into his mouth. She wiped out the sink and pretended not to notice.

Keeping her pregnant had been the main problem. Seven months before, during their final pregnancy try, she had been put on strict bed rest. She couldn't even sit up to read or type, and holding things overhead made her arms ache. Clive went out and bought two small flat-screen TVs, one for the bedroom and one for her study. They hadn't owned a television in years, since the last one exploded in sparks.

From the start, most shows bored her, particularly the reality ones with their trumped-up animosities and alliances. True crime, though, fascinated her. The lengths people went to, only to get caught. Take the novelist on trial for murdering his wife by pushing her down the stairs. Years before, another woman, a family friend, died the same way. The novelist had been the last to see her alive, too. Such unoriginality and poor planning. Then there was the Naughty Girl Bandit, who wore a T-shirt imprinted with the word "Naughty" to rob three banks in the Boston-Cambridge area, one in Hannah's very own neighborhood. She slid notes to tellers, once showed a handgun in her bag. Fairly commonplace, as bank robbers went. But how silly to wear a memorable shirt and no mask, though her features were blurred in surveillance tapes. She was sure to be apprehended.

Clive didn't approve. "It's morbid," he said, "obsessing about the worst parts of life." And look how jumpy she had gotten, suspicious of even the grocery store clerks.

But it was exhilarating to be fearful, to feel something other than an endless cycle of impatience, hope, grief, rage. Even after she was allowed out of bed, she watched true crime programs until dawn, shivering on her study couch as she mentally cataloged clues: *open window, unlatched door, abandoned car, corpse in a field, a river, an abandoned water main.*

Now there was Rune. She moved in that weekend, bringing a knapsack, a few boxes, and her scooter. Their computer and stereo equipment remained untouched, as did the cash in their wallets. (Hannah counted it every night the first few days, her cheeks warm with shame.) Rune just wasn't the criminal type. She lacked an iota of stealth, and her emotions dwelled close to the surface, as flamboyant as her tattoos. Once she roused herself (she tended to sleep until noon), she either bounced around the house with enthusiasm or draped herself across a chair in despair. And there was that moment on the first day, the battle between hope and futility on her face as she envisioned the constellations she'd left behind. The need in that gaze was too unguarded to be feigned.

There were oddities. Small, silly things disappeared, a magnet from the refrigerator, a set of rusty keys from the mud room junk drawer, things that Hannah herself could have misplaced and wouldn't have noticed missing if not for Rune's presence. Her behavior was a little strange, too. Before leaving the house she peered outside from behind the dining room curtains as if checking for suspicious characters. She kept her bedroom door shut, and no letters arrived for her, no bills or magazines. During the first week, Hannah asked casually whether she'd had a chance to forward her mail. She kept a po Box, Rune explained, because she moved so often. Hannah found herself mulling over these details, trying to make them mean something.

"It's strange, her keeping the door locked, like we might rob her," she said to Clive one morning at the end of Rune's second week. They sat at the kitchen table. There was a cherry Danish by his elbow. She dug into her grapefruit. They were supposed to be dieting. A show of solidarity wasn't too much to ask. "Or she could be hiding something, drugs maybe."

"You wanted a tenant," he said.

He stood and nuzzled her ear. She sat up straighter.

"Rune might come down."

"So what? I'm kissing my wife."

But he stepped away. She felt cold where he had kissed her, oddly abandoned. They hadn't made love since she went on bed rest. Before, they had desired each other with a deep, satisfying necessity that showed itself with comforting regularity, like hunger for a scheduled meal. Sex seemed superfluous now, something other people did, younger people with less to lose.

"I ran into Eugene," he said. "You haven't returned his calls about whether you're teaching next semester."

"It's barely June. He doesn't need an answer yet."

"You'd feel better if you were busy again."

She whirled around. His arms were crossed, his face stern.

"I'm busy. I got the spare room ready, for one thing. We need the money, remember?"

"If that were true, you'd be teaching. That's not what this is about."

"Then what? Tell me what this is about if you know so much."

Clive frowned at the doorway. There was Rune, her spiky hair mashed, her drawstring pajamas askew.

"Am I interrupting?" she asked.

"Yes," he said. "Give us a minute."

It wasn't like him to be so brusque. Hannah said, "It's all right. You must be hungry."

The girl walked in and opened the refrigerator. "Can I drink some juice? I'll replace it."

"You don't have to," Hannah said just as Clive said, "Please do." What was wrong with him? She nudged his pastry toward Rune. "Have some breakfast," she said.

Rune smiled gratefully. Clive frowned.

"So, you're a graduate student in my department." His lecture voice again. "Who's your advisor?"

"Actually," Rune said, carefully, "I'll be a sophomore."

"That class of mine you said you took. It's only open to grads."

"I audited. I'm thinking about majoring in anthropology."

"Ah," he said and cocked his head, as if about to bury her in questions.

"Clive, she just got up. Leave her alone."

The relief on Rune's face was reward enough for the annoyance on Clive's. So what if the girl seemed jumpy. That just might be her way.

Hannah took to dawdling in her study each morning, half-listening to crime shows while she reviewed course materials. She could revive her class on the evolution of marital law. Or there was her seminar on China's one-child policy. The debates about fairness and the right to have as many children as you wanted, government be damned. Those didn't seem bearable.

More and more she found herself stretched out on her study couch watching television as she listened for signs from upstairs that Rune was awake. Sometimes she waited until Rune came down and then sat with her while she ate. Other times she knocked on her door. "I'm

doing laundry," she would say. "I could fit some things if you'd like."
Rune never invited her inside. Still, she would say thanks and bring
out some clothes. Hannah rejected her offers to help, which would
have spoiled her sense of purpose. Occasionally, Rune followed her
to the basement and settled in a worn armchair near the washer to
tell stories about traveling the world with her father, who played
trombone in the army marching band, and her mother, who built
a nest egg reading tarot cards to other military wives. Or she talked
about her plans for the school year, or her job at a Central Square
burger joint. The dinner crowd tipped better, she said. Hannah had
been there a few times after faculty meetings. It was dark and over-
heated; sawdust and peanut hulls scratched underfoot.

"I could help you get a job at the law school," she surprised herself
by offering one day. "Clerical work, maybe. Better hours for studying."

"Are you a professor too?"

"I've been on sabbatical. We were trying to have a baby," she found
herself saying. "It didn't work out."

"That's sad. I'd love a baby someday." Said with an odd yet touching urgency.

The tattoos, Rune explained over lunch another day (breakfast for
Rune, whose socked feet had whispered downstairs at one o'clock),
caused her broken engagement. She rolled her sleeves to her shoulders; the tattoos swirled upward and beyond.

"They're not permanent. I had them done in Kenya. Bishop is an
anthropology grad student. Professor Jacobs might know him. He
got a fellowship this summer to study Kenyan wedding rituals. We
were supposed to get married there."

She thrust her hands across the kitchen table. Up close, the tattoos
were lovely, a rich earthy red, like the Sedona clay Hannah knew
from childhood. Terrible for growing anything but perfect for mud
makeup. She and her friends used to make a sludgy paste and paint
each other's cheeks with flowers and curlicues much like these. A
memory she had planned to share with a daughter.

"They were only supposed to do my hands and feet for the wedding, but I thought, when's the next time I'll have the guts to tattoo this much of my body? It'll fade, right? Bishop went ballistic.
Told me I was bastardizing a sacred tradition. I always take things
to extremes, he said. I have no self-control. He put me on the next
plane."

Hannah glanced at Rune's twisted mouth and damp eyes, then tentatively patted her hands. "Let me make you some pancakes," she said and stood.

Rune wiped her eyes and curled her knees to her chin. Hannah could feel her gaze tracking her around the kitchen. Clive was wrong. She was just a child starved for attention, a lost soul in need of sympathy.

❀

Clive's adoption book was the first thing that Hannah was certain disappeared.

He showed it to her one morning when Rune had been there a month. Hannah was making breakfast, which she had started doing every day, Belgian waffles and biscuits heavy with buttermilk and lard, food that could withstand the oven until Rune got up. For Clive and herself she served protein shakes or oatmeal topped with Splenda and fruit.

"I assume that's not for me," she heard him say as she checked a frittata in the oven. She turned. He stood there, smiling slightly, holding out a thick, spiral-bound book that felt weighty when she took it. It looked like something he had compiled for a class. Typed on front was "Chinese Adoption." Inside were articles about the general pros and cons of adoption as well as about Chinese adoption, including a list of agencies specializing in the region and a copy of the voluminous application materials. It must have taken months to compile. Clive always was a careful researcher.

"Maybe if you knew more," he said, "you'd see how this could be good for us. We could still be a family."

If only he would stop looking at her. "Clive, I'm not sure—"

"And it could be a good seminar topic," he hurried on. "Eugene agrees. You could ease back in with the one class."

"You talked to Eugene about this?"

"Someone had to."

"He's my dean, not yours."

"I know." His face reddened, but he kept going. "Look. Teaching makes you happy. I want you to be happy again."

How dare you, she wanted to yell. But the hope on his face.

"Read it," he said. "Please."

She nodded, not trusting herself to speak. He kissed her and left quickly for work, as if she would change her mind if he stayed. At least he still knew her that well.

All week the book lay by the coffeemaker. Crumbs collected around the borders; wavery rings from damp glasses marked the cover. Clive glanced over but said nothing whenever he walked by. Each day he ate his healthy breakfast without complaint. Instead of candy he snacked on grapes. His resolve almost made her read the book. But a child in the house, someone else's child. A breathing, healthy, growing child.

"Is this for a class?" Rune asked on Friday when she was pouring herself coffee.

Hannah tried not to flinch as Rune turned pages. "Something Clive's working on. He thought it would be an interesting seminar for when I go back."

"Is he kidding? This is probably the last thing you want to think about." She gave Hannah's arm a squeeze. "Guys can be such jerks."

The next morning the book was gone, its crumb borders wiped away. Hannah assumed Clive had taken it (finally, he'd realized his folly) until he came down for breakfast and saw the empty counter. "So you read it," he said. "It made you see, didn't it, how such an intense process would commit us to a child."

"I don't have it," she said. "Maybe Rune borrowed it."

"Borrowed what?" Rune was standing behind them, fully dressed, her hair spiked with gel. As if she had armored herself, it occurred to Hannah.

"The book on the counter is missing, honey," she said, the endearment slipping out. She liked the smile it produced from Rune.

"Oh." Rune thought a moment. "I haven't seen it."

"You might not have realized what it was," Clive said.

"I try not to touch other people's stuff."

His laugh was caustic, totally unlike him. "Except for food."

"Hey, I'm happy to get my own."

"Clive, what's wrong with you?" Hannah said. To Rune, she said, "Ignore him."

"I'm not doing it, Hannah," he said. "I'm not fighting with you."

He stalked out the back door. She should follow him, apologize. He was grieving, too, and trying to move forward. But still wanting children, after everything. It felt like a betrayal.

Rune sat down. "He doesn't like me."

"He'll get over it." Hannah pulled some waffles from the oven and sat to watch Rune eat.

※

More of Clive's things vanished, of no real value except the annoyance their disappearance caused: a dry-cleaning ticket, a backup flash drive, extra seminar materials. Whenever something went missing, Hannah hid in her study and listened to him rush around murmuring, "I was in the car, then I came inside and put it on the counter . . ." Once, she heard him say, "Damn that girl!" A swell of protectiveness almost pushed her out of hiding. *Leave her out of this*, she was tempted to say.

But it could be Rune. Hannah meant to talk to her. The timing just never seemed right. Rune had become such a comfort, especially with Clive around less and less. In the weeks since the book disappeared, he left for campus earlier and returned later, rarely pausing outside her study, where she lay on the couch clicking through channels. (How long had it been since they'd slept in the same bed?) Often the only traces of him were the candy wrappers that reappeared around the house.

She didn't let them bother her. Instead, she read cookbooks or watched television (the shows flowing through her now rather than reverberating in her brain) or spent time with Rune, not even pretending to work anymore. She went hours, at times, without thinking. Some days after Rune woke up, later and later it seemed, they chatted until Rune left for her evening shift. Or after work Rune might show up in Hannah's study with some pie from the restaurant and they'd eat and watch TV until the airwaves filled with reruns and paid programming. She noted how Rune asked advice about the smallest things and turned away if Clive walked in. She imagined the growing list of pilfered items stockpiled in Rune's closet, the girl's sly satisfaction as she listened to Clive search. *That's what you get for upsetting your wife*, she would be thinking. There was comfort in imagining that this girl understood what hurt her better than her own husband did.

※

In mid-July, she caught Rune in a lie, a small one, involving a time when she and her mother got lost in Amsterdam's red-light district looking for somewhere to buy saxophone reeds for her father. Rune was helping Hannah fold laundry.

"I thought he played trombone," Hannah said, placing a towel on Rune's pile.

Rune's face stilled; then she looked puzzled. "Nope, sax. Alto, tenor, bass, you name it." Her tone was overbright, reckless. Hannah hesitated before pulling another towel from the dryer. She could have misremembered. Such a silly thing to lie about, and for no apparent reason. Still, part of her whispered, *What is true with this girl?* and, louder, *She is no substitute.*

That night, while Rune was working, Hannah stood outside the bedroom door and contemplated picking the lock. She knelt to peer in the large, old-fashioned keyhole, which revealed only darkness. Tingling with guilt, she hurried away, into their bedroom. This girl trusted her, relied on her even, and she was about to invade her privacy. She had no proof, just a sense, probably misguided, spurred by too much crime TV and her growing anger at Clive. His disapproval of Rune was palpable. How dare he judge her.

She started flipping through his closet, snatched a velvety suede jacket, his favorite, and then she was yanking buttons—*tearing scratching ripping*—until her breath came in gasps. Somewhere, a keening wail. Her own. Her face was wet with snot and tears. She had to get hold of herself.

After she stopped panting, she spread the jacket on the bed, tried to smooth the ruined suede that turned his eyes the color of honey. It couldn't be fixed. She finally buried it in the trash.

When Clive noticed the jacket missing from his closet the next morning, she told him the dry cleaner lost it.

"Stop pretending," he said. "We both know she's responsible."

"That's ridiculous," she snapped and started to walk out.

He grabbed her arm. "Dammit, Hannah—"

"Stop blaming me!"

"What's happening to us?" he said and let her go.

He sounded so lost. To feel his solid, heavy warmth against her; to rest her head in the hollow of his throat. She took his hand, as familiar as her own.

"Do you ever wonder what they would have been like?" he asked.

She dropped his hand, backed away. "No. Never."

"So now we can't even talk about them? It's like you're pretending they never existed."

"They barely did," she said and immediately regretted it. What she'd meant to say was that if she let herself think about them, she couldn't do anything else. She had to let them go or they would consume her. But he would never understand, she could tell by his horrified look. It had been so long since they understood each other.

At the end of July, when Rune had been there almost six weeks, Hannah helped her decorate the bedroom ceiling. It was the first time Rune invited her inside. The few scattered possessions made the room look abandoned, like a motel after a hasty checkout. A book on the end table, an empty glass. Hannah held the stepladder while Rune dotted the ceiling with star and moon stickers. Yellowish white, they were barely visible, but Rune assured her they would glow brightly at night.

"They'll look like a tornado in this long sweep," Rune said. As Rune reached up, Hannah noticed how much her tattoos had faded. When Rune paused to rest, Hannah touched her wrist.

"They're almost gone," Hannah said. Hard to believe so much time had passed. The decision about whether she would teach in the fall had been made for her. The schedule had been set, said a message from the dean's assistant (not from Eugene himself, which was its own message). A relief, really. Teaching was part of a past that she was finally letting go.

"I'll probably have them redone," Rune said. "Come with me. You could get some, too."

"I'm a little old."

"You're only as old as you let yourself be. That's what Bishop says." She climbed down the ladder. "It's like I'm giving in to him if I let them fade."

"Have you two spoken?"

"He doesn't know where I am, the asshole," she said in a cold, flat voice so unlike her that Hannah shivered. Rune handed her a packet. "You try," she said, her normal voice restored.

"I'm no artist." But Hannah climbed the ladder. At the top she reached up with a sticker. Her C-section scar tugged. Such a small incision required to take them. She made a circle, added stars for eyes, a mouth of moons, a crescent nose. When she looked down, Rune was grinning.

"The Smiley Constellation, discovered by Professor Hannah Arnett," Rune said and handed up another packet. The stickers looked fresh and new, like the beginning of something.

"I'll do it," Hannah said. "I'll get a tattoo."

They went that day, picking a place on Brattle Street near campus. It was surprisingly peaceful, New Age music playing softly, dim lights, blinds pulled against the afternoon glare. There was a low-slung couch and a coffee table littered with magazines. They were greeted by a man covered with tattoos and piercings. When he asked what she was interested in, Hannah impulsively unzipped her jeans low enough to reveal her scar. Even Rune looked surprised.

"Can you tattoo this?" Hannah asked. "Real, not hennaed."

The man crouched. "May I?" he asked and gently prodded the scar. The coolness of his fingertips raised goose bumps on her belly. He stood.

"It'll hurt a lot," he said as she zipped up. "I'd have to go extra deep. Scar tissue doesn't take ink that well. And it fades pretty fast. You'd need lots of touch-ups."

She must have winced because Rune said, "Start somewhere easier, maybe. See if it's worth the effort."

The man pointed at the couch. "Think about it while I do her hennas. Let's take a look." He examined Rune's arms. "Nice, clean work. Easy to trace. Jusneet over at Cambridge Body Art, right?"

"I had them done in Africa," she said.

"Huh. Looks just like Jusneet's stuff." He went to set up.

Rune sat next to Hannah and flipped through a tattoo design catalog. She looked absorbed, but Hannah knew with sudden force: Rune was lying. Now was the time to confront her. *You don't need to steal from Clive,* she could say. *I know you care about me.*

Rune pointed to a Chinese symbol in the catalog. "Naked," the caption said it meant. "How about this?"

Rune shifted closer. Her narrow shoulder felt fragile against Hannah's. People lied all the time, to themselves and others, to hide pain, to seem like more than what they were. Hannah was as guilty as anyone. Those tiny nails and fluttering chests would never leave her, no matter what she told herself. But there were other ways to diminish the ache. She wouldn't say anything to Rune, she realized and felt a slight thrill. Not now or ever.

"Maybe that one," Hannah said and pointed to a yin and yang circle, one half light, the other dark. Together, they paged through designs.

⁂

"Those aren't for you," she said the next morning when Clive tried to take a waffle.

"How could I forget?" he said. "Egg whites and low-fat toast for me." He took one anyway, biting it as he walked to the fridge.

He wasn't going to rile her. She adjusted her shirt to cover the new tattoo on the small of her back. It didn't hurt, but she kept touching it, hoping to evoke the needle's exacting intensity, in and out, demanding her attention. Rune got the same one on her left shin. Definitely worth the effort, they had agreed. Already Hannah felt different.

Clive peered in the refrigerator. His stomach strained against his shirt buttons. He kept glancing over.

"What's that?" he asked when she reached for a glass. He walked over and lifted her shirttail. She went to push him away, but his expression was bemused, playful, like the man she used to know. He brushed his fingers across the tattoo. A chill shot through her.

"You like it?" she asked. God. She sounded like a flirty teenager.

"It's sexy."

He crouched down, his breath warm on her back. She closed her eyes.

"When did you get it?"

His hair, soft beneath her hand. "Yesterday, on a whim. We found this place—"

"We? As in you and Rune?"

Her eyes flew open. He stood staring at her. Her back still tingled where he'd touched her. She opened her mouth to tell him: *Touch me again.*

"Let me get this straight," he said. "There's no time to work or to read the research I slaved over so that we could maybe have a shot at staying together, but there's more than enough time to pamper some stranger and go off with her to mutilate your body?"

Maybe have a shot at staying together? He'd leave her?

"You said you liked the tattoo," she said.

"Don't change the subject."

"What's our subject, then, Rune? She's not a stranger, she's—"

"She's a liar, dammit!" He took a step back. "I checked with the registrar," he said more quietly. "There's no record of a Rune Zapata ever taking a class."

"Maybe you spelled her name wrong."

"A grad student of Sid's came by my office yesterday. Bishop something. They're married. She left without a note, nothing, just disappeared. He said she's pregnant."

That couldn't be. She looked the same. But some girls hid their bellies until birth. The constant sleeping, the bounces between lethargy and enthusiasm. They could be signs. Who knew what was true with this girl? Her breath caught; she heard herself gasp. The satisfaction on Clive's face made her want to hit him.

"If it's true," she said, "she needs support. She needs me."

"She needs to use you."

"You've been awful since she moved in."

"I'm sorry if I can't settle for bringing home strays."

The bowl slipped—or did she throw it?—and shattered at his feet. They stared at the mess. She couldn't get herself to move. Finally, he stepped over the shards and walked to the door.

"What about what I want?" he said, so quietly that the effort to hear him felt like it would split her.

After he was gone, she cleaned up and walked to the staircase. Upstairs, the shower was running. She had imagined herself posed this way, one hand on the banister, her head cocked, listening before she called, "Candace and Matt"—or Portia and Brad, or Rowena and Jake—"time for school!" She stood there, listening.

During the last pregnancy they had picked out cribs. Clive held the catalog over her head while she lay in bed. They kept the doors open so they could call to each other while he worked on the room. When he was done, he lay beside her, his hair and arms speckled with paint, and showed her photos. The bright ochre walls, the cribs end to end, matching rockers framing the window. Beneath the crown molding, a decorative border of cows leaping over moons, Clive's surprise for her. He had been so eager. Careers came and went, books were written anytime or not at all. A family endured. It hadn't occurred to her that her body would fail them. She had never let herself imagine what it would be like, the daily, crushing weight of knowing that her own deliberate choices—to wait until her next book was published, until she got tenure, until she lectured at one more conference, rather than make the time, take the risk, reprioritize—had led her to this place.

The extra key to Rune's room required jiggling before it worked. Down the hall the shower was still running, but it would stop soon. She walked inside, climbed on the wing chair to check the closet shelf. Empty. She wasn't sure what she was looking for. Not just Clive's things. Something to prove him wrong about Rune.

She stepped off the chair and hurried to the dresser. Jumbled clothes in all three drawers. Crumbled behind the bottom drawer was a tank top with "Naughty" printed across the chest. That female bank robber. Notes slipped to tellers, guns in purses. It didn't mean anything for Rune to have this shirt. Lots of girls did, at least three in her intro family law class the last semester she taught. And it wasn't necessarily hidden. It could have gotten stuck by mistake. But what if?

Sneezing from dust, she felt around the box springs cover and found a hole. Clive's swim goggles were there, and his reading glasses. Farther back, two manila envelopes. One was filled with cash, tens and twenties secured with thick rubber bands. Tips. This was tip money. But so much of it, and such big bills. The other envelope was sealed, its contents stiff, squarish. Passports, maybe, fake IDs. Or pictures of Rune and a man, the two of them hamming it up, brandishing pistols maybe, or simply smiling and cradling her belly with their clasped hands.

"What are you doing in here?"

Hannah shoved the envelopes under the bed. Behind her, Rune stood in the doorway wrapped in a towel, her bare arms tensed. Hannah tried to imagine her wearing the "Naughty" shirt. News reports hadn't mentioned tattoos. Still, she could have gotten them afterward, cut and dyed her hair. Appearances were so easily altered.

"We should talk," Hannah said, still crouched awkwardly by the bed.

Rune grabbed some clothes from an open drawer. "Would you mind?"

Hannah nodded, mute, and left to wait in the foyer.

When Rune came down, she was dressed, her bulging backpack slung over her shoulder. What was inside? Stolen clothes and jewelry? Hannah stepped between her and the front door. "Do you want to tell me something?"

"You should have something to say to me. Like an apology." Rune unzipped her backpack and pulled out a jeans jacket, which she slipped on despite the heat outside. The backpack looked deflated, unincriminating.

"You could have told me the truth about Bishop," Hannah blurted. "I would have understood. And I don't care that you took Clive's things—"

There was something in Rune's face, embarrassment or regret. Too fleeting to be sure. Then Rune snorted. "You break into my room and call *me* a criminal." She pulled out a scrap of paper, scribbled on it. "That's my PO Box. Mail me my deposit. I'll get my stuff later." At the door she paused. "I thought we were friends."

Hannah ran outside after her.

"What about the baby?" she called.

Rune spun around. "I can't help it if you can't have a baby."

Hannah stood gasping as Rune sped away on the scooter. Then she watched the empty street until her breathing calmed. She could follow Rune, find out where she went, what she really did with her time. Her midsection throbbed. From the new tattoo, the C-section scar? It didn't matter. Whether the girl was a student or a bank robber, whether she was pregnant or not—none of that mattered, either. Imagining her possible incarnations wouldn't bring her back. But Clive. She found herself wondering where he was. When he was coming home.

She walked down the porch steps, across the lawn. The tattoo parlor was a ways, but not too far to walk. She reached the sidewalk, let herself touch the ridge on her abdomen. The needle in and out, deeper and deeper, helping the grief settle in and find its place. Afterward, she would walk back home and lie on the bed to wait for him. *They existed*, she would tell him. *They did. He might have been a soccer player or a chemist, she a sculptor or novelist, something creative and volatile.* The needle, its precision. She would coax him to stretch out beside her and she would take his hand and trace his fingers across the design. *The boy,* she would say. *The girl. Touch me. Cyclist. Journalist. Concert pianist. Touch.* Her feet stepped forward, tapping out the possibilities. She would round a corner soon, and the tattoo parlor would be there, waiting for her.

Daredevil

Every Sunday during Mass, Grace stared at little Noreen Baransky—at her swollen joints and wasted limbs, her bulging, watery eyes, the discolored fingernails. Grace wondered what was wrong with her. Maybe a rare chromosomal disorder with a complicated Latin name. Sometimes her eyes strayed from the girl's wan profile to her son Aiden's sweet—though sullen—face. He wouldn't say the recitations unless she handed him a hymnal, and she had to prod him to kneel. At least he *could* kneel. Noreen usually stayed hunched between her parents, her chapped skin mottled an odd hue by the sunlight streaming through the stained glass windows.

Forgive me, Grace prayed sometimes after receiving Communion, *forgive me for being thankful she's not mine.*

It was Noreen's mother who explained the little girl's condition on the first day of Sunday school, a mild September morning. Noreen had been assigned to Grace's class. A hole in her heart kept her blood from being properly oxygenated—hence her purplish skin, which wasn't a trick of the stained glass as Grace had assumed. Up close, the girl's breathing rattled like a faulty steam radiator, and there was something sour about her expression. As her mother talked, Noreen picked at one scaly elbow and regarded the other children at their kidney-shaped desks with a faintly proprietary air. Her gaze settled on Aiden, who sat in back. Promise, he'd said, no goofy names, no kissing hello, no hint they were related (they were new to Beverlywood and Grace had started using her maiden name, which worked in his favor). He had an image to maintain, he told her. An image, in third grade. She had almost called Kyle to say, *Can you believe our son?* But she wasn't ready to be friends just yet.

"I want that seat." Noreen pointed at Aiden, who didn't budge. Grace gestured to a desk up front. "This one's empty."

Noreen's skin flushed a shade deeper; her chest heaved. "Mom, why won't he move?"

"Please. She's not supposed to get upset," Noreen's mother said. Harriet, she'd asked to be called, but the assumed complicity in her request annoyed Grace too much for informality. Where was the sympathy she should feel for someone with such a sick kid?

"You can sit up here," Grace said to Aiden, biting back the "sweetheart" she would normally add. He scowled but moved.

Noreen's mother helped the girl settle in, then beckoned Grace into the hallway. "Her inhaler's in her backpack. If she feels faint, there are fruit rollups. We got her a cellphone and programmed my number on it if you need to call me."

Grace felt like she should be taking notes. She must have looked nervous because Noreen's mother said, "Everything should be okay. Really, she's a sweet girl."

Back in the classroom Grace walked to the blackboard. "Welcome, I'm Ms. Cole," she said as she wrote her name. Behind her, an insistent humming rode an undercurrent of whispers.

"Let's quiet down," she said. The whispering stopped, but not the humming. Grace turned. The children were darting glances at Noreen, whose head was on the desk. She hummed loudly as she thumped her heels against the chair legs.

Grace walked over and touched her shoulder. It felt bony and insubstantial, so unlike Aiden's body, which was a coil of muscle and energy, constantly flexing.

"Noreen, we're starting."

The girl stared up at Grace. "Sorry," she said, then put her head down again. Her heels kept thumping, but at least she'd stopped humming.

The other children, including Aiden, were looking from Grace to Noreen. Grace walked back up front and smiled. "Let's talk about things we're thankful for. Open your books to page 3."

They all did, except Noreen. Grace ignored her. Better to pick battles wisely.

After Sunday school, Grace and Aiden worked on the playhouse in the backyard. She had been planning it since they'd moved in three months ago, after the separation. Aiden slumped on a wood pile while Grace set up the table saw. The floor was done, a sturdy rectangle of two-by-sixes topped with plywood. Next, the walls. Almost all the two-by-fours for framing them were cut and stacked in four piles. With the saw in place, Grace arranged the other tools in a row. She had always been the handy one, who finished what she started. The orderliness should have pleased her but didn't.

"It's all dusty and hot back here," Aiden said.

"Since when do you care?" she said, although he had a point. The scruffy lawn was more dirt than grass, and the beds overflowed with weeds. But fixing up the yard felt like she meant for them to stay. Maybe they would. Neither she nor Kyle had much desire to reconcile. "Once we finish the playhouse, it'll be nicer."

"Can I use my PlayStation?"

"No, but you can check how many more two-by-fours we need."

He groaned but started counting wood. She knew he would prefer a tree house. He had cried when she'd said they couldn't take his, a slapdash affair (typical Kyle) mounted in the magnolia behind their Topanga Canyon cottage. They had left Butchie too, a bulky lab-shepherd mix prone to digging. He would destroy the yard, which wasn't theirs, she'd told Aiden, who had buried his face in the dog's bristly coat and sobbed harder. Which had made her want to cry too, her face pressed beside Aiden's against Butchie's stoic back. Maybe the playhouse—complete with a shingled roof and shutters for privacy—would help make this shabby Westside rental feel more familiar to Aiden amid all the newness: new school, new friends, newly separated parents.

"One more piece," he said, finished counting the wood.

"Coming up." She placed a two-by-four on the table saw.

He scuffed his heels in the dirt. "Dad lets me cut stuff."

"You're eight. This thing's heavy, and dangerous."

"You always say no."

He looked just like Kyle when he frowned.

"Fine," she said, "but only if I help."

Together—her arms around him, her hands steadying his—they cut the final piece. The end clattered to the ground.

"Told you I could do it," he said.

He paraded around, bowing, happy for once. She couldn't help clapping. Immediately he stopped. Still, he picked up the two-by-four when she asked and helped her carry it to the piles.

Halfway there, he stumbled and dropped his end.

"Ouch!" He wouldn't unclench his hand when she tried to look.

"Let me see." She coaxed open his fingers. A large splinter protruded from his thumb, the grayish tip embedded in the skin. He flinched, but she held his hand firmly and plucked. "There," she said and held it up.

Like that he was glaring. "I never get splinters with Dad."

Of course you do, she almost said. That and worse. She had memorized the number for urgent care and had learned to dread whenever Kyle proposed a new adventure: skateboarding in empty swimming pools or biking down the steepest mountain trails. Worrying invited disaster, Kyle said if she objected. They couldn't live their lives expecting the worst. And the worst happened anyway, he would say now. Their family was in ruins.

She pointed Aiden toward the house. "That needs soap."

"Dad would rinse it off with a hose."

"I'm not Dad." She could see him getting impatient, but there was an order to things he had to understand. "Your thumb could get infected if we don't clean it and then you'd have to go to the doctor. Now move."

Suddenly, he stomped his foot. "Leave me alone!"

Before she could stop him, he ran inside and slammed the door.

Jealousy, not faith, had driven her to join Saint Timothy's.

It was early on a hot summer Sunday a few weeks after their move. Aiden planted himself by the living room window half an hour before Kyle was due and pretended to read the final *Harry Potter,* which he'd read countless times since it had come out the previous year. "He's here!" he shouted when the car pulled up, and then he dropped the book and ran outside without saying goodbye. Still carrying her coffee mug, she hurried after him onto the porch for a fierce hug that made her slop a little coffee on his backpack.

"Mom," he protested.

"I'll miss you." She waved like crazy as he slid into the passenger seat and the car pulled away.

Back inside, she tried to work at her drafting table tucked in a living room corner. She was a landscape architect with her own small practice, and there were always blueprints to draft. She drew and erased and checked the clock every few minutes. They could be bungee jumping or racing Quarter Midgets, though even Kyle knew better. More likely they would drive up to Malibu so Kyle could teach Aiden to surf. No matter what they did, Aiden would come home pulsing with excitement. Maybe this time he would announce that he really, really wanted to live with Dad and Butchie and she shouldn't mind since then she could stop worrying about whether he'd cleaned his room or finished his science projects. Dad was better at science anyway.

She fled to her car and drove aimlessly before heading for a coffee shop, straight past Saint Timothy's. She'd noticed it before, its stone facade like her childhood church back East. This time she veered into a parking space. The Sundays of her youth, daydreaming beside her parents in a pew. The security of her own innocence.

Inside, she sat in back. The prayers were so familiar she could recite them without thought. Then the march to the altar for Communion, the wafer stiff and flavorless, dissolving quickly, along with her anger at Aiden, at Kyle, at everything.

She returned every weekend that summer until the priest who said High Mass greeted her by name afterward. It seemed natural to respond to the request for Sunday school teachers at summer's end.

"Why do I have to go?" Aiden demanded the night she announced she'd enrolled him. He was already in bed, the covers pulled up to the belligerent jut of his chin.

She leaned against the doorjamb. *Because you might like me again if you see that other kids do.*

"Aiden, look—"

"You can't make me," he said.

"Wanna bet," she said and flicked off the light.

"Who can define *agapē*?"

Hands shot into the air. It was the third week of Sunday school. The children had proven to be bright and eager. She always brought snacks and played at least one game. To her relief, the material was more ethical than religious: offer forgiveness instead of revenge, be thankful for the gifts you receive.

The boys still hung back (Aiden scowling among them), but the girls crowded around her before class, vying to be her helper. Noreen, though, sprawled across her own desk as if too weary to sit upright. Which could be true.

The other kids liked Noreen. She had a way of telling stories— *Missy's new dog is as big as a pony,* she might start out, her eyes wide with conviction—that made her classmates listen eagerly. And they jumped to help her, fetching tissues or a sweater when she sniffled. A far more generous response than the resentful clench in Grace's chest.

Noreen's hand with its oversized nails waved in response to Grace's question.

"Noreen, tell us what *agapē* means."

"It's when someone's mouth opens real wide, like this." She stretched open her purple lips until the other children giggled.

"That's *agape.*" Grace kept her tone neutral, although Noreen's grin made her suspect the flub was intentional. "You were supposed to read about *agapē* for this week. Can someone else define it?"

"How come we get homework in Sunday school?" Noreen's voice was muffled, her head buried in her arms. The other children stayed silent. No one raised a hand.

"We're learning about how God loves us. That's worth some effort." Still no raised hands. She settled on Aiden, who was coloring his book jacket. "Aiden, maybe you can help."

"Teacher's pet." The words were a hiss, barely audible, like a swift breeze off a frozen lake. The classroom filled with titters. Aiden flushed. His eyes flew to Noreen, who had laid her cheek on her arms. Her purplish scalp showed through her thin blond hair.

"Noreen—" she said and saw Aiden shake his head. But she would reprimand her no matter who she teased. "There's no name calling, Noreen."

Noreen looked up with wide eyes. "I didn't say anything."

"I heard you—"

"My dad says there's no God," Aiden burst out, his gaze fixed on his book. "He says there's nothing in the sky but the solar system."

My dad, as if she didn't know who that was.

"Everyone's entitled to an opinion," she said curtly to Aiden. "Now, please read us the first paragraph on page 11."

The classroom was quiet except for pages rustling and Aiden reading aloud the definition of unconditional love.

❁

She finished the playhouse over several weeknights and Saturdays while Aiden was with Kyle. Inside she put a battery-operated lantern and a crate of Aiden's favorite comics bookended by beanbag chairs. As a favor, her crew cleared the flowerbeds and planted a fledgling olive tree that would eventually cast a comfortable shade.

The day of the unveiling she covered the playhouse with a tarp and waited by the living room window for the school bus. It was unreasonable to expect much reaction, but she couldn't help imagining how Aiden would hug her and grin like he did when Kyle's car pulled up. Their old tree house listed and was furnished with sleeping bags. Still, she used to have to coax Aiden and Kyle down after a night spent eating corndogs and reading *Harry Potter* together with flashlights. "No girls!" they shouted if she climbed up to check on them, Butchie whining below; then they pelted her with corndog sticks.

The bus was late. As she stepped outside to check for it, it rounded the bend. Reflexively she waved, then realized her mistake. Aiden didn't want her waiting outside. Some Sunday school kids went to his regular school and rode his bus.

Aiden got out and stood by the curb until the bus pulled away. Once it turned the corner, he trudged up the walkway, past her, into the house. She followed him to the kitchen.

"How was school?"

He opened the refrigerator. "They all saw you."

"Everybody has a mom, Aiden. So what if kids know I'm yours?"

He kept gazing in the refrigerator. Maybe he was ashamed of her.

"I've got a surprise," she said.

He looked over. Finally, a grin.

She made a production of the reveal, blindfolding him, guiding him out back, where she uncovered his eyes and swept off the tarp.

"Voilà!" she said.

He stood staring.

"It's not like ours at home. I mean, at Dad's house," he said. "Thanks, though."

He walked inside and sat carefully in a beanbag chair as she tried to smile.

❀

Noreen's mother was late. Again. Grace read a magazine while Noreen sat at her desk. Aiden drew on the chalkboard. Usually he ran ahead and waited by the car. But Noreen's mother had been picking her up a little later each week. She always arrived flustered and apologetic. Maybe this was her only time to herself. Even so, Grace disliked the idea of Aiden alone in the parking lot for who knew how long.

"Why is he still here?" Noreen sounded peevish and tired.

"She's driving me home," Aiden said before Grace could answer.

She turned pages and eyed the children. Aiden focused on his skateboard drawing, but Noreen kept peering at him from the nest of her arms.

"My birthday party's next Saturday," she finally said. "You can come if you want."

"Nope." Aiden glanced at Grace. "I mean, no thanks."

Noreen's mouth pursed.

"Cheryl thinks you're cute," she said. "Lanni does, too."

His ears flamed. Grace pretended to read. The poor guy.

"Oh yeah?" he said. The flush spread to his neck.

Noreen stared. "I think you've got a big nose."

"Noreen, be nice," Grace said.

"What does she know?" Aiden said, still drawing. "She's butt ugly."

Grace's mind whirred, searching for any thought other than the one—*God, yes*—that filled her head. Noreen's hands were clasped tight enough to whiten her purplish nails. How many taunts had it taken for her to learn to be so different that other children's stares hurt less?

"Aiden Mitchell, apologize!"

"But Mom, she started it—"

"She's your mom?"

Noreen's eyes darted between them. Aiden gaped as he realized what he'd said. He looked miserable. Grace half-stood, but he'd already turned away to scribble tight, dark circles across the skateboard, the chalk shrieking.

✿

Fall turned to winter. Noreen started waiting in the hall for her mother. A cluster of little girls, including Cheryl and Lanni, took to waiting with her. They all went to Aiden's regular school, as did Noreen. Every Sunday after class, the girls peered into the room at Aiden. Grace could never quite catch what they were saying. Slime eyes, maybe. Potato nose. Aiden didn't race ahead to the car anymore now that everyone knew his secret. Noreen had made sure of it. Instead, he drew on the blackboard (witches riding flaming broomsticks, monsters with talons and bulging eyes) and frowned at the door, which Grace longed to shut but couldn't. She had to keep an eye on Noreen, whose expression turned angelic whenever Grace strolled over to eavesdrop on the little girls' whispered conferences.

There were phone calls, too, in the early evenings, a few in quick succession with giggles on the other end. Once, when Aiden beat her to the phone, he listened, then shouted, "I'm not!" She couldn't help snatching the receiver. "Stop calling here," she said and hung up, but not before hearing a piping voice (not Noreen's, though probably a girl coached by her) chanting, "Mama's boy, mama's boy!"

She told Aiden that this was how girls acted when they had one-sided crushes. They got silly and mean but eventually they stopped. "I could have her class switched," she said. "Or call her mom."

"No!" he said, so loudly she flinched. "Can't I spend Sundays with Dad and Butchie, like when you first made us leave?"

"Dad and I agreed together—" She stopped herself. "Look, honey, she's a sick little girl who wants your attention. Try to be the bigger person."

"I gotta finish my homework," he said, this boy who fought for every last minute of playtime, and he trudged to his room.

She shouldn't have been surprised when the principal started calling. She should have suspected Aiden would act on his frustration. This teasing was new. He had been well liked at his old school. One day he was sent to the principal's office for shoving an older kid. Grace gasped when she saw his swollen eye. "He started it," was all he would explain. Another day he sneaked into the main office at lunchtime and shredded half the papers on the secretary's desk before getting caught. Another day he jumped from the top of the jungle gym.

"They're only bruised," he said about his ribs when Grace yelled that he could have gotten a concussion or broken an arm or worse. He shrugged when she took away his PlayStation privileges. "Dad'll let me use his," he said. It wasn't true—Kyle had been equally worried when she'd phoned—but just his saying it made her wonder.

The principal called late one afternoon to say she thought Grace should come see what Aiden had done this time.

At school, Aiden sat in the main office with two bigger boys who stopped poking each other when Grace rushed in. Aiden stared at the floor. He looked pale and frightened. She crouched beside him.

"Honey, are you okay?" she asked, but he wouldn't look up.

Someone coughed by the doorway. Noreen stood holding a "restroom" placard. Her shirt cuffs didn't reach her bony wrists. She stared at Aiden.

"That was mean," Noreen said to him. She frowned, her expression suddenly fierce. "But it doesn't change anything."

"Leave me alone," he muttered.

"What's going on?" Grace asked.

The principal—a brisk, decisive woman—emerged from her office. "Noreen, you shouldn't be here." She guided the girl into the hallway. When she returned, she gestured to Grace. "Let's go see your son's handiwork," she said and led Grace outside.

There it was on the kickball field, chiseled into the dirt: "Noreen sucks cock."

The *e*'s were crooked, the *s*'s squat and sluggish, like Aiden's. Beneath was a remarkably accurate rendition of Noreen's bulging eyes and toothy grin.

"He doesn't even know what this means," Grace said. She clutched the chisel the principal had found, the handle neatly labeled with Grace's own initials. The playground was deserted, as if everyone had fled the ugly taunt.

"Some fifth graders told him what to write," the principal said, "which doesn't excuse him. They'll all have two weeks of detention. Frankly, Aiden's getting out of control. Something needs to be done."

Grace nodded. This was her fault. He had been oozing anger and hurt for so long. Noreen was an easy target. Grace followed the principal inside. She had to help him.

❀

A week passed, then another with no phone calls from school. The principal had recommended a therapist. Aiden didn't talk much during his first two sessions, which the therapist said was normal. He was also quiet at home, but in a peaceful way, as if he'd resolved an interior battle. Grace grounded him for a month and took away his screen privileges. Even so, he seemed content to sit with her in the evenings, doing homework or listening to her read *Harry Potter and the Deathly Hallows* aloud. One night she woke to find him curled against her, asleep. She held him close, breathed in the musky scent of his hair. He was finding his way back to her.

It could also help to fix up the house, make it feel more like home. Kids needed a secure environment, the therapist had emphasized. So, the weekend after the playground incident, Grace planted a garden. Wires strung with bougainvillea crisscrossed the fence in a hatch pattern, and she punctuated the beds with succulents and grasses hearty enough to withstand the winter chill. Rose bushes, spiky and denuded of buds, filled the back bed, where eventually they would flourish in the southern exposure.

The next weekend, early Sunday morning, she tackled the sprinkler system. A few heads needed replacing, as did a length of leaky pipe. Next, she used wire mesh and stakes to fence off a patch for vegetables. She and Aiden had planted them every year since he was big enough to hold a spade. He loved watching the plants push through the dirt. Last year he had set up a stand and sold Armenian cucumbers and snap peas to the neighbors, though Butchie had gobbled most of the peas. She and Aiden could plant this vegetable patch together in spring. He would be feeling better by then, more like himself. They both would.

She had just finished the fencing when she heard the front door slam. It was early for Aiden. Kyle usually returned him at the last moment, right before they had to leave for Mass and Sunday school.

Aiden entered the yard.

She brushed off her knees as she stood. "What're you doing home?"

"Dad wanted to go out for brunch. I didn't feel like it." He wandered to the potting bench. "He was meeting some girl."

It wasn't surprise, exactly, that rocked her backward—this moment was inevitable—more a piercing jab of grief, and resignation, at the permanence of this broken incarnation of their family. If she felt this way, what about Aiden?

"It's good that your dad has someone to keep him company," she said, carefully. "You must feel strange, though."

He shrugged and started scooping potting soil into a container.

"Wanna talk about it?" she asked.

"Nope."

She wanted to hug him, but his shoulders looked so rigid. She settled for rubbing his neck. "Later, when you're ready," she said and went to rinse the tools behind the garage.

As she finished, she heard a guttural cry and a cracking sound. She ran back to the yard. Aiden was attacking the olive tree with pruning shears. Silvery leaves rained down as he chopped viciously.

She grabbed him, but he jerked away.

"You're not even trying to fix things!" he shouted and kept chopping.

She bear-hugged him, but he was strong, so much stronger than she'd thought, and they fell to the ground, wrestling, and she felt a blade slice her palm, feet kicking her thighs, an elbow in her gut, winding her, bringing tears, and then she wrenched away the shears, rolled onto her back, still gasping, her wounded hand an excruciating pulse.

"I hate you!" Aiden yelled, his voice muffled by his arms.

"I hate you too!" she spat and immediately kneeled beside him, trying to pry apart his arms, her bloody hand staining his sleeves. "Oh, baby, I didn't mean it—"

He curled away from her.

Late that night, when she couldn't bear watching the clock anymore, she wrapped herself in an old robe of Kyle's and wandered outside. The stitches in her palm itched as she contemplated the playhouse. Inside it was comfortable, orderly. Totally unappealing to an eight-year-old boy.

She eased open the door, felt her way to the lantern, turned it on. There in a beanbag chair was Aiden, his knees pulled to his chest, his face hidden.

She settled on the floor and hunkered close. Then she heard him, so quiet, so defeated and old: "We're not going home, are we?"

The church's winter festival buzzed with people hawking prizes at game booths and children screeching on whirling rides. Sizzling oil prickled Grace's hands as she drizzled funnel cake batter over the fryer.

The night air filled with a sugary swoon that almost made her forget her stitches, which still itched after a week. Whenever kids from her class ran up to her booth, she gave them an extra funnel cake. A few boys walked over to where Aiden sat drawing at a nearby picnic table. He brightened as he spoke to them, but when they gestured to the rides, he shook his head and huddled over his drawing pad as if he couldn't risk enjoying himself. He'd barely spoken to her all week.

She piled some funnel cakes on a plate and walked over after the boys left. Aiden's drawing swirled with colors, in the middle a small dark figure, arms extended as if in flight. She sat on the bench and offered him the plate.

"I'm not hungry," he said.

"You should go explore with your friends."

He shrugged. "Don't feel like it."

She slid closer. "Honey, things seem bad now—"

"Why are you sitting here?" said a nasally voice.

There beside them stood Noreen, bundled in a puffy down coat. She hadn't been to Sunday school since the playground epithet. Her mother had been kind when Grace phoned to apologize. "At least no one got physically hurt," she'd said. Grace cringed thinking about the conversation. She wasn't sure she would have been as forgiving.

Aiden started scribbling on his pad. Grace stood.

"Nice to see you, Noreen," she said. An excusable lie. "Would you like a funnel cake?"

Noreen regarded her seriously. "I'm not allowed. Anyway, I'm talking to him. Want to ride the Tilt-A-Whirl?"

Aiden kept drawing. "Nope."

"The Flying Saucers?"

"Nope."

"The Shrieking Snake?"

"Nope."

"Fraidy cat."

He glared at her. "I'm not!"

"Prove it," she said, an odd smile twitching her livid lips.

She was behind everything, Grace understood with a sickening jolt. The shredded papers, the jump from the jungle gym, each dare more outrageous to prove he was no mama's boy but the opposite, his father's son. The slur carved into the playground must have been his attempt to rebel.

"He's not proving anything—"

"Who's selling funnel cakes?" she heard behind her.

"Hold on," she called. Aiden slumped over his pad and chewed his lower lip. She fixed on Noreen, who considered her with those unblinking, owlish eyes. "Stay away from my son."

"You can't tell me what to do." Said with a phlegmy hiss. How gratifying it would be to shake those puny shoulders.

"Mom, stop!" Aiden's voice startled her. He stood by the table, his face flushed, his drawing forgotten. "I don't need you," he said.

"I'm trying to help—" She stopped. It was in the ball of his fists, the sheen of tears in his eyes that she knew he wouldn't let fall. She couldn't protect him without making him into what Noreen kept telling him he was: a mama's boy, a boy without his own place in the world. Her boy. Her sweet, sad, heartbroken boy.

There was a crash behind them, a startled shout. Grace whirled around. A man with a huge pot belly stared into her booth, where the fryer hung by its cord, dripping oil. Funnel cakes littered the ground. The man sheepishly held one up. "Sorry," he said.

"Don't move," she said to Aiden and ran to pick up the fryer. She looked back at the picnic table.

Aiden and Noreen were gone.

Grace dashed from the booth, calling Aiden's name. He couldn't have gotten far. Her thudding heart left her wheezing. She pushed through the crowd searching for Aiden's face, Noreen's with its purplish glow, but they were nowhere.

At the fair's outskirts she paused, gasping, at a soccer field. Bleachers loomed in the field's floodlights. On top stood two small forms, one sturdy and straight, the other hunched in a puffy coat. "Aiden, don't!" she screamed.

Their heads turned to look at her. The smaller figure leaned closer to the taller one as if to whisper something. They joined hands, bent their knees.

Don't, don't, don't, echoed in her head, *don't be so protective, don't leave him without choices, don't let him go, don't, don't, don't, don't.*

She started running again, her limbs horribly heavy, as if she were struggling through glue. Even her shout—"Aiden, no!"—sounded sluggish. The figures jumped, seeming to hang in the air forever even as they plummeted to the ground.

Extra Precautions

Someone is killing cats in Claire's neighborhood. A cop shows up Sunday morning to examine the nearly decapitated tabby on Claire's front lawn. Its eyes are milky, its head thrown back. There's a triangle of blood-soaked grass between its neck and body.

"Probably a machete," the cop tells her.

He crouches by the dead cat and squints up at Claire, who shivers in shorts and a tank top that just covers her gently mounded belly. A house key is tucked in her running shoe. She was about to go on her daily walk when she found the cat. Looking at it makes her want to gag.

"You should be more careful, ma'am, especially in your condition. Carry a cell phone for emergencies," the cop says. He's got misshapen ears, a lipless mouth. She's pretty sure he's the guy who testified against one of her assault cases last year (a homeless kid who took a swing when the cop woke him up in an alley). He seemed like a blowhard then, too. With his baton he prods the cat's head, tearing the gristly bit of connective tissue. "Third decap around here. Seems like the modus operandi"—prod, prod—"although there was a skinned cat near Fairfax"—prod—"and one chopped up on Miracle Mile, guts spread out all fancy, like the killer was being arty."

The gristle rips completely, freeing the little head; it rocks blindly toward Claire. The cop wipes his baton on the grass. The bully. Fairfax and Miracle Mile aren't even that close to here. *Poor pregnant girl can't stand a little blood*, he's probably thinking. She nods and feigns indifference.

"He was trying to scare me," she tells Duff later that morning. He's reading the arts section in their tiny breakfast nook. She stands at the kitchen counter mashing bananas for banana bread.

He grins. "Fat chance." His newly bleached buzz cut glows in the sunlight. Dead cats, burglaries, occasional shootings—all are normal in Los Angeles, even in this Westside neighborhood, which is quieter than where they used to live in Hollywood. Just last week, a Radio Shack a few blocks away got held up by some crackhead. But she and Duff can live with that. They're city people, they reminded each other after the cop bagged the cat carcass and Duff hosed down the lawn until there was no trace of blood. They've seen everything.

She takes the bowl of mashed bananas to the breakfast nook window and looks outside. She's gaining too much weight for the second trimester, but lately all she can keep down are sweet, bready things. Her stomach feels queasy again, her skin prickly. It's the adrenaline from this morning, and the increased blood flow from being pregnant. The combination intensifies smells, sounds, colors, tweaking her perceptions. The sidewalk outside seems more broken, the surrounding duplexes—old, stucco Spanish-styles like theirs—more cracked and peeling than before. On their lawn a patch of damp grass glistens in the sun. Most of her clients are guilty of what they're accused of. It's never bothered her before.

"Remember my client who killed those prostitutes downtown?" she says. "Growing up he used to catch birds, break their wings, then boil them alive."

Duff keeps reading. "That's something I'd rather forget."

"Animal torture is the first step to becoming a serial killer." She thumps down the bowl on the table. He stares at her. She feels herself trembling. "This cat killer could graduate to people. We'd be stuck here with a baby."

"Whoa. I didn't know you were freaked out." He takes her hands. "We can always move."

"I'm not freaked. Not really. Besides, if we move now we lose our security deposit."

"Screw the deposit. I could pick up extra gigs at the foundry or teach another seniors class."

"The job market sucks and you know it."

He pulls her onto his lap and hugs her. She could sit like this forever, his heart steadily beating beneath her palm, his close-cropped hair bristly against her cheek. She misses his dark curls, but he likes to mimic the aesthetic of whatever sculpture he's working on. The new one is his first commission, for a law firm lobby. He's chiseling it from a creamy marble block, a spare, angular woman yearning toward the sky—what Claire used to be, and needs to be again. That's why she still walks every day now that she's not allowed to run. She's got to stay fit. There's no one to help once this baby is born. She and Duff are on their own, both only children, both parentless, more or less—his died when he was a kid, she gave up on hers years ago. She couldn't wait to flee the East Coast after law school graduation five years ago. Her parents barely noticed she left, they're so mired in their own dramas. Her mother is too busy holding a grudge against her philandering father instead of divorcing him, and her father, a real estate lawyer, chases his next deal almost as hard as he chases his next conquest.

Claire and Duff are each other's family, and the only family their child will have.

"I just want to keep the baby safe," she says.

"We'll get a big-ass dog that only bites guys with machetes."

She laughs, links her fingers behind his neck. "And cops with batons."

"Now you're talking."

When she kisses him, she lingers on his lips, their warmth and give. It's her day off, the first one in ages. Maybe they'll go to the park down the street and lie in the sun, swing on the swings like children, and she'll forget about her clients—the rapists, the druggies, the bangers, the meth dealers. Maybe she'll even forget about the cat killer.

They spend an idyllic afternoon lazing in the park that's over all too soon. Before she knows it, she's in bed reviewing case files. Duff surfs the net beside her on their laptop. She'd rather be curled against him watching *Leno*, enjoying the last easy moments of the day, but there's work to be done.

"This could come in handy on your walks," he says after a while. He's staring at the computer screen, which displays a close-up of a Taser with a lightning bolt etched on its side.

Bloody whiskers, sightless eyes.

She shuffles through her files. "Great. Give an attacker something to use against me."

"True. Dumb idea." He closes the computer. "Maybe pepper spray. Just to make me feel better."

"Common sense, that's all I need," she says and kisses him.

❀

Monday morning, she and her cocounsel Judith drive out to Eastlake Juvenile Hall. They've been assigned a new client, a fourteen year old who killed his grandparents. The ADA filed against the boy in adult court, which requires an immediate objection. Claire usually welcomes the investigating and strategizing involved in a new case. Today she dreads the details. It's a relief when Judith drives for a while, whistling resolutely, before sharing what she knows.

"He called the police after he did it." Judith steers the car toward the freeway exit.

"Did he give them a typed confession, too?"

"Just his knapsack with his grandparents' hands and feet. Their heads were in the oven."

Claire can't help gagging. She grips the dashboard. Judith glances over.

"Morning sickness? Or have I finally succeeded in grossing you out?"

"I'm okay." Claire unwraps some crumbled banana bread from her bag and chokes down a bite. Her skin still feels clammy, but her stomach stops heaving. "This case sounds impossible."

"We'll figure out an angle." Judith brakes for the exit ramp. "Savvy was sick constantly her first few months. Said it should be called all-day sickness instead of morning sickness. Or strike-me-dead sickness."

Judith's smile makes her plain, freckled face luminous. Her wife, Savvy, gave birth to a baby boy two weeks ago, which has made Judith even more upbeat than usual. She's always whistled when she's anxious, to raise her spirits, and now she's added countless nursery rhymes to her repertoire. Claire tries to emulate her positive attitude, especially about work. The system can't function unless people like her and Judith defend it. They have to forget about guilt and innocence and focus on protecting their clients.

From outside, Eastlake Hall could be a rec center or a school. The front is a wall of gleaming windows, with palm trees and flower beds flanking the entrance. Inside, there's no mistaking it's a prison. The metal detector by the door has guards at either end. Posted nearby is a large sign listing visitor rules: "No blue or gray or khaki clothing, no weapons, no drugs, no alcohol, no gifts, no backpacks, purses, briefcases, hip pouches, packages, or parcels; limited paperbacks, magazines, notebooks, and postage stamps allowed, subject to inspection and approval." As always during visiting hours, there's a long line of people waiting to be patted down. Claire usually uses this time to jot questions, consider options. Today she can't look away from the visiting children with their unbridled energy, the way they play hide and seek behind the grown-ups' legs. They could be anywhere.

Once Judith and Claire get through the metal detector, they sign in at the reception desk manned by a guard behind bulletproof glass. Then they are led through several locked doors to the visitation center, where they wait in a tiny soundproof side room that smells strongly of disinfectant and more faintly of mildew. They take the chairs closest to the door and window overlooking the visitation center, leaving the chair by the cinderblock walls for their client. Claire has braced herself for his youth, but she still isn't prepared for the hulking boy who shuffles in, his hands and feet shackled. His name is Zeke. He's well over six feet tall, but his face is splotchy with picked-over acne and his features are softly rounded. Floppy brown bangs fall into his eyes. His pupils are so dilated he looks like a startled animal. Fear or drugs, maybe both. Judith said he's on a mood stabilizer, which could bolster an insanity defense. He's probably textbook abused, too. There's a story to be woven here. They can defend this kid.

A guard removes the shackles before he leaves, shutting the door behind him. The boy is within arm's length. He staggers when he tries to sit. An urge to flee surges through her. She reaches out anyway, but Judith grabs him first.

"Your meds could be too high," Judith says to him. "Our shrink will adjust them after she interviews you. And we'll work on transferring you to a psych ward."

Her tone is casual, as if they're discussing what he had for lunch. She looks tiny next to him, breakable. He barely glances up, grunts as he steadies himself on the spindly wooden table. His hands are chubby, the nails bitten below the quick. The hands of a child. But what he's done. What those hands have done. Claire hasn't seen the crime scene photos yet, but she knows enough from three years in the Public Defender's juvenile division to envision the spatter pocking the grandparents' cheeks, the ragged meat beneath their chins.

"We'll get you through this. Right, Claire?"

She looks up to find Judith frowning at her: *Pay attention.* She tries, but for the rest of the meeting she barely registers the boy's slow, stumbling responses to Judith's questions. Instead, she keeps imagining him holding a knife, slicing through flesh and fur.

A week later she finds another cat.

It's early, the sky just brightening. No one else is around. A low-fat bran muffin is tucked in her jacket pocket. She's a few blocks from home on her way to the park, which she will lap several times at a brisk stroll, her iPod blaring to distract her from the achy protests in her ass and thighs. Until recently she ran this route with ease. The doctor has been urging her to walk. Running overheats her body, which taxes the fetus. At first, she simply decreased her usual brisk clip to a jog; then, a few weeks ago, she came home spotting. The bright drips of blood in the toilet alarmed her enough to start walking.

This part of the neighborhood is quieter than hers, uncluttered, no apartment buildings or duplexes. One after another she passes small, neat, single-family bungalows with trim lawns and higher-end cars parked in the driveways. Large leafy trees line the streets, unlike the saplings on her block. She's thinking about how she'll leave work early tonight no matter what to make Duff a special dinner, chicken thighs braised in tomato sauce, oven roasted broccolini, something chocolaty for dessert. A secret apology for the thought she's had more than once: *We could move if you got a real job.* She doesn't really want to move, and she doesn't really want him to change jobs, which have been scarce anyway since investment bankers tanked the economy last fall. Besides, they're both doing what they love. That's what matters.

She is near the park entrance when she notices the cat beneath a house's box hedge. It looks like it's sleeping. But the odd angle of its neck. She averts her eyes, then, dry-retching into her cupped palm, crosses the lawn to the cat. A fluffy black and white split from sternum to anus. The intestines piled nearby steam in the chilly air. This cat is newly killed.

"What're you doing?" she hears behind her. Her heart pounds hard and high.

A man on the front porch squints at Claire. His sparse hair is mussed and he's wearing a bathrobe. He peers past her. "Gus?" he says, then he races over shouting, "What did you do to him?" He shoves by her to get to the cat and she falls, her face and neck raking the hedge. She hears the man puke before he yells, "Brandi, call the police!"

Claire lies on her side clutching her stomach; there's a faint shifting, a cramping. The cat is inches away, its insides flayed like bloody steak, the intestines a slimy coil. The air reeks of shit. In the distance someone laughs.

The scrapes on her throat are the worst. For the rest of the week she covers them with a scarf, which she takes off when visiting clients in lockup, so an inmate can't reach through the bars and choke her with it. Duff wants to confront the cat owner, who begged her forgiveness once the cops calmed him down. Afterward, she spent the night wearing a fetal monitor in the hospital. Whenever a technician did an ultrasound, she and Duff searched the screen for signs of distress, but the fetus floated peacefully in its murky sea. Once, it started sucking its thumb, lips gyrating in steady pulsing motions that should have reassured her. This should be the easy part, keeping the fetus safe while it's inside her.

"That guy could have hurt you," says Duff the third morning in a row. He's sitting on the bed watching her dress. She's in her underpants, her breasts swollen and heavily veined, her belly jutting out like a little shelf. He likes to admire it, stroking its widening expanse, but the past few days he's been obsessed with her neck. "He could have hurt the baby," he says, his hands clenched.

"He thought I killed his cat." She sits beside him, unclenches his hands, places them on her stomach. "Besides, we're fine."

She's not fine. The laughter she heard when she found the second cat: she hears it as she falls asleep at night; it wakes her in the morning hours before her alarm, makes her long, fleetingly, to call out, "Mommy, Daddy, I'm scared," like when she was little and heard creaks in the night and still thought her parents could protect her from anything.

Instead, she untwines herself from Duff's sleepy warmth and rises for her walk. The laughter she heard when she found the second cat—it was probably a neighbor laughing at a talk show. She doesn't frighten easily. In law school she had to be dragged off a guy twice her size who tried to grab her backpack in Harvard Square. She reacted instinctively, jerking back so hard that he fell, still pulling, and she fell too, and then she was pummeling him, blind to everything but his surprised, bloody face. Even afterward she didn't feel afraid, only a pumping rush of certainty: *Screw you. I did it.* Duff prods her to tell the story at parties. "The police threatened to arrest her just to get her off him," he always finishes for her. "This woman is *fierce*."

Duff starts waking up early with her, to put in extra time on the new sculpture, he says. "The sooner I finish it, the sooner I get paid." But she doesn't like the way he plants himself at the picture window as she leaves to walk, how he's waiting in the same spot when she returns. He calls several times a day, with the same questions: *How're you feeling? How's the baby? Where are you, where to next?* "Stay safe," he says instead of goodbye, instead of "I love you."

One morning when she's tying her running shoes, he emerges from the bedroom wearing sweats.

"Thought we could make this a family thing," he says, yawning.

He's only a few inches taller than she is, and as lean as a boy. He's strong, though. She's seen him sling a marble slab over his shoulder like it's nothing. But a stranger could think he's just some skinny kid.

"Go sculpt," she says.

"It wouldn't hurt to have some muscle along." He flexes his arms and growls.

She laughs the way she knows he wants her to, but his concern feels overbearing. He used to trust that she'd take care of herself. He used to brag about it.

"I don't need a bodyguard." She gives him a quick kiss, then she's out the door, alone.

❀

She and Judith work overtime on the double homicide, making numerous trips to Eastlake, where Zeke is cooperative but quiet. The preliminary reports from the shrink and the PI reveal a grim history: the father has been in prison since before Zeke was born for beating a man to death during a burglary; the mother is an addict who's lived in halfway houses since Zeke was five. He was shuffled between foster homes, which resulted in a series of suspicious burns, bruises, and fractures, until the grandparents took him in last year. Despite everything, he's had no other brushes with the law and he's an outstanding student with a genius IQ.

Over the past few weeks he's emerged from his stupor: his chewed fingertips drum the table; his knees jiggle in their institutional blues. He's put on weight, from the meds and the starchy food. His hair has been shaved so close he might as well be bald. It makes him look more menacing, a better fit with the other boys and their flat, cold faces. Always he is polite, his speech littered with pleases and thank yous, but there's a watchfulness about him, like he's waiting for them to reveal something that will give him an advantage. Each time he sits down across from them, Claire is startled by her urge to bolt from the room.

One day he arrives wearing glasses with thick lenses that magnify his eyes. When she asks where he got them, he says, "My grandma. She always bugged me to wear them." He picks at an acne scab. "She was pretty good to me."

"Then why?" Claire asks.

He regards her steadily.

"I wanted to know what it felt like to cut somebody up."

She freezes over her notes. Beside her she senses Judith stiffen.

"It was a lot of work, especially their hands and feet. I got pretty sweaty." He pushes at his glasses with a raw-looking index finger.

Judith's wife, Savvy, thinks they'll lose his objection. She says so over brunch at her and Judith's house that weekend. Claire and Duff are there to meet the baby, who is asleep on Duff's chest.

"You haven't got a chance," Savvy says.

Judith stands to gather dishes. "You're entitled to your opinion, as wrong as it may be." Her hands full, she knees open the kitchen door.

"That monster deserves to be tried as an adult," Savvy calls after her, but without much conviction. She's a prosecutor, and a good one, known for her ruthless cross-examinations. Her eyes are puffy from lack of sleep, and her full, finely etched mouth is tensely pursed.

Judith reenters, whistling along with the steaming kettle. She glances pointedly at Duff, who smiles down at the sleeping baby. "Enough about work," she says.

Savvy blinks like she's waking from a dream. "Sorry. I don't get much chance for shop talk lately."

Judith sets the kettle down, offers Claire a cup. "You were pretty sick of the DA's office by the time you went on maternity leave."

"Nothing to miss about dealing with scumbags all day," Duff says.

Claire sets down her cup. "I thought you admire what we do."

Duff shrugs. "I'm starting to see the downside."

Savvy gazes across the table at the baby. "Funny how you change. Last week, I was driving on the freeway with Luca and someone cut me off. Nothing major, didn't even deserve a honk. But I started shaking so much I had to pull over. All I could think was how I could have killed Luca. Judith had to come get us. I haven't driven since."

Judith sits and takes her hand. Duff holds the baby close as he nods his understanding.

Later, Claire sits on the floor of Duff's garage studio with a baby carrier in her lap. Duff is chiseling a tall marble block marked with careful gridlines. A hyperslender woman has emerged in places: elegant arms extended overhead, delicate face in profile. It's going to be one of his best pieces, maybe kick his career into overdrive. Usually, she loves to watch him work as she daydreams about their future successes, but today she can't stop fiddling with the baby carrier. It's from Judith and Savvy. There are sturdy shoulder straps, a padded chest pouch for the baby. She slips on the straps. "I'd be back on the freeway already."

Duff glances at her. "Maybe. Or maybe you'd wait, too, until the baby was bigger and less defenseless." He takes a pad and starts drawing.

"That's crazy. There are other ways to feel safer. Get a better car seat."

She stands to look over his shoulder at his unfinished sketch. It's her wearing the carrier, a baby nestled inside. On her face is an unfamiliar, gentle expression.

"Parenting isn't always a rational process," he says. "Or so I've heard."

She lengthens her morning walk to include an additional lap around the park, the house with the tidy box hedge in her periphery each time she nears the entrance. There's no trace of blood or intestines by the hedge—of course there's not, there wouldn't be, weeks have passed—but the spot still draws her eyes. She tries to think like a predator, to keep herself alert to potential danger. Sometimes the bushes rustle (an animal? a person?) or she passes someone walking or running or cycling, but mostly she is alone. Whenever she sees something questionable, she forces herself to investigate. Just a dried-up lizard, or a possum smeared in the road. She relaxes a little.

As she's leaving the park one day, she sees a dead squirrel by the curb. It's intact, no sign of what killed it. Maybe hit by a car. Or maybe strangled and left by someone who wants it found. When she crouches down—slowly, her belly is bigger—she notices that the squirrel's front paws, twisted and wizened like arthritic hands, are clasped as if praying. *What did it feel like?* she finds herself wondering.

She flees, her body awkward and heavy, a sound like faint laughter buzzing in her ears.

Their first afternoon in the duplex, she and Duff took a blanket to the park. She wasn't showing yet. They spread the blanket under the trees and watched some guys in hoodies and low-slung jeans playing basketball. She saw kids like them every day in lockup, separated by gang to avoid fights. These guys in the park just bumped chests when they disagreed over a play. Children swarmed the jungle gyms and counselors organized circle games and a bicycle cop patrolled the chain link perimeter. Claire felt lazily self-satisfied sprawled next to Duff.

She leaned against him. "See? A real neighborhood. Perfect for a baby."

He stayed quiet for a while. He still had his curls and looked closer to fourteen than thirty-four. They could only afford the new apartment if his money jobs stayed steady. But they'd find a way, like always. Take her pregnancy. They hadn't planned it. When the test stick changed color they were still living like kids, picking their apartment for its proximity to their favorite clubs and using beach chairs for furniture. But they went out and found the new place—all on their own, without help from anyone—a second-floor unit near Beverlywood with its good schools and nannies pushing strollers along the sidewalks. Their street had more skateboarders than strollers, and occasional bums scouting junk, but it was still better for kids than Hollywood, where music from the Strip sometimes made their walls vibrate.

"What if the foundry closes?" Duff said. "Or the seniors center lays me off?"

"We've eaten ramen before."

"But it was just us." He raised his face to the sun. "A baby, man."

He helped her up, and, arms laced, they crossed the park so she could pee in the surprisingly clean public restroom. She smiled as she washed her hands. They may not have planned this pregnancy, but they could plan everything else.

When they returned to their spot under the trees, their blanket was gone.

She orders a Taser on the internet the weekend after they meet Judith's baby. The website says it's small, the length and width of a dollar bill, and it doesn't look like an actual gun the way some Tasers do, which is comforting. Less risk of getting shot by someone who thinks she has a gun, although she has no intention of using it. It's for reassurance, that's all.

Duff is showering the night she orders the Taser. By the time he's done, she has shut the laptop and turned on the television. Her heart is pounding as he lies on the couch, resting his damp head in what's left of her lap.

"I managed to set up an interview," he says. He looks tired. Every night this week he has stayed up late job searching online. "A prosthetics company's looking for fitters. There's a training program and everything. Decent money. I'll bet we can rent a house right in Beverlywood soon, maybe near Savvy and Judith."

"What about sculpting?"

"The job's nine to five. I'll have mornings and evenings, weekends." He reaches up to stroke her face. "I even found a listing for a white-collar defense firm. The pay's outrageous. You'd be perfect."

"I'd be bored."

His face is solemn. She takes his hand, examines it, the thick, rough fingers, two knuckles uneven where he broke them carving headstones one year, the burn scars from chasing bronzes at the foundry. The odd jobs, the money jobs that get them through, help her stay a public defender instead of droning for some corporate law firm the way her father always wanted.

"Aren't you ever afraid of those kids?" he asks.

"I thought this was about money."

"It's also about knowing you're coming home every day in one piece."

The baby moves inside her. She finds herself hoping for a boy. A girl would be more vulnerable and difficult to protect. The Taser is small; it will fit snugly in the palm of her hand. She should tell Duff, let him remind her that they agreed it wasn't necessary. *My woman is fierce.*

He sits up. "I felt something." He presses his hand against her stomach; the baby bumps up against the pressure.

She puts her hand over his, feels a steady thumping from both outside and within. "I've been thinking. Maybe it's time I took some precautions."

He grins, his first real smile all week. "Finally. For starters you could take prenatal yoga instead of walking."

"That's not exactly what I had in mind—"

"You're almost six months pregnant. You shouldn't be wandering around alone in the dark. After what happened with those cats—"

"What, you think I can't take care of myself anymore?"

"I didn't say that. But why take any chances?"

"Living my life is not taking chances."

She picks up the television remote to channel surf. She senses him watching her, but she stays fixed on the TV.

"Okay," he says, "live your life."

She feels him shift position on the couch, so that he's just out of reach.

❀

She and Judith lose Zeke's objection on Monday morning. His case will be transferred out of juvenile court. He'll be tried as an adult. He shrugs when they tell him.

"I'm not sure you understand," Claire says. "You could wind up in an adult prison for good."

He chews his thumbnail cuticle, examines the wet, raw spot. "Could you bring me some comic books? Nothing bloody or they'll get taken away."

On the drive back to the office Judith says, "He belongs in a psych ward."

Claire stares out at the squat warehouses lining the traffic-packed freeway. They'll enter an insanity plea soon. If they win, Judith will get her wish: Zeke will be placed in a prison psych ward, his release contingent on him getting better, which isn't likely. He's a sociopath, Claire is certain even without a final psychiatric report. People like him don't get better. Still, there would be the possibility for his release. She thinks about the baby inside her. He'll have Duff's curls, her long-fingered hands. If he was playing in the park, if some bangers got in a fight; if someone pulled a gun and stray bullets flew. There would be nothing she could do. *Daddy, Mommy, help me.* Her clients' crimes used to feel distant and theatrical, like ghost stories told at slumber parties.

"Maybe he should stay locked up," she says.

Judith shakes her head. "He's just a kid. Someone has to help him." She grips the steering wheel and starts whistling an off-key, determined tune.

During a lunch break that week, Claire trades in her ancient cell phone for a sleek new Blackberry and immediately programs 911 onto speed dial. She puts the Taser in her glove compartment when she's in court or at Eastlake visiting Zeke. Otherwise she carries it everywhere.

She works from home on Friday so an alarm system can be installed. It's the most expensive kind, with a digital touch pad, window screens that trip the alarm when cut, a panic button to hang by the headboard. The landlord objected until Claire agreed to pay the difference between the cheaper system and this one. She tries not to think about her credit card balance creeping toward its limit. Just a few extra precautions. She can still take care of herself.

When Duff gets home, she's putting alarm company stickers on the kitchen windows.

"I didn't know we were getting an alarm."

She glances over her shoulder. He's holding a grocery bag.

"I thought I told you."

He puts down the bag. "It's a good idea, with the baby and all."

"It's no big deal."

"Hey, I'm agreeing with you."

Behind her she hears him rummaging through cabinets. She smooths out a sticker on the window over the sink, where she can see it while she's washing the dishes that accumulate so quickly lately. When she's not working or walking she's baking, trying out low-fat recipes to keep her weight in check. Even that makes her achy. Her ligaments and joints are already loosening for birth.

Duff says, "I got the job with the prosthetics company. Training starts in a few weeks."

She turns around. He's holding two champagne glasses. A bottle of sparkling cider sits on the counter.

"You're sure that's what you want?"

He puts down the glasses. "I thought it's what we both want."

"You insisted on this job, not me."

"Because you refuse to even contemplate changing jobs."

"Why should I? We're fine the way we are."

"Alarm system and all."

"I never said I wouldn't make adjustments."

She affixes a sticker to the breakfast nook window. When she turns back around, he's gone, the glasses abandoned by the sparkling cider.

Usually, once she's this far into a case, where most of the investigating is done, she's all business. Pick a strategy, stage the defense most likely to create reasonable doubt. She spends hours preparing exhibits, scouring evidence files for facts she may have missed, prepping and reprepping witnesses to ensure they'll withstand cross. Sometimes she doesn't see the client for a month.

She sees Zeke several times a week, driving out to Eastlake alone, bringing comic books and rolls of quarters for the visitation center vending machine. He points to what he wants and she slides quarters into the slot. He's not allowed to take money from her. Then they retreat to the tiny interview room with the table between them and she grills him: *What's your earliest memory of your mother, your father, your grandfather, your grandmother? Have you ever even met your father? Did you have friends? Did you have pets? Did you hurt them? What toys did you play with, what cartoons did you watch, what books did you read? Who touched you, where did they touch you, how did they get the chance?* She fills one notebook, another. Cautionary tales about how not to raise her child. What to protect him from.

The baby is so big he's crowding her lungs; she gets winded climbing out of bed. Still, she walks. Nothing dead or maimed for a while now. Every morning she leaves the duplex a little bit earlier; it's a little bit darker. Her jacket pockets are weighed down with her Blackberry and her Taser. On the mornings after she visits Zeke, she feels fully equipped, like she's done everything she can to protect herself. There is no faint laughter in the distance.

Duff starts training for his new job. In the evenings he spreads manuals and prosthetic limbs across the dining room table and pores over them. Often he doesn't finish until she's asleep. He's already studying when she wakes up. They haven't really been talking, a few clipped sentences—"Pass the creamer," "Want to shower first?"—but nothing more. Whenever she asks how the new sculpture's going, he says, "Moving along," without looking up.

He's not inside when she gets back from her walk one morning. She finds him out back in the studio examining the marble block. It hasn't changed much, the woman still mostly merged with stone. Duff is dressed for work, pressed khakis, a new polo shirt. His hair has grown out, the ridges of his skull softened by thick waves, dark at the roots, that aren't nearly as luxurious as his curls.

"I was getting worried," she says.

He polishes the marble with a drop cloth. The file cabinet filled with sketches, the metal shelves lined with drawing pads, sculpture tools, mallets, chisels, blowtorches, boxes of wax and modeling clay—everything is coated with dust.

"This will make a good playroom," he says.

"Where would you work?" When he doesn't answer, she says, "You can't just quit."

"One of us has to start sacrificing."

He won't look at her, fixing on her jacket. She should hug him, remind each of them what they risk with a poorly chosen word.

"I'm the one renting out my body for nine months," she says. "Even my toes feel bloated."

"This isn't about you anymore."

"You think I don't know that—"

"Claire, what's in your—"

He grabs her jacket pocket, and she's so startled she grabs too, it's reflex, she's imagined so often pulling out the Taser to stun an attacker.

Duff gets it first.

"Are you nuts?" He shakes the Taser at her. She's never seen him so angry. "If I can take this away from you, someone else can too. Someone can use it on you. Isn't that what you told me?"

"That won't happen."

"Why, because you say so? You can't control everything."

"I'm protecting myself—"

"So go to the gym instead of walking alone. Or get a job that doesn't lock you up with rapists and murderers every day—"

"You mean I should give up, like you."

"No, you should get realistic."

"My whole life doesn't have to change just because I'm pregnant!"

"Christ, Claire, grow up! Everything already has changed!"

He throws the Taser at the sculpture; it hits the shoulder, chipping the marble. She stands staring at the chip, listening to his ragged breaths.

Zeke is being transferred to the adult county jail. They file a flurry of motions, but there's nothing they can do. Given the violence of his crime, the court thinks he's too great a risk in a less secure juvenile facility.

The last time Claire sees him at Eastlake, his fingertips are bloody crescents, the nails barely visible in the ravaged flesh.

"Can I go to school there?" he asks.

She shakes her head. "But you can do correspondence courses."

"I've gotta have books." There is panic in his voice. He sounds like a kid. He is a kid.

She's outside the duplex about to start her morning walk when Judith texts to say the transfer's done. The text message glows in the murky dawn light. "Now he'll get a crash course in Murder 101," it says. Claire imagines Judith's whistle, a short, thin sound with nothing musical about it.

Her vision blurs as she stows her phone with her Taser in her jacket pocket and starts walking. They bump rhythmically against her taut, heavy belly. Zeke will probably lose everything, and there's not much she can do about it. That boy, his bitten nails, those smudged glasses, his fear so palpable and childlike. She failed him. What's worse, she's relieved to have failed. What kind of person does that make her, to be happy she couldn't help a kid?

Before she knows it, she's reached the park, which looks empty and quiet in the slowly brightening sunlight. Anyone could be lurking behind the handball court or beneath the play structure. She shivers, zips her jacket to her chin. No. This is her neighborhood, her park, which she laps every day, as consistent as clockwork. Soon, she'll be pushing a jog stroller while the baby coos and gurgles, a cap covering his wispy curls, a blanket tucked around him. Her responsibility. Hers to guide, to protect.

Once inside the gate, she hears mewling. Several yards away stands a small gray tabby, one paw raised as if deciding whether to flee. It sniffs the air, its neck extended, and mewls again, steps toward the shadowy trees.

There's movement beneath the trees. Claire freezes. The cat creeps forward. A hooded, slender figure shifts out of the shadows, one hand extended, holding something. The person crouches and gently shakes whatever's in hand at the cat. An odor reaches Claire, a fishy stench that almost makes her retch. He's coaxing the cat over, maybe to feed it. Probably.

As the cat creeps closer, the person digs his free hand into his hoodie pocket. Maybe he's grabbing a knife, the tabby another victim. The Taser is in her own pocket, within reach. She could use it, knock him on his ass, worry about the consequences later. But she can't get herself to move.

Light glints off whatever he's holding out to the cat. It's a can. Claire breathes, a slow, long breath. Food. Feeding. Fine. Everything's fine.

The cat reaches the outstretched hand. Swiftly, the guy drops the can, grabs the cat by its scruff, pins it down. It yowls, flails, claws until the guy lets go, cursing, and the cat races up a nearby tree.

"You little shit," he shout-whispers and stands to look up at the wailing cat crouched on a branch.

His hood falls off. It's a girl, not a guy. Pony-tailed, wide-eyed, heart-shaped face. A girl who might live down the street. A girl Claire might ask to babysit without a thought.

"Don't," Claire tries to yell, but it comes out a choked, wordless cry.

The girl sees her and smiles, slowly, slyly. "Wanna help?" she says and leans over to pick up whatever she dropped. The can stinking of cat food. But what if it isn't, what if she's reaching for a knife or some other weapon?

Claire takes one step backward, another. The Taser. The phone. Get them. Fend off the girl, call the police.

She turns and stumbles out of the park, the Taser and phone pounding against her belly that she supports with both hands. The baby kicks inside her; a tiny limb presses against her palms. The treed cat keeps yowling, but she doesn't look back. She can't be fearless anymore. Her body isn't only hers. Nothing will ever be solely hers again. She cradles her stomach and runs.

Lamb

Any other day I wouldn't have answered the door. I would have checked the peephole, seen who it was, and hidden. But lack of sleep had addled my brain. So when the bell rang, I got out of bed, as blurry as a sleepwalker, with Luca clasped to my shoulder, my only concern that please, God, don't let this child wake up. He'd nursed most of the night. My nipples were raw. There was bottled breast milk so Judith could help, but she'd worked late again preparing for a trial and then had left at dawn, leaving me alone with Luca. Again. The house felt empty, terrifying, Luca a kamikaze of demand that I couldn't satisfy. Clutching him, I stumbled down the hallway and opened the front door.

On the porch stood my mother with two large suitcases. Not a word in two years, yet there she was with enough luggage for a month.

"You don't look like you just had a baby," she said, her voice more gravelly than I remembered. Too dumbfounded to protest, I stepped aside as she picked up the suitcases and brushed past.

"Where's Pop?" A safe question. *Why are you here?* could too easily turn into *How dare you come here?*

"Home. Someone has to run the market." Her trim, sturdy figure, the fitted serge dress, impenetrable as a coat of mail—unchanged. But her neck was wattled and her careful French twist more salt than pepper. The suitcases thumped against her dress as she put them down. The bigger one left a damp splotch. She walked to the baby grand in the living room. "Fancy-schmancy," she said and tapped a key.

"Judith plays."

"Ah." The slightest wince, but it was there. She closed the lid and sat on the couch to scrutinize me. "Skinny after six weeks," she said. "Just like my family. Once we have the baby, poof, it's like we were never pregnant. Your father's side, they blow up like balloons and never deflate." She lifted her chin. "This must be my grandchild."

"His name is Luca." I sat in an armchair across the room and shifted Luca to my other shoulder. She looked so small, her hands clasped like a child waiting for confession. The Rose DiCorscia I knew would have taken the baby already. "What are you doing here, Ma?"

She drew herself up. "It's my only grandson's first Easter."

"He still confuses night and day."

"Start early with tradition, they'll have it always. Besides, you can't ignore the holiest day of the year. Too tempting for *il malocchio*." She laughed a little as she shook her fist with her pinkie and index fingers extended toward the floor, to ward off *il malocchio*, the evil eye. A nonsense childhood habit, she claimed, even though my whole life she couldn't resist shaking those horns at the ground whenever she felt threatened.

She stood up from couch and walked to the bigger suitcase. A puddle had formed underneath. "Ach," she clucked and wiped it with a handkerchief pulled from her sleeve. "I told the butcher, it's a long flight from New Jersey to California, use extra plastic wrap. We'll need a pail and some bags of ice. The meat will get tough if we defrost it too fast."

Already she was listing demands. What could possibly need defrosting? I clutched Luca tighter. His eyelids fluttered. He frowned, as if deciding whether he knew me, and wailed. It seemed like he'd just fallen asleep. Reflexively, I checked the mantle, where a clock lay face down, then the shadowed circle on the entry wall. That one was in the closet. I'd hidden all the clocks. Better not to count the minutes Luca refused to sleep. He screamed louder. Judith could get him to stop with a nuzzle.

"Savina, don't look so panicked." My mother walked over, prodded Luca's diaper. "Wet," she announced and took him.

I almost snatched him back, but he wasn't a wishbone to be tugged until he broke. My mother touched his nose and murmured. His wails faded.

"He knows his *nonna*," she said. She tucked him into the crook of her arm. "I'll change him. You rest. The lamb I'll take care of later."

I trailed her into the hallway. "Lamb?"

"In the big suitcase." She opened a door, peered inside, shut it again, all the while expertly jiggling the baby. Another door, opened and closed. "For Easter dinner." She found the nursery and disappeared inside.

I used to be known for my powers of concentration. Pinpoint, they called me at the Los Angeles DA's office. I got so focused on my work, I tuned out everything else. The district attorney himself had once stood outside my office—cramped, immaculate, clockless—and called my name twice before tossing a book on my desk. I didn't look up or even flinch, he said later.

After Luca's birth, I couldn't focus long enough to read the newspaper. The evening of my mother's arrival was no different. Judith stood in the kitchen beside an ice-filled garbage pail and muttered something, but I couldn't make myself listen. I leaned against the counter and gazed at the pail. Inside was the lamb, which my mother had packed in crushed ice after putting Luca down for his nap and settling into the guest room. The lamb's muzzle was barely visible beneath an icy veneer. It was smaller than Luca's downy skull.

"Savvy, you haven't heard anything I've said."

Judith was grinning at me. No point in lying.

"Not a word."

"This thing weighs at least fifteen pounds. She must have checked it to get through airport security. I can't believe it stayed frozen."

Judith sniffed the pail, her nose wrinkled, her pale, freckled face haloed by curls. Typical, her interest in how this had happened instead of why, the inner forces that had pulled my mother relentlessly toward our new family, which was still tenuous and untested. The frozen lamb might be a peace offering, a gesture of acceptance, even. *Sinning against nature, that's what you're doing.* More likely a decoy.

"The cold packs did their job," I said. The little blue pouches— thirty altogether—lay sweating in the sink. Earlier, my mother had piled them there matter-of-factly, tsking at the fully melted ones. As if carting a carcass from Newark to Los Angeles should have been trouble free, easily conquered by the likes of Rose DiCorscia. I walked to the pail and swept away some ice. The muzzle stuck out, the eyes clearly visible. They looked reproachful.

Judith adjusted her rumpled suit jacket. "She really thinks we're going to eat this."

"We had a whole lamb every Easter. A bigger one without the head."

"Ah, Easter. The day we Jews killed the Christ child so we could use his blood to make the matzo."

"Very funny. Even my mother's not that extreme. And Easter is about the resurrection, not the crucifixion."

"A fine-line distinction for someone who's skipped church since high school. Is this thing"—Judith gestured at the pail—"staying here?"

"Meat belongs in the kitchen."

"Savvy, we don't celebrate Easter, remember? You can't let her walk all over you. All over us."

Static, like a burst from a walkie-talkie. My mother stood by the door holding the baby monitor. Her graying hair hung loose to her shoulders and spit-up stained her bathrobe lapel.

"Ma. Judith's home."

"I have eyes. I can see."

Judith extended her hand. "Nice to meet you again."

My mother stayed put. Judith kept her hand outstretched. She would stand there until Christ rose again. So would the old Rose DiCorscia. All day she had behaved. She'd played with the baby while I'd pumped breast milk; she'd changed him, rocked him to sleep, refrained from correcting me or warning me about going straight to Hell. *God won't pretend He doesn't notice just because you've got a good track record. Vatican II is horse manure. He can still be merciless when He needs to. No more protecting you from il malocchio.*

My mother touched Judith's hand—"Yes, hello"—and strode to the pail. She dug in up to her elbow. "A little give to the flesh. Good. Tomorrow we'll take out some ice, the next day some more, and so on." When she stood, her sleeve was damp. "I made a grocery list. There's nothing but dust in the pantry. I guess you haven't been cooking, Savina, what with a new baby and no help. We'll need wood for the fire pit, a spit, some support forks. You must know a good butcher who can thread the lamb. Although I'm not above doing it myself. Your great-grandmother used to butcher her own lamb, did I ever tell you that? She raised it in our barn with the cows. When it was time to kill it, I used to hide under my mother's bed, but I could still hear the poor thing bleating. Such a ruckus, all the other animals joining in. And then silence, like the cows and chickens were afraid they were next. Though the cows shouldn't have worried. My grandmother loved them more than she ever loved us, at least according to my mother. After Nonna skinned and gutted the lamb, she'd skewer it, push through the skull like it was an eggshell." She looked at Judith, whose face wore something between a grimace and a smile.

"We don't have a fire pit," Judith said.

"The gardener can dig one. Although I'm not above doing it myself."

"No gardener either. Anyway, there are too many low-hanging trees for a fire."

My mother drew herself up. "It's tradition."

I stepped between them. "We'll cut it up and cook it in the oven."

They both frowned.

"It won't taste the same," my mother said.

"Ma, stop."

That stare, measuring how much further she could push. "All right. I'll check your pans tomorrow. By the way, Luca is sleeping like an angel. I gave him a bottle around eight, I think. I couldn't find a clock." She picked up one overturned on the counter. "Still with this habit, Savina. I've told you, time doesn't stop just because you can't see it passing."

A surprised laugh from Judith. "That's what I say."

"Whenever she had a paper due, she'd hide all our clocks in the basement."

"We can't program the coffee maker because she won't set the clocks on the appliances."

Both women were smiling. I made myself smile too. "Enough."

Judith kissed my cheek. "We're joking."

My mother scowled and repiled the ice packs in the sink.

Judith picked up her briefcase. "I've got to research an objection anyway, for that transfer motion on Monday morning."

"The double homicide?" I asked. Each day I questioned Judith about work, hungry for details despite a resentful twinge. For two weeks after Luca's birth, she'd rushed home to help. Then she landed the defense of a fourteen-year-old honors student who dismembered his grandparents while his mother honeymooned in Mexico.

Afterward he called her and announced, "Honeymoon's over." The state wanted him tried as an adult.

Judith nodded. "Our expert says Zeke's brain wasn't developed enough to understand his actions had consequences."

My mother dried her hands on a dish towel. "That's right, you're a lawyer, too. You defend guilty people. My daughter puts them in jail." Before I could object, my mother gave a little laugh. "Now's not the time for a moral debate. I'll say goodnight." Stiff-backed, she marched out.

Judith turned to me. "How long's she staying?"

"I didn't ask." Then, at Judith's deadpan gaze: "Probably only until Easter. That's what, a week?"

"Nine days."

"Try to get along with her."

Judith hugged me. "You'll barely know I'm here."

I rested my cheek on Judith's shoulder. *You're never here*, I wanted to say. As we walked down the hall, I avoided looking at the guest room door.

The bris had been my idea, but when the time came, eight days after the birth, I had been too sore to help much. Judith suppressed her inner slob and did everything. A hot buffet, a gift table in the entry, programs with "Lior: My light, I see" printed on the cover—Luca's Hebrew name and its meaning. The mohel came early with supplies, including the razor-sharp *izmel*, which he placed on the baby grand. Judith hurried around arranging and rearranging (and still leaving things disarrayed) while I watched from the couch, Luca fussing in my arms. "Can I at least fold napkins?" I asked, but Judith waved me off. "Enjoy the baby." As if caring for him were my only function.

As soon as the guests arrived, I handed him to Judith and started making adjustments (antipasti drizzled with olive oil, a frayed throw pillow hidden away), ignoring Judith when she called me over. Such luxury, to bend and stretch without Luca on my hip.

Finally, light-headed, I surveyed the crowded room. By the piano, Judith held the baby as she talked with the mohel and the rabbi, a lesbian wearing a yarmulke on her platinum crew cut. Our temple was beyond progressive. Joining was also my idea. With two mothers and a data file for a father, Luca would need to believe in something. *Sinning against nature.*

Catholicism wasn't an option.

When the mohel beckoned to everyone, I found a seat in back. Judith would hold Luca during the service, we'd agreed. I was too sore to stand for so long, and blood made me queasy, I'd reminded her. Really, though, I wanted to sit and enjoy my empty arms.

"Blessed is the one arriving," the mohel began.

The baby burped as loud as a man. I imagined the spit-up on his chin and shifted, vaguely nauseated. Everyone else tittered.

"I taught him that," Judith said and beamed at him, completely, effortlessly in love.

It hit me then: the wrongness of my choice. Bearing Luca and staying home with him—also my idea. Pinpoint. Those powers of concentration. I was built for success, my mother used to brag. The highest conviction rate since starting in homicide two years prior; before, in Manhattan, the most billable hours in the firm for five years running. But my body had protested with ulcers, IBS, shingles. And the exhaustion. I could catnap standing in an elevator. Parenthood offered a graceful exit and seemed easy by comparison. Bliss, to focus on something so sweet and oblivious to achievement.

But when Luca cried, I cringed; when he spit up, I had to put my head between my knees. And that immediate adoration mothers supposedly felt—I didn't. A distant affection, yes, and fear, that I couldn't soothe him, that I'd rather be anywhere else. But the surety of love I'd felt with him inside me—that had disappeared.

The mohel slipped a wine-soaked handkerchief into Luca's mouth. I closed my eyes. When I opened them, I was slumped, Judith crouched beside me. "He barely cried," she said. "Sit up, love, we have to do the naming. Please, come hold the baby."

Lior, our son. My light, I see.

Judith holed up in the study all weekend. Whenever she emerged, I tensed. My mother might lash out at her, or they might compete over who knew Luca best. Worse, they both might notice how he preferred them to me.

But my mother behaved herself. At night, she fed Luca and let me sleep. The freezer overflowed with marinara and homemade gnocchi. The lamb thawed, its eyes bluish and dilated. Tight-lipped my mother surveyed our dented roasting pans before borrowing one from our neighbor with the loud, barrel-chested dog and the little boy in the wheelchair. I avoided them whenever possible; the mere sight of them disturbed me. If I happened to be on our porch when the woman wheeled her son with his vacant gaze down their driveway, I waved and ducked my head as I hurried back inside.

When my mother returned from Mass on Palm Sunday, she didn't lament my absence, only the traffic and the twisting city streets. "I kept getting lost," she said as she placed a jar of palm frond crosses on the kitchen table. "Even New Jersey's traffic isn't this bad." Judith ignored the crosses but dragged the lamb into the laundry room while my mother watched.

I slept uninterrupted two nights running. The sky seemed crisper, the baby more alert and cuddly. He even managed a crooked smile, his first.

"Gas," Judith said.

"Definitely a smile," said my mother. I had smiled at two weeks, she said, the earliest of all three children. "Always my overachiever." I'd hiccupped when crying, like Luca. His long, thin thumbs were like Dommy's and the fuzz on his ears like Connie's. I welcomed the ghostly presences of my brother, my sister, my own baby self. Luca had a history. His habits could be predicted. "Watch how easy," my mother said as she sprinkled his bottom with cornstarch. His diaper rash improved within hours. I put back the clocks and didn't ask when she was leaving.

Sunday evening, Judith settled on the couch where I was burping Luca. My mother sat nearby, folding laundry. Quiet coos but no burps. She and Judith shook their heads. My throat clenched. Judith took him and draped him face-first over her knees, then firmly patted his back. A huge burp; the baby squawked.

"Works every time," said Judith.

"Good trick," my mother conceded.

Neither mentioned my failed attempts, and they were being civil, better than I had hoped. My panic faded.

Early Monday morning, my mother borrowed the neighbor's pruning shears to tame the backyard, a postage stamp of ragged sod framed by tangled vines and weeds. She'd already pruned the date palm, leaving a fan on top. The cypress was a perfect triangle. From a lounge chair I watched her chop at the bougainvillea covering the back fence with precise, ferocious swoops.

Whistling tunelessly, Judith stepped outside with her briefcase. Her hair was neatly combed. Her only dress pants that didn't bag at the ankles bore faint scorch marks.

I shaded my eyes. "What's the occasion?"

"I told you Friday. I'm trying to keep Zeke's case in juvenile court where it belongs."

"The kid's a sociopath. You'll never win."

"No history of violence, and he looks like an overgrown cherub. He barely has hair on his balls. I've got a shot."

"I'd make sure he rotted."

"Glad it's not your case."

We watched my mother sift weeds from dirt clods.

"She's been at it since dawn," I said. "Obsessed."

"Reminds me of someone." Judith grinned and called, "Fast work, Rose. You shouldn't bother, though."

My mother savaged another weed. "Gardening relaxes me. And I've cleared a spot for the fire pit. Grace, that nice lady next door, recommended someone to dig it. Although I'm not above doing it myself. She said I can borrow any tools we need. She's got plenty, poor thing. All alone with a disabled boy. He had an accident last year. She doesn't have time to garden anymore. I made friends with their dog so he'll let me into the yard."

Judith's smile stiffened. "You know our neighbors better than we do," she called before muttering to me, "Tell her no or I will. Again."

"A fire pit could be nice." When Judith frowned, I said, "I'll talk to her. Will you be late?"

"Depends on what happens with Zeke."

"Why should it depend on anything?" My voice carried; I could tell by the way my mother's hoe paused.

"I'll try to be earlier." Judith touched my shoulder. "Let's not make a scene."

She leaned down for a kiss. I couldn't help but turn my cheek. She sighed. "Have you asked yet when she's leaving?"

I glanced at my mother, who stared hard at the dirt. "No. Soon."

With a brisk wave, Judith trotted out the gate. My mother watched her go, her hoe raised as if poised for attack.

❀

Later that morning while I napped, I dreamed of the bris, Judith sitting in a wheelchair holding Luca, the mohel helping her undo the baby's diaper, the flashing *izmel*, and then Judith stood with a bigger boy in her arms, his face hidden against her chest and his pants stained red. She held him close as she whispered through a confessional grate that appeared beside her. Suddenly she looked at me and shook her horned fist at the ground. *You wanted him to believe in something*, she said. *A lot of good that did.*

Then I was awake, my pulse racing. I kicked off the covers and walked outside to the garden. My mother was digging in the far bed. Luca slept in his Moses basket on the patio. I crouched beside him. His soft spot pulsed beneath my cupped palm. A swell of emotion—something like love.

My mother knelt beside me. "He stops your heart, he's so beautiful."

"I shouldn't have slept so long."

"That's why I'm here, to let you rest." She brushed back my hair. "Judith left early."

That underlying disapproval. Days ago, it had rankled. Now, it seemed fair. Luca was only eight weeks old. Things could continue this way, Judith home to kiss him goodnight, for a few hours on weekends, most of her time spent strategizing defenses; me relearning the alphabet, arguing about undone homework, my own knowledge of courtroom tactics stale and outdated. How appealing that all had seemed when I'd assumed I could excel at anything. What if Luca sensed my resentment, reflected it back on me like sun off a puddle until his rage exploded like that boy Judith was so staunchly defending? The boy's image came into focus: floppy bangs, an uncertain smile, his eyes buggish behind thick glasses. He could be anyone's son.

"Judith hasn't been much help," I said slowly.

"You can't expect her to have the same maternal feelings. He's our blood."

"She loves him as much as I do." My face felt hot. I'd responded too vehemently, almost like I didn't believe myself.

My mother regarded me, then stood. "I'll stay as long you need me. My ticket's open-ended. Come. Some exercise will do you good."

She led me to a rectangular clearing centered by a shallow hole.

"This better not be what I think it is," I said.

"You used to love my Easter lamb. It won't be the same." She held out a shovel.

I hesitated. My mother had cut all the overhanging branches. The hot coals, the scent of roasting meat, palm frond crosses tucked around the platter. Heads lowered over folded hands. *Bless us, Father, for these thy gifts.*

I took the shovel and started digging.

Once the pit was dug, wider than it was deep, we bundled Luca into his car seat and the lamb (marbled and bloody in an oversized cooler) into the trunk. First to Home Depot for a skewer, iron support forks, stones to line the pit. Then to a butcher shop my mother had noticed on her way to church. Bouncing Luca on her hip, she persuaded the owner to gut the carcass, sever its head and hooves, and skewer it by Good Friday, four days away, all for free.

At home, we worked into the afternoon, stopping for Luca to nurse. My tender breasts barely ached as he squinted up at me, his fist batting my chest. Almost easy, almost natural. Then back to digging, hauling, digging some more, positioning the supports, the U-shaped cardboard wall covered in tinfoil, until the fire pit resembled the one from my childhood.

When Judith got home, my mother and I were making a teepee of wood.

"We're almost done," my mother called. "Come look."

Judith paused, then walked into the house. The door slammed.

My mother sat back on her haunches. "Someone's in a bad mood."

I could feel her staring as I followed Judith inside. I stopped to peek at Luca, who slept in his Moses basket with his fists against his cheeks.

Judith was sorting mail in the kitchen.

"How did the motion go?"

An envelope slapped the countertop. "We lost."

"I'm sorry." Though I wasn't. He deserved to be catapulted into adulthood, this boy who could commit such a horrific act just to spite his mother. "You shouldn't have won."

"He's a child, for God's sake, and he's being tried as an adult. They could lock him up for life. Every time I see him, I think, what if that were Luca? Would we want everyone to give up on him?"

"How can you mention Luca in the same sentence as that monster? Who, by the way, you see more than our son."

"So that's what outside is about."

Fraying my consciousness, a thin cry. A heaviness in my breasts, a letting go. "Why does it matter where we make the damned lamb?"

"What matters is that we're celebrating at all." Judith shook the jar of palm frond crosses, which rustled like whispered threats. "We agreed. No Christmas trees, no Easter egg hunts."

"Your family had a tree."

"That's not the point, and you know it. We decided together how to raise him. You can't unilaterally renege."

"What about my being stuck alone with him? Doesn't *that* go against our agreement?"

"It's this case. When it's over—"

"There'll be another."

"I'm doing the best I can!"

"If this is your best—" *we're screwed* was my finish, but I stopped. Judith should be helping more, but at least the baby loved her. I was the one who couldn't cope. "How could I be such a bad mother so fast?" My nose was running. When had I started crying?

Judith hugged me. "That's what you think? Savvy, it's not true—"

"Savina, what's this about no Christmas trees?"

My mother stood by the back door with Luca fussing in his basket. I stepped away so quickly Judith staggered. She looked between me and my mother.

"We're raising Luca Jewish," Judith said. "Savvy didn't tell you?"

"What? You can't."

"We can, Rose." Each word a terse missile.

"How dare you—" My mother stopped. "Savina, you're his mother. Of course you'll raise him Catholic. Savina?"

Outside a breeze fluttered the weeds piled near the fire pit. The anger, the disappointment certain to be on my mother's face. The counter felt cool beneath my grip as I stared out the window. Finally, I heard rustling behind me—my mother setting down Luca's basket.

"He's hungry," she said.

The back door shut.

I turned to Judith. "You should have let me tell her," I said.

She stared at me, her freckles stark against the pale, angry landscape of her face. "You're afraid to tell her anything that matters."

The kitchen door creaked as she left the room. I picked up Luca and looked outside to watch my mother retreat across the yard.

❀

Lamb had never been part of my family's daily diet. When the pastor came for Sunday dinner we might have his favorite, *stinco d'agnello*, stewed until it fell off the bone. Sometimes at Christmas there was a rack of lamb served with lemon balm pesto instead of mint jelly. Once a year my father attended a *capozella* feast at his Italian-American club, each man presented with a roasted lamb's head, the brain, eyes, and tongue intact. The one time I tagged along, I burst into tears when my father dug out an eyeball and popped it in his mouth like an olive.

Every Easter, though, there was a whole lamb, its legs hugging the spit in an upside-down double curtsey. It roasted all day over the fire pit by the boarded-up barn where my great-grandmother had kept the milking cows. First thing in the morning, my father would pyramid wood, arrange the giant iron supports, and set the lamb to roasting. An uncle or a cousin turned it while my family attended Mass.

At church, Dommy stood beside the other altar boys and swung a brass urn smoking with incense that stung my nose. My father paced in back while my mother sat beside me and Connie in a front pew. My mother's lace mantilla was always pinned in place, her hands a perfect steeple. A glare from her was enough to keep me from poking Connie or pleating the hymnal pages. On the altar drowning in lilies the priest preached atonement and loyalty to God for sacrificing His beloved Son. *What might we sacrifice for Him, who rose on this day so that we could be forgiven?* I drifted on the tide of his booming voice and imagined the lamb turning on the spit, my mother polishing serving platters, the Easter eggs and chocolates hidden in the yard.

The guests always arrived as my family pulled into the driveway: aunts, uncles, cousins, friends, anyone who had no place to go on this, the holiest of days. The men were sent to watch the meat. Better they should pass a sambuca bottle around the fire, my mother said, than get in the way. The women set out the antipasti, my mother repositioning each shining platter and palm frond cross. Then the Easter egg hunt began.

So much more than eggs to find. I raced my siblings and cousins around the yard, filling my basket with picture books, stuffed animals, candy, hardboiled eggs dyed in rainbow hues. The satin of the bright shells, the scent of chocolate, my mother beaming as she pointed out a missed egg, a hidden bag of jellybeans. One year, a warm, late Easter, Dommy found a journal with a little latch and key. My mother took it, gave him some candy to keep him from crying, then handed me the journal. "For you," she said. "Special."

When the hunt was over, the other children retreated behind the barn to barter marshmallow chicks for cream-filled bunnies. I took my basket under the table where the women were gathered. Their new spring sandals shifted around me. Wedged heels for the younger women, squat ones with thick straps for the *zias* and *nonnas*. My mother, as always, barefoot. I pulled out the journal. The cover, purple velour, bled on my sweaty palms. Mine alone. Special. Above, the women's voices, my mother's soaring over the rest. "Savina's such a thinker. She needs somewhere to write things down." I stretched out, the book pillowing my cheek. My mother peeked under the tablecloth. "My little genius," she whispered. The obligation of being her favorite. I couldn't let her down. The women kept chattering above me. The heat of the day. The lull.

Then my mother crawled under the table to hug me awake. "Sweetheart, dinnertime." As I emerged, rubbing my eyes and yawning, one cheek purple with ink (Connie would tease me later, tell everyone I had a hickey), my mother called to the men to hurry, the children had to be fed. The men huddled around the pit, poking the carcass to see whether the juices ran clear. Ready for carving, they finally declared. I clutched my book and watched them carry over the lamb. My mouth watered at the thought of the sweet, succulent meat.

My mother sat by the fire pit until dark. Then, all night, she paced, slippers whisking, from kitchen to nursery. The study door remained shut, Judith bunkered behind it. I tossed on the couch. By the time I drifted off, it was dawn. I didn't hear Judith leave, barely noticed when my mother crouched beside me. "Sleep, I have bottles," she whispered. "Luca and I are going out."

I awoke to quiet. Even the dog next door was silent. In the kitchen, there was a note in my mother's tidy print: "Be back soon." No cars in the driveway. All the clocks faced forward, but I hadn't bothered to check when my mother had left. Too woozy and worried, wondering whether, how, to apologize. And to whom—my mother, Judith, Luca?

Half an hour. My breasts ached. I pumped a few ounces, stored them in the refrigerator. There had been several bottles on the top shelf, enough for the whole day. They were gone.

Judith sounded tinny on the phone. "She's probably lost. Stay there, she might call. I'll check the parks."

An hour. Anything could have happened, an accident with irreversible consequences, like what happened to the neighbor boy listing in his wheelchair. He'd fallen from something, hit his head. I'd never asked for details. I'd actively avoided knowing. This heaviness, this dread flooding me. This must be what his mother felt daily. I had to shake it off.

The sun rose higher. Judith called from her cell. Once more around the neighborhood and then home. "We'll find them, Savvy."

I paced the living room, watched the street. Maybe my mother had bundled him up and boarded a plane. Her suitcases were in the guest room, but her purse was gone, her wallet and ID. By now, they could be halfway to New Jersey.

Another hour. Judith came home. I tossed clocks in drawers, turned them face down, to the walls. I circled the fire pit, took one stone, another, and threw them at the house. Judith joined in. The chips in the stucco became a gaping hole. Each stone hit the house like a gunshot. The neighbor's dog started howling.

Tires squeaked in the driveway.

"Let me," I said when Judith tried to follow.

Out front, I raced to the car as it stopped. "Where have you been?" I yelled and flung open the back door. Luca's eyes darted behind thin, closed lids. Gently I unlatched the car seat. He looked fine. When I touched one small fist, his fingers unfurled. He whimpered, arched his neck, his eyes shut. A baby dream—of what? Shadows, voices. His mother's—my own—scent.

My mother stepped out, smoothing her dress, the impenetrable serge. She held up a pamphlet. "Baptismal Rites, Saint Timothy's Church."

"Ma, you didn't."

She clutched the pamphlet. "It took three churches, but I finally found a priest through Grace, your neighbor. What if Luca had an accident like her boy, God forbid? Or worse. Luca would've spent eternity in Limbo with the other unbaptized babies."

"We don't believe in Limbo."

"Of course we do."

"No, Ma. Judith and I. His parents. If we want to shave our heads and become Hare Krishnas, or raise him Buddhist or Muslim or Jewish, that's up to us."

"There's more at stake than your unnatural lifestyle with that woman." The words spat out like a taste of rancid milk. She shook her horned fist at the ground, as if to ward me off my own child.

I steadied myself against the car. She hadn't changed. How had I allowed myself to believe such a miracle could occur?

Behind me, the front door banged. Judith cautiously walked over. "Everyone's home safe."

I hugged the car seat tight. "No. My mother's leaving. She's not welcome anymore." Then I marched past Judith, inside.

A musky aroma filled the house, had filled it since dawn. In the bedroom I lay reading, Luca's Moses basket within reach. Since yesterday's fight, I'd kept him close and avoided my mother, whose suitcases were in the entryway awaiting the red-eye. I even strapped him to my chest in a carrier when I returned my neighbor's gardening tools earlier. I made sure to look straight at my neighbor—Grace—and to smile at her little boy, Aiden. He sat motionless in his wheelchair, though he shot me glances when I placed his hand on Luca's head. That small, damp hand with its surprisingly steady grip, the only thing that seemed steady about this broken boy. It almost made me seek out my mother when I got home. *Life is fickle*, I'd almost said. *Please stay.* Instead, I'd retreated to the bedroom.

Now, I set down my book on the bed beside me and sat up to look outside. The sun dipped below the treetops, staining the yard with a pinkish glow. My mother sat on a bench by the headless lamb suspended above the coals. The head was cooking in the oven, the eyes gelatinous, the tongue leathery in the gaping mouth. After our fight, she'd reassembled the fire pit and convinced the butcher to finish late last night. "Of course, if you can't make time," I'd heard her say on the phone, "I'm not above doing it myself."

Outside, she stood to turn the burnished carcass, both her mitted hands grasping the skewer, then hushed the dog barking next door—"Butchie, *basta!*"—before walking toward the house. I lay back against the pillows, one hand grasping the Moses basket.

Soon, I heard footsteps in the hallway. The bedroom door clicked as my mother opened it. "I thought I heard him crying," she said. "All that barking woke him up, I thought. I didn't know you were here."

"Where else would I be?"

"Of course. That was a silly thing to say."

She stayed in the doorway, waiting to be invited inside. This woman who never waited for anything, who took what she felt was hers, heedless of the consequences. I turned away and opened my book.

Behind me, the door clicked shut. Soon I saw her cross the yard and resume her seat. Judith walked into view carrying two glasses. The pockets drooped out of her cutoff shorts. My mother patted the bench. From this distance, her expression was unreadable. Judith hesitated before she sat and passed my mother a glass. All day, I'd heard them talking in sporadic bursts, more forced civilities. Now, their voices skimmed the air, halting and staccato, then weaving together, a melody in need of tuning but recognizable. To anyone else, they might be friends exchanging confidences. Judith looked at the house. I flopped back down. My face burned, as if I'd been caught peeping in a window.

After a while, Judith walked into the bedroom and sat cross-legged beside me.

"Your mother keeps saying hello unprompted. I think she's lonely."

I studied my book. "Too bad."

"She gave me this."

I glanced over. Judith held out a gold medallion. On it was a monk surrounded by squirrels and birds.

"Your mother said it's Saint Francis, the one who protects animals. For Luca, but only if we want him to have it, she said."

The silence felt leaden. I scanned pages.

"Savvy, she's trying. Maybe she deserves a break."

"After what she did—"

"I know. She's impossible. But she was convinced she was doing the right thing for him." Judith gazed at Luca. "She adores our son. Maybe that's what matters most."

I sat up and scooted over. Luca was sucking on his fist. Yesterday he couldn't connect hand to mouth. Today, look at him. That small hand. Steadier now. I gathered him up, sniffed his crown. Milky, sweet. Mine. This certainty of love, so out of reach before my mother came. I felt a shift inside, an opening to possibility.

Cradling Luca, I stood and walked outside, the grass prickly beneath my bare feet. I sat beside her. She kept staring at the lamb.

"They shrink less if you cook them slowly," she said. "Your great-grandmother taught me that."

"You've told me that since I was five."

"A little reminding never hurt anybody."

"You have to trust me. About Luca, Judith. Everything."

She laced her fingers over her knees. "In sixth grade you decided to make a log cabin for a history project. I told you, use those Lincoln Logs that clip together and, poof, you're done. But no, you had to use twigs, they looked more authentic, like logs cut by pioneers. And no Elmer's glue. You made your own mortar from mud. A solid week trying to get the thing to stay together and you wound up with a pile of twigs. My straight-A student would have gotten an F if I hadn't convinced the teacher to let you do extra credit, paint a picture or something."

"I wrote a poem." Which had taken me almost as long. The teacher had hated it. I hadn't told my mother that part, or that it had taken several more extra credit assignments to save my grade. Let my mother keep her version. One day I might need such a story to convince myself I was doing what I could to protect my son as he flung himself down some seemingly disastrous path.

Luca was sucking his fist again. My mother watched. Coming to Los Angeles, staying in the same house with Judith—huge concessions for this proud woman, and not just made for her grandson. I wouldn't have made them. At least, not before Luca. I inched along the bench and laid my head on her shoulder.

"I've got more than a pile of twigs, Ma."

She hesitated before smoothing my hair, then stood to turn the spit. Together we watched the lamb rotate over the coals.

F-Man

That voice. Gravelly, loud, insistent. "Fuck you, fuck you, fuck you!" yelled over and over outside Mila's building, six-thirty sharp, mornings and evenings. God knew who it was, maybe one of the homeless guys who slept in the storefronts up on Pico and searched the dumpsters of shabby, Spanish-style multiplexes like hers. His hair was probably scraggly, his palms grimy, with long, crooked lifelines that helped him survive the streets of a city as sprawling and anonymous as Los Angeles. Maybe Mila's own life-lines would lend her the same resilience, more even, assuming Peter didn't find her. Although she wasn't really worried. He would never hurt her, not physically. Even the accident that had sent her into hiding had been her fault, not his.

Pillows couldn't block out the shouting, not even earplugs. In her old life she would have praised a student for projecting his voice with such conviction. One particularly loud morning she kicked off her covers and sat up. A revelation, to no longer feel sore. Only some stiffness in her neck remained from the car crash over a month ago. That and the rough hideousness of her voice. She got up to dress. Around the corner was a twenty-four-hour café with seats in back, far from the windows, one reason she'd rented this apartment last month, along with its hardwood floors and first-floor location near the building's rear exit to the alley. She kept her car there for a quick escape, just in case.

When she stepped into the hallway, Rune, the building's young manager, stood in the opposite doorway. Rune stretched and smiled at Mila. "He woke you up too, huh, Mary?" she said.

Mary Gordon, not Mila Genaro, was the name on Mila's lease. Rune didn't believe in credit or reference checks. She went on gut, she said. She kept her door open whenever she was home, sometimes late into the night, to encourage tenants to stop by. The other tenants ignored Mila whenever she hurried by, her face averted. According to the doctor, she should be "engaging in regular vocal activities," but she still avoided speaking whenever possible. She hated the way she sounded. Besides, why make friends? She might need to move on a moment's notice. But Rune, with her rust-colored hair and round, plain plate of a face that belied her fluty speaking voice—a coloratura, maybe, or a flowing lyric—possessed a determined cheer that was difficult to avoid.

Mila locked her door. "He seemed louder today," she said. Her voice sounded scratchy, low. Awful.

Rune yawned and retied her bathrobe. "It's just Harvey. He lives a few buildings down. He dresses like he's homeless, but he's just strange."

Rune's little boy stepped out from behind her. He had his mother's rust-colored hair, but his large eyes were fringed with extravagant lashes and his skin looked milky and flawless in the hallway's dim lights. He held a docile kitten face-forward in his arms, its back legs dangling.

His mother stroked his head. "Fender found a kitten in the alley by your parking spot. Paw-Paw, he named her, all by himself."

Fender held out the kitten for Mila to pet.

Rune startled, her chin jerking. "Look at that. Usually he's so shy."

"Allergies. I shouldn't touch," Mila lied.

The child stared at her. She'd never heard him speak. Sometimes she wondered what he sounded like, whether his voice was high and sweet like his mother's or grating like the shouter's, or something else altogether. Still, his silence was appealing. She craved silence lately. Before, she had spent her days inundated by sound, the swoop of her students' vocalizing, Peter's blaring baritone lecturing, lecturing, lecturing as they ate breakfast or dinner, dressed for work, undressed for bed, or, on bad days (there were a lot, near the end), yelling, berating, belittling. Silence had been a luxury. Now, she lolled in it, found herself protective of it.

Her cellphone rang. She pulled it from her jacket pocket: the caller ID was blocked. Not even her parents had this number, though she'd gotten it using their New Jersey address so it wouldn't have an LA area code and give away her current location. But Peter could be resourceful, especially if he thought he'd been robbed of the last word.

Mila forced herself to smile at Rune. "Has anyone been asking about me?"

"Nobody."

"If someone does, could you say I don't live here?"

Rune considered her, then nodded. "Tenants deserve privacy."

"Thanks." Mila waved at Fender. "Cute cat." She trotted down the hallway, out of the building.

Her hair was different—a pixie-short chestnut cap instead of her long, tawny mane—and she dressed in baggy shirts and nondescript jeans, tinted-lensed glasses shielding her green eyes. She made a point of slouching and walking slowly, not clipping along at her usual impatient pace, with her posture impeccably straight and ready to support her voice, project it to the rafters. But if anyone who knew her really looked, she was still herself. Except for the voice. That was different. Completely, irreparably different.

Of course the call was from Peter. She listened to his message at the café. "Hey, sweetheart," he said, as if no time had passed, as if she hadn't moved out last month while he was away overnight with the debate team. He taught history at the same New Jersey Catholic school where she'd taught music. They'd met there, had planned to marry in the chapel.

Maybe he was here already. It would be just like him to take time off and track her down. "After all I've been through," she could imagine him telling their principal, a grandmotherly type who would embrace whatever sob story Peter concocted to explain Mila's sudden resignation and disappearance. She listened to his message again. He could find her if he tried. This must be what women felt like after escaping men who beat them daily: relief tempered by constant anxiety. But that wasn't her and Peter. She wasn't afraid of him, not really. The accident had just woken her up. It had taken something away but given her something too: the realization that she should start over. She was barely thirty. It wasn't too late. He would leave her alone eventually, once he understood. Once she made him understand. She should call him back, convince him she needed to cut herself off from him to move on.

No. Convincing him wasn't her job anymore.

Days of picking up the phone, dialing, hanging up. Finally, one evening while curled on her Goodwill couch, she let herself call back. One call. Just one.

"I can't find the Cuisinart," he said without waiting for her hello. Her new number was probably already paired with her picture on his cell. "You used it last, right? Where'd you put it?"

"Try the pantry behind the soda."

Like that, she was answering to him again.

There was rustling in the background, as if he was searching shelves. "I'm making pizzelle for the fall festival," he said. "It's easier with the Cuisinart. Which is supposed to go back in the same place every time." Creeping in, that lecturing tone, which usually arrested her with its authority. He had twelve years on her, he reminded her often, twelve years of knowing more about how life worked. *Like you know anything, like you know how to do anything.* "I'm sure I'll find it," he said, brighter, friendlier, as if he sensed her clenching. "But I'm used to you helping."

"You're a good cook. You can do it alone."

"I'd rather do it with you."

The silence stretched out, demanding to be filled. Soon he'd say something: *This is your solution, to hide like a baby?* or maybe *I never thought you'd be such a quitter.* She picked at a tear in the couch. Her own words began to bubble up: *I'm sorry, forgive me, I'll come home.* But he was counting on her guilt. "I'm hanging up now," she said.

"Don't. Not yet. You sound great, like yourself. Maybe I can visit wherever you are. Knowing you, it's someplace warm, right? Or you could stop all this bullshit and come home."

Outside, the yelling started in the distance, approaching rapidly: "Fuck you, fuck you, fuck you!" She walked to the living room window, but the street was barely visible beyond the neighboring building. The strength in that voice, the certainty. Her hoarseness was permanent. Tiny hairline fractures in her larynx had healed improperly. She had waited to see a doctor a few days, which proved to be too many. She was fine, she kept telling herself. Just a little accident. She'd rear-ended someone while arguing with Peter and the steering wheel had caught her in the throat.

"Fuck you! Fuck you!" Louder, more insistent.

"Mila, what's going on? Is someone threatening you? I knew it, you're in trouble—"

"You're wrong. I don't sound anything like myself," she said and hung up.

❁

Sometimes the urge to sing still hit, usually in the shower, hot water cascading over her, blocking out thought and sound. She always stopped herself before she got past a low hum.

She needed something to do. The disability checks plus her savings would sustain her while she figured out how to earn money. Teaching wasn't an option. It was too taxing to stand in front of an auditorium talking in a loud, overenunciated voice so that even the rowdiest kids paid attention. In choral singing, blend and focus mattered more than natural ability, she told her students. They would excel if they worked hard and followed her instructions. Sometimes she turned sideways to demonstrate how to fill the lungs, even the lowest regions, even the tips above the clavicles, how she could puff out her abdomen to double its size, then slowly release the air to create a steady stream of notes. Singing, like anything else, was about constant striving, to strengthen, to deepen, to make each tone more pure and lucid. She was demanding, a perfectionist, but she got results. Over the years her choirs had won championship after championship. She was useless now, without a voice.

Her fault. Hers alone.

The library around the corner was looking for volunteers. Her teaching background would help, the head librarian said when she accepted Mila's application. The kids who hung around after school occasionally needed managing. Mila found shelving books relaxing, shushing children a refreshing change. She hardly ever had to talk.

Except to Fender. Whenever she stepped out of her apartment, there he was: standing in his doorway, hiding beneath the stairs, in the vestibule by her mailbox. The kitten was always hanging from his arms. Fender never spoke, even when she said hello and gave what felt like a big, fake smile. He and the cat just stared, as if they were waiting for her to slip up and reveal her secret.

She nearly tripped over him one day while taking out the trash. It was early, before F-Man's morning round. Fender was crouched down peering under her door when she opened it. She shrieked, then clutched her throat. The cat sat nearby, its tail swishing.

"You startled me," she said. Across the hall, the open door revealed Fender and Rune's cluttered living room. Where was Rune anyway? "Are you spying on me?" Mila asked Fender.

He sat and leaned against the wall. Beside him the kitten yawned and stretched out its spindly front legs. Mila had never seen it out of the boy's grasp. The orange starburst shape on its chest was matted from where Fender's arms rubbed. The boy gathered it into his lap, the cat once again a fluid, boneless mass. Mila held up the garbage bag like a shield.

"Let's find your mom," she said.

"Fuck you, fuck you, fuck you!"

Close, like he was out front, waiting for her. She jerked around toward the sound. The cat shot out of Fender's lap and through Mila's partly open door.

"Dammit," she yelled. She stepped inside and looked around. The cat had disappeared.

She and Rune searched the apartment twice.

"Where could it be?" asked Mila. She stood in the hallway by the empty linen closet, surrounded by towels and sheets.

Rune walked in from the kitchen. "She hides sometimes, for a little breather from Fender."

They went into the living room where Fender sat by the coffee table drawing in a notebook. He didn't look up when Rune settled beside him.

"Baby, Paw-Paw won't come out and it's time for daycare." He kept drawing. Rune held out her hand. "We'll find her later. Let's go."

She tried to pull him up. He let out a guttural moan, then started kicking and crying, his small, perfect face twisted with rage. Mila sat, startled into helplessness, while Rune grabbed him in a bear hug— "Fender, breathe!" she commanded—and whispered in his ear until he relaxed. She sank to the couch with him. Damp faced, he leaned against her and pointed at his drawing, a surprisingly detailed cat with a starburst on its chest. Rune whispered again, then stood.

"Can we talk?" she asked Mila, who nodded and followed her into the kitchen. "The thing is," Rune said, "fighting him out of here without Paw-Paw will make me even later. You're off today, right? Can you watch him?"

"Why doesn't he talk yet? He's what, four?"

"Five. And he talks a little, to me. He talked more before his dad left last year. When he's ready he'll talk again." She looked tired, and young, much younger than Mila.

"Look, I don't think—"

"Please, Mary. He really likes you. He'll be okay as long as he knows Paw-Paw's here. It's just a few hours. I can't miss this shift. We need the extra money. There's this great school for kids like him, but it costs."

Mila looked past Rune into the living room, where Fender sat on the couch with his eyes fixed on her. Like he was making a wish, or hoping for something. Peter would tell her to say no. Strangers' problems weren't hers to fix. *Fix yourself*, he'd say. *You've got enough shit of your own.*

"Fine," she said. "He can stay."

Rune was gone longer than a few hours. When she called to say another waitress was sick and she'd volunteered to cover the shift, Mila let Fender examine her pantry, where he picked boxed macaroni and cheese for lunch and dinner. They ate at the coffee table, then drew pictures and played cards—crazy eights, go fish, war—using simple pantomimes. After dinner he stretched out on the couch to watch cartoons, his head on her lap. A quiet, restful day. When Rune's knock woke Mila, he stayed asleep. The kitten curled in a purring ball against his stomach. It gave Mila a pang to realize they both would be going home.

They fell into a rhythm: after F-Man's morning round, Rune would send over Fender and Paw-Paw with doughnuts and milk. Mila would watch them until Rune returned from the gym or grocery store. While Rune was gone, Mila, Fender, and Paw-Paw would sit on the couch, Mila perusing the news on her iPad, Fender with a ragged stash of comics inherited from his dad. "The only other thing the guy left was one of his old guitars," Rune said. "That was a shocker. He lived for those damned things. At least I got a hundred bucks for it."

After Rune collected Fender and the kitten, Mila would walk to the café to drink coffee and read until her library shift. Then a few hours reshelving books or manning the checkout counter, referring questions to the real librarians. Evenings, Fender would sometimes reappear with Paw-Paw, followed by Rune. "You're a lifesaver. I forgot what it's like to have a break," Rune would say as she hurried out. Mila didn't mind. She knew she and Fender would sit side by side engaged in their own silent tasks. Even F-Man's chants were almost soothing, part of the fabric of this new, more peaceful existence that was devoid of calculation or thought.

Often, though, during a lull at the library, or after Fender had gone for the day, Mila spent time wondering whether he could be drawn out, whether his voice could be made to soar. One afternoon, she sat Fender by the speakers housing her iPod. "What do you think of this," she said and played a recording of herself singing "Little Green" from Joni Mitchell's *Blue* album. The song suited Mila's old voice, a bright, supple lyric with a nimble upper register. Peter loved when she sang. She would be famous if only she would try, he insisted. He kept pushing her to tackle Manhattan. Still, whenever she performed at local clubs, he sat up front cheering. Afterward he would whisper so only she could hear, "That voice is like a miracle."

Fender sat motionless until the song ended, then looked at her with eyebrows raised and mouth pursed as if to say, "So?"

"That was me. I used to sing," she said.

Peter started calling most evenings around six. The first few times she let him go to voicemail. "Checking that you're okay," went the message, or some equally mild variation. She could change her number, but he'd just find that one too. Better to convince him to stop. Better, at least, to try.

"I talked to a lawyer," he announced when she broke down and answered. "He thinks we should sue the manufacturer for your air bag failing."

"Suing won't solve anything."

"Don't be stupid. Of course we'll sue." His most blaring baritone. "You've got to make people pay for their screwups. You let them off too easily." He paused. She pictured him raking back his dark hair, his shoulders tense as he paced their sunroom with his long stride, figuring out how to convince her that she was the one who needed to prove herself, like always. "We'll talk more once you're home." Quieter, more mellow. "Oh, and Jeannie and George invited us for dinner. Ben's reading already and he's only three years old, can you believe? They asked for your chess pie, but I said you'd surprise us."

"I'm not making chess pie. And Jeannie and George are your friends, not mine."

"Well, there's custard or banana cream, or whatever you want, just something good that they'll remember. I'm making suggestions, not telling you what to do. I'm trying."

He couldn't understand the problem. He never would. He would keep hearing what he wanted to hear, viewing her through the prism of his own demanding standards. She checked her watch. Almost time for F-Man, her alarm clock, her talisman, her reminder of this new life without Peter. "Listen to me. I won't be there for dinner or anything else. I'm not coming back."

The words were out. In response, silence. No bullying, no rush to prove her wrong. She picked at the couch tear, letting the silence extend, wrap its peacefulness around her.

"If I could change everything, I would," he said. "I would give you your voice back. I'm sorry, Mila. Desperately." And he did sound sorry, his rich, dark voice clotted with sorrow. He'd never said those words in seven years together, and now here he was apologizing for something that was her fault. Dear God, her fault. If he had kept talking, maybe he would have pointed out that all the blame was hers, as if she needed reminding, and she would have hung up. But he let another silence linger until she found herself yielding and saying, "I'm sorry too," until she found herself staying on the phone, even after F-Man started shouting.

Fender turned out to have an ethereal, fluty singing voice, along with perfect pitch. She discovered this one day when she was playing him a Gregorian chant. She had taken to playing him music whenever he visited, recordings of her various competition choirs, of adult choirs, pop musicians, world music lullabies. Sometimes he would hum a little while he drew, but it wasn't until the Gregorian chant that he sang along quietly. He sat cross-legged at the coffee table coloring, Paw-Paw curled in his lap. No words, just vocalizations, each note matched to the recording. Mila sat on the couch behind him and pretended to keep reading, though her heart pounded.

When the music stopped, she tapped his shoulder. "That was beautiful," she said when he looked at her. "You sing beautifully."

He cocked his head, almost as if he didn't understand, then smiled before he went back to coloring.

She started leaving out her electric keyboard when he came over, then noodling around, playing scales, waiting until he cautiously sat on the bench with her. At first she just played while he hummed along, until one day he stopped and pointed at her. "Me?" she said and shook her head. "I can't anymore." He nodded and tapped out some notes on the keyboard, humming as he went. She hesitated, then said, "You've got to breathe correctly to really sing." She stood and inhaled from her diaphragm. Awful. It would sound awful. But he stood beside her, filled his lungs like she had. She sang a short, raspy arpeggio. Her throat felt tight, her face hot. Fender sang it back, then herded her to the keyboard and put her hands on the keys. "More?" she asked. He nodded vigorously. "Really?"

He tilted his head and waited.

More. More.

Every day she taught him simple vocalizing exercises that didn't require much use of her own voice with its catches and dead spots. She blew raspberries to make him laugh, then made a game of showing him how to buzz his lips while singing scales. When she discovered he could roll *r*'s like a champion, she taught him how to do that while singing as well. He resisted anything that involved recognizable words, though. So far, words seemed beyond him. But when he sang, he let Paw-Paw go, stood straight and tall beside the keyboard while Mila played, his feet planted firmly apart as if he knew intrinsically that singing required the support of his entire little body, each muscle focused on sending his voice surging through the air.

"Do you ever miss me?" Peter asked one night. F-Man's round had long since passed. It had barely registered for Mila. Peter hadn't even made his usual joke about how she really knew how to pick a neighborhood. She was alone. She had started turning Fender away on the evenings Peter called (Mondays, Wednesdays, Fridays, and random Sundays, to keep her guessing). Rune had looked stricken the first night Mila couldn't watch Fender. "But he's used to spending time with you," she had said. "Change is tough for him." Mila had apologized before hurrying inside, shame fluttering her stomach. Talking to Peter felt like a betrayal of Fender, Rune, of Mary Gordon. But Peter was trying, maybe enough to dispel the need for Mary Gordon entirely.

"You must miss me by now," he said on the phone, his voice the low, teasing rumble that he used during good times, that she could trust. "It's been almost three months."

"Yes, I miss you, it's just that—"

"What, sweetheart?" The promise, the expansive tenderness. *Sweetheart, lover, voice of my soul.*

"I'm different," she said. "I want a different life, where I get to make some decisions."

"I can let you do that. Give me a chance."

She pictured him sitting on their bed with its comforter they had picked out together. The soothing purplish blue with thin dark stripes that he kept assuring her wasn't too masculine, that it reflected both their tastes. Which it sort of did. She had chosen something similar for herself in Los Angeles, the comforter on which she now lay. But maybe that was just conditioning. Years of yielding to him made it difficult for her to tease out her own likes and dislikes.

"I don't know, Peter. Maybe."

She waited for his voice, its embracive warmth.

"We both know you need me," he said, flatly.

Her fault. Hers. She climbed under the comforter and listened as he listed the things they would do once she came to her senses.

Slow down. Test his sincerity. She left a voicemail ("Let me call you when I'm ready"), then made herself set the phone to vibrate. On a calendar she checked off the days: one, two, three, four. He didn't call, not once.

Maybe it was over. Maybe he was releasing her. *Careful what you wish for, idiot.* She grabbed the phone once or twice but never did more than dial.

There was more time for Fender again. Rune started bringing him over instead of letting him come alone. Her smile was guarded.

"You're sure he's not too much, Mary?" she asked once, gripping Fender's shoulder. He wriggled away and ran inside to plunk on the keyboard. She stuffed her hands in her back pockets and watched. "He's getting really attached," she said before leaving.

I'm just a babysitter, Mila should have reassured her, but she was too eager to start. The music was what mattered, drawing this child out through the music.

Each day his voice sounded fuller, stronger. Each day, he projected farther into the room, extending his range until he could vocalize through two full octaves. "I'll bet your mom would love to hear you sing," she said to him after three weeks. Three weeks, phone call free. Three weeks of blessed silence except for this supple, young, wordless voice.

"What do you think, Fender?" she said. "Do you want to sing for your mom?"

He stood up tall and nodded.

That evening when Rune arrived, Mila positioned herself at the keyboard. "Fender has something to share."

Rune looked surprised when he handed her the kitten and stood beside Mila. He sang a simple chant they'd practiced many times. Mila kept glancing over at Rune, who sat on the couch with her fingers dug into Paw-Paw's fur. When he finished, Rune jumped up clapping. The cat thudded mewing to the floor and skittered off down the hall.

"That was great, baby," Rune said. "I haven't heard you sing in ages." Fender let her hug him before chasing after Paw-Paw. Rune turned to Mila. "You're amazing."

"It's all him. Community centers have cheap music classes for kids, but he's so talented, you could find someone to teach him privately for almost nothing."

"Oh. I thought—" Rune shoved her hands in her pockets. "You're so good with him. He won't even look at most people. Can't you keep teaching him?"

Staying, teaching this child, making a life here. She could. The phone calls had stopped, maybe forever. But what if Peter hadn't given up, what if he was respecting her wishes and waiting for her to call? She could become Mila Genaro again, a stronger, better version of herself.

"I may not be here much longer," she said. "But the way Fender sings, it's a gift. It's how he communicates. You've got to pursue it for his sake."

"So you're leaving." Rune pushed back her hair, drew a breath. "You know, Fender sang with his dad sometimes. His dad would play the guitar, they'd harmonize. Fender glowed, he loved it so much. But that guy lived for his music. He couldn't handle anything else, especially Fender being, well, different. Me, I'm tone deaf. I never understood the fuss. I just know my kid needs someone who'll stick around." She stood there blank faced before flashing her customary smile. "It would mean a lot, if you kept teaching him. Think about it, okay?" She walked to the front door and called, "Fender, bedtime."

Fender sprinted into the room carrying the cat and followed Rune out, leaving Mila alone at her keyboard.

A few nights later. It was late, so late. She didn't even remember answering. Someone was yelling at her. Peter.

"How could you do this to me? Over something that was your fucking fault."

She pressed the phone to her ear, her body hunched around itself. The dark room came into focus. Her fault. Yes.

The night of the accident she had been trying to hurt him, to jerk the car and make his head snap back, something small but startling that would shut him up for once. They were arguing about the mail. She always left it in the kitchen, he wanted it in the office. "Who cares where I put the goddamn mail?" she yelled, surprising them both. He started yelling again, louder than her, he was always louder, the familiar litany of why she was wrong, everything she'd ever done wrong, until finally he punched the dashboard. "You never listen, you stupid cunt!" That ugly word. No more. No. She slammed the brakes, skidded into the car ahead. Blinding pain; she couldn't speak, swallow. Beside her, he wiped his bloody nose. "Look what you did," he said with something like wonder. Then he'd gotten out, smiling and apologetic, to talk to the other driver.

On the phone there was a crash, then muttered cursing. "I came by the choir room a few times afterward," he said, "and listened to you lead rehearsals. You sounded fine. But once I knocked, you let yourself get all scratchy, like you wanted to make me feel bad for something *you* caused."

That reckless, angry act. She couldn't change it; she had to let it go. But he would use it to define her, to justify everything he did as saving her from herself. *Look what you did. Look what you fucking did.*

Another crash. "Don't you dare blame me, you dumb bitch, you dumbass, stupid—"

"Stop it!" she said loudly enough to shut him up. "Stop calling me." By the time she hung up, he was yelling again.

Rune started keeping Fender home. At first, Mila thought he was sick, but when she knocked on the door after a few days, Rune said, "We thought Fender shouldn't come over so much, since you're moving and all."

"Nothing's definite," Mila said and peered past Rune to where Fender sat inside on the couch holding the kitten. He glanced at Mila, then scowled down at Paw-Paw. "Fender, don't you want to sing anymore?"

He kept scowling and petting the cat.

Rune stepped into the hallway and pulled the door shut behind her. She gave Mila her most determined smile. "If you decide to stay, I'll send him right over for a lesson."

Mila put away her keyboard, the speakers, and the iPod. At the library, she didn't shush the after-school crowd's whispers, which rose to a loud buzz that the reference librarian had to silence. Mila didn't care. The quiet was uncomfortable now. Any noise seemed preferable.

She especially welcomed F-Man's shouts. She had managed a few glimpses. He was tall and emaciated with bushy, graying hair mashed under a baseball cap. Whatever the weather he wore a heavy parka and stained dress slacks that he held bunched above his waist. He lived two buildings down in a boxy complex with carports under the front apartments. Mila saw him leaving a downstairs unit one morning when she was out getting coffee. She rarely slept more than a few hours lately. To talk to someone, to look directly at a person; to look directly at *this* person, this foul-mouthed, odd, aggressive stranger. *Say fuck you to my face,* she'd tell him. *Say it's my fault. I dare you.*

When he walked by her muttering, she stopped and held out her hand. "I'm Mila, your neighbor," she said.

He glanced at her hand, then the ground, then took her fingertips gingerly, as if afraid to catch something. He smiled, revealing strong, yellowed teeth. "Harvey, I'm Harvey. Going to the center today. How about you?"

"The library later. Now, just home."

He adjusted his pants, glanced up. "Gonna be nice today. You think? A nice day."

"Probably."

"Nice. Yeah. Nice. Glad to meet you, Mila." He ducked his head, took few steps, stopped. "Thanks for saying hi," he said into the air and continued on his way, muttering.

The next morning, Rune caught her as she was leaving for the library. "It's probably nothing," Rune said, worrying her uniform collar, "but some guy was nosing around yesterday."

Mila's heart beat triplets against her ribs. "Did he leave a name?"

Rune shook her head. "But he showed me a picture. Didn't look familiar, I told him. I think he believed me. Is he the one you're avoiding?"

Breathe. Deep, steady breaths. "Maybe," she said.

Rune watched her. "Even if it was him, that's what restraining orders are for."

"It's more complicated than that."

"Not really. Either you live your life or you let yourself be chased." She tugged her collar again, not looking at Mila. "Fender would love it if you stuck around."

Mila took off her glasses and polished the fake lenses. "Maybe I will," she lied.

She'd reached the vestibule when she heard Rune call, "I guess I was right about you." Behind her, Rune stood in the same spot.

"Right about what?" Mila asked.

Rune walked closer. Her mouth was a grim line. She looked ready to cry. "You've got no staying power." Arms crossed she trudged back down the hallway.

That afternoon Mila found another apartment miles away, down-town in an anonymous-looking high-rise with security cameras and a keycard parking lot. She forwarded her mail through two different PO Boxes and had her disability checks sent to a check-cashing place in Echo Park. Peter would have to work hard to find her again.

Moving day, Fender came outside as she finished packing the car in the alley behind the building. His arms hung at his sides, kitten-less. He was crying. She knelt and hugged him. It took him a while to hug her back. *Keep singing*, she wanted to say, but she sensed some-one nearby. Rune stood watching from the rear exit. Mila rose, found the electric keyboard in her car. "For Fender," she said, pulling it out.

Rune waved her away. "It'll just get dusty."

Fender's quiet sobs shook him. He walked over and clutched his mother's legs.

"I wish I didn't have to go," Mila said.

Rune stroked Fender's hair. "Paw-Paw ran away. Maybe it's better. Fender starts school soon and the cat would've been all alone." She patted Mila's shoulder. "Sorry I have to keep your security deposit. You were one of my nicest tenants."

She walked back inside, tugging Fender along with her.

When Mila checked her mailbox in the vestibule one last time, she heard Harvey making his evening round. She stepped outside and peered down the street trying to see him. Walking toward his building she passed a furry heap by the curb. It was Paw-Paw, sprawled on her side, unmoving, like she'd been hit by a car. Mila crouched down and smoothed the matted starburst. The body was already stiff. This animal. It wasn't hers. Time to leave all this behind, to start over somewhere she couldn't be found. Still. She sat on the curb, felt tears dripping down her chin when she propped it on her hand. The cat purring in a corner, Fender's voice soaring around her. Those small intimacies, enveloping her in possibilities that felt new and right, like something to strive for.

She would sit here a while longer, keeping guard. Then get a gar-bage bag from the car, bring the body to a vet for cremation. She could keep the ashes, or send them to Fender. Or even bring them to him in person. Someday. When she was herself again.

"Fuck you, fuck you, fuck you," Harvey chanted, somewhere close.

"Fuck you!" she shouted, still seated on the curb. Raspy, harsh, but strong, tinged with bright remnants. She stood, breathed from her diaphragm. "Fuck you!" she shouted. "Fuck you!"

Jump

The fire drill was Winston's idea. No way Marney would have done it alone. This was in '78, during summer break. She was ten, Winston eleven. Irish twins, their mother called them. Back then, Marney ached to be his actual twin. She settled for wearing his hand-me-downs and imitating his grin; she would do anything he suggested, as long as he did it first.

"Finish eating already," their mother, Gwen, begged the morning of the fire drill. "Mom" was for old ladies, Gwen claimed. Marney ate even slower and picked a fight with Winston about whether to bike to the creek by the horse farm later. Gwen lit another cigarette and checked her watch. "I'm going whether you're done or not," she said, gesturing broadly, scattering ash.

Her eagerness to leave was like another body in the room. In this mood she would be gone all day, then return in the evening smelling weird and mumbling baby talk. Last week, she'd fallen asleep holding a lit joint. Winston doused the smoldering couch cushion, then hid it from their dad while Marney watched, paralyzed. A fire. There could have been a fire.

But Gwen wouldn't stay that morning, even when Winston pleaded, "You could paint our portraits," and Marney showed what she'd written on her calendar: "Gwen stays home." "You promised," Marney said, ignoring Winston's glare.

Gwen ground out her cigarette. "God, you're a stickler. I said I'd *try*. Your brother understands. Right, honey?" Then she smiled at Winston, only Winston. Always Winston.

At the front door she kissed them—"Do something worth telling me about"—and fled.

"You should've shut up," he said, fists clenched, once their mother's car was gone. "She listens to me. I could have stopped her."

"You didn't last week," she said. "What if there's really a fire this time?"

His fists unclenched. He chewed his lower lip. "An escape plan," he said. "That's what we need."

His idea was to toss blankets from the roof onto the lawn, then jump into the pile. They carried a full laundry basket upstairs to Marney's bedroom, which overlooked the back porch, the roof's lowest point. He climbed out first, barefoot and dragging the basket of blankets. She watched from the window. Outside, the shingles stretched like a gray, pebbly beach. If Gwen had stayed, Marney would have tagged along while the other two chased each other with squirt guns or painted the garage walls with crazy symbols only they understood. Marney wouldn't be having this adventure. Follow Winston's lead and everything would be fine.

She climbed up on the windowsill. "What if we get hurt?" she said.

He blew a raspberry at her from the roof's edge.

The shingles prickled her feet. She sat and scooted to him, tar plucking at her shorts. The landscape swayed below. She shut her eyes, felt him stand, maybe to help her back inside.

"Easy peasy," she heard him say.

When she opened her eyes, the blankets lay scattered on the lawn. It really wasn't that far down. Still.

"Let's just hang off the edge," she said, "and drop into the bushes."

"Do what you want," he said. "I'm jumping." He bent his knees, swung his arms; readied himself.

She couldn't let him jump alone. She wouldn't.

Winston keeps jumping into everything first: the first to go to college, the first to become successful, the first to move far from home for good, the first to stop speaking to their parents; the first to sleep with a man, to marry one, to get divorced.

Marney is successful too, as a developer of publishing websites, but her Chelsea loft is a short train ride from their childhood home in New Jersey, and she visits their mother often. Someone has to. Winston hasn't spoken to their parents since he came out after college and escaped to Los Angeles, where he produces highbrow, arty films that Marney rarely sees. His divorce is mere months old. He's forty-one and living alone for the first time in fifteen years. "Who knew I'd miss his clutter?" he emails Marney about his ex, Lou.

Email is how Winston communicates these days. God forbid he call or visit, although she used to visit him a lot until their fight two years ago. Since then, she's claimed to be too busy, either working or helping out their mother, who, she emails Winston, has started wandering the house sometimes, uncertain of her surroundings.

"Flashbacks, maybe," Marney writes. "That acid she dropped when we were kids might finally be catching up."

"That was once," he writes back. "She's seventy-two. Forgetfulness comes with age. Speaking of, did I mention that Lou and I were thinking about having a baby when he left? We wanted a girl. I did, at least."

She writes, "Maybe you're better off. A baby's a huge obligation, especially for a single parent. Gwen's enough work. I'm always there lately, the 5:55 from Penn Station to Westfield, then I cab it over. Same cabbie every time. No chitchat, and he's so Jersey chewing that toothpick. Mostly Gwen's fine, but sometimes I have to remind her where the pantry is, or that the Newels moved away. Their dog loved to dig up Dad's flowerbeds. They left a year ago, right after Dad died. Gwen's tirade about how all that digging killed her husband may have influenced their decision."

Nothing that she writes about their mother is true.

Gwen still has a steel-trap memory that refuses to relinquish the most ancient flaw—except with Winston—and a teenager's lungs despite her lifelong penchant for pot and cigarettes. And she no longer tirades, preferring carefully chosen barbs. "You'd make it an English tea garden, just like your father," she said when Marney recently offered to tame the wilderness overtaking the backyard. They were sitting on the roof outside Marney's old bedroom, where Gwen likes to smoke sometimes. "Winston would know what to do, if you asked," she added, surveying the scruffy yard. Not a chance, Marney wanted to say. "Nothing wrong with tea gardens," she said instead.

There are other things she doesn't tell her brother, things he would know if he bothered coming home. She doesn't tell him, for instance, that after she's done visiting their mother, her regular cabbie is waiting outside to push open the front passenger door, take out his toothpick, and kiss her hello. "Whose place tonight?" he always asks.

His name is Dominic DiCorscia. After a year of dating, it still thrills her to see his waiting cab. He's thirty, ten years younger than she is, but looks older, his lean face heavily stubbled, the skin leathery from working landscaping jobs with his brother-in-law. Nights he cabbies. He's saving for his own restaurant, which will be a small family place with a few signature dishes. On his evenings off, she takes the PATH to Hoboken to watch him play baseball in Sinatra Park by the Hudson River, or they pick up food at the Italian market run by his mother, father, and sister. His mother—a small, elegant woman with a formidable chest and watchful eyes—fusses over them, offering the choicest pancetta or guanciale despite Dominic's reminders that Marney doesn't eat meat. Then he cooks for Marney in his kitchen with its crowded pot rack and professional range, so different from her own spartan kitchen, where she uses the stove for storage. He likes to feed her spoonfuls from the pan, food that fills her with a tingly warmth and leaves her wanting more.

"Time to up my cardio," she says one night after second helpings.

He grins. "My mother thinks you're too skinny."

"So she's told me."

He toys with her hand. "Maybe somebody should feed you better. I'd cook every meal if we lived together."

She stands to gather dishes. She's lived alone since college. She likes uncluttered surfaces, cabinets and closets empty except for essentials. Her schedule requires solitude: up early for meditation and exercise, then hours in her office loft above the kitchen, building the intricate author websites that have made her name in publishing. But this man, he makes her forget all that.

"So that's your plan," she says. "Fatten me up to make your mother happy. Strange tactic, but it could work."

"Is that a yes?"

"It's a definite possibility." She kisses him, then carries the dishes to the counter.

❀

A few evenings later, Dominic is helping his sister move boxes at the market when his mother, Rose, corners Marney in the pasta aisle. Something about her tight, determined smile makes Marney glad they haven't spent much time together.

"I thought you don't cook," says Rose, her hands clasped.

Marney holds up a pasta box. "Just grabbing a high protein brand."

"Pasta isn't meant to be protein. Let's find something Dommy likes." She puts back the box and scans the shelves. "We still haven't met your mother. I keep telling Dommy to invite her to Sunday dinner, although lately he's too busy for us on weekends. With your family, I assume."

"Actually, no. My mother doesn't get out much."

"I'll go to her. We're almost in-laws with you and Dommy always together. Keep in-laws close, I say."

"Like enemies." It's out before Marney thinks. Dominic's mother stares. Marney feels herself flush. "You know the saying. 'Keep friends close, enemies closer.' Never mind. Dinner sounds nice."

"Soon, I hope. Nobody's getting younger, including you." Before Marney can respond, Rose hands her a crinkly bag of small, cuplike pasta. "Orecchiette, Dommy's favorite. 'Little ears' it means in Italian. My *nonna* used to shape them on her pinkie tip. She was nobility in Italy, did Dommy tell you? Became a milkwoman here in New Jersey after my grandfather drank himself to death. They lost seven of nine children to flu. Delivering milk was the only way she could support the kids who lived. She treated those cows like family, better even, but she had to. They kept us alive. The women in our family will do anything to protect their own." She gestured at the ground with her fist, two fingers extended.

"Ma, how many times can you tell that story?" Dominic says as he walks up.

She puts her fist behind her back. "Mandy should know where we come from."

"You'll make sure of that."

Marney waits for him to add, *Her name's not Mandy*, but he doesn't. Finally, she says, "It's 'Marney,' not 'Mandy,' Rose."

"That's what I said."

"You didn't, actually—"

"No big deal," he says and puts his arm around Marney. Placating her. She almost shrugs him off her but notices his mother watching, as if hoping for just such a reaction. Nope. She won't give her the satisfaction. She smiles at him instead. His mother's lips tense before she smiles too.

"What kind of name is 'Marney' anyway?" she says. "It sounds like something from those society pages with people named Buffy and Scamp."

"Ma, come on—"

"Rose, leave her alone," says a rumbly voice.

Dominic's father stands in the aisle. A massive man, he wears a stained apron that strains across his wide chest. Marney has barely heard him speak until now.

"I'm joking," says Rose.

He wipes his broad hands on his apron. "Stop."

"For goodness' sake—" She forces a laugh. "I can't have a friendly conversation without Gabe reading in nonsense." She waves—"Don't be strangers"—and marches off. Dominic's father rubs his face before following her.

Marney stares after them as Dominic hugs her.

"She means well," he says.

There are other things Marney could write to Winston: *Gwen's kept your room the same even after all these years. Mine's an art studio now. She's used it maybe once.* Or: *She still writes you letters that she hides in the old hat box where she used to keep her pot. When the box fills up, she piles everything in a trash bag and tosses it in the basement. Fifteen years' worth of letters takes up a lot of space.* Or she could write: *When Dad got sick, that anger he wouldn't let go of, it morphed into regret. One afternoon near the end, when I was pushing his wheelchair in Tamaques Park, he tapped my hand and said, "I know you tried, honey, but I said some terrible things when he went gay, and your brother's not one to forgive. He's like his old man that way."*

She could write to Winston about all those marathons they ran together after college, until veins stood out on their sculpted arms and people started noticing again how much they looked alike, the same small, stern features, the narrow torsos and piston thighs. Or about when they were kids, how she wore her hair chopped short like his and both their bodies were angular and ropy and as tawny as hazelnut shells; about their fire drill when the only casualty was her broken collarbone, or swimming in the creek by the horse farm, making forts from Gwen's discarded canvases, shooting cork guns at neighborhood cats. The late nights curled together on the basement couch, far from the fighting upstairs, when they would huddle under a blanket and chant "It'll be over soon" to keep from crying.

Instead she writes: "Gwen got stuck in the bathroom yesterday. She forgot how to unlock the door. 'Soon I'll be in diapers anyway,' she said after I got her out. Then she laughed like crazy."

❀

Dominic is easy to love, like Winston used to be. Marney's mother adores him. Since Marney's father died last year, Gwen rarely leaves the house, preferring to spend her time painting murals on the walls. So Dominic comes by with bags of food that he prepares with a flourish. They eat what they can before Marney packs the freezer with carefully labeled leftovers.

"What a doll," her mother says one night while Dominic is taking out the trash. He's just finished rearranging the living room so that she can continue her mural onto a second wall.

Marney can't help smiling. "A regular Kewpie," she says.

Gwen holds an unlit cigarette in one hand, in the other a drippy paintbrush that she dabs at the living room wall. Furniture huddles under faded sheets. At the hearth Marney lays a fire to ward off the spring chill. It's frustrating, how drafty the house has gotten.

"This place is like a wind tunnel," she says. "I could get the windows caulked."

Her mother steps back to contemplate the new wall. "Don't bother," she says, then adds, with some satisfaction, "The state of this place would kill your father if he weren't dead already."

"Christ, Gwen."

"I'm kidding." She sniffs her cigarette without lighting it. "Dominic certainly knows his way around the kitchen. It's almost like having your brother home."

Marney sits back abruptly, scattering kindling. "Winston can barely turn on a stove."

Dominic walks in and crouches beside her. "The backyard needs work," he says to Gwen as he collects the kindling. "Let me at least mow it."

Gwen waves the paintbrush at him, flinging paint droplets everywhere. "How sweet. You really do remind me of Winston."

"Who?"

Gwen flicks paint at Marney. "You haven't mentioned your brother?"

Dominic keeps arranging wood. "She has, a few times. I'm bad with names." Bless him for inflating a passing reference. "I'd like to meet him next time he's here," he says.

"Pigs will hula first," Marney says as she stands to gather paint cans.

"You could ask him to visit," Gwen says, "now that your father . . . well, you could ask." She stabs her paintbrush at the wall.

Marney focuses on stacking the cans. "We don't talk anymore," she says, which is technically true.

Dominic lights the kindling. It crackles to life. "You'll regret it if you don't try to make up. Believe me."

"Maybe I should call," Gwen says.

Marney stops stacking. "You're kidding."

"Why not?"

"Because he didn't call even after Dad got sick. Because he skipped the funeral. Need more?"

Gwen raises her cigarette, lowers it. "He's my son. We have to forgive each other eventually."

It would feel so good to send the paint cans flying. Instead, Marney finishes stacking them.

"He wants nothing to do with you," she says. "He told me so himself."

This is what she should write: *It wasn't my fault, that fight we had the last time I saw you, right after Dad got sick two years ago. All I asked was that you call him, just once. Instead you claimed either I was on your side or his, even after I pointed out it was ridiculous to still have sides. Then months went by without a word from you. Months of Dad dying, of Gwen spiraling, of my needing your help. I shouldn't have had to email you Dad's obituary for you to start talking to me again. You shouldn't have ever stopped.*

Instead she writes: "Sometimes I catch Gwen talking to mirrors. Once, when I asked what she was doing, she pointed at her reflection and said, 'Why's that woman in my house?'"

A few days after starting the second wall, Gwen decides the living room mural can wait. Instead, she has Dominic rearrange the dining room so she can start another one. She stops mentioning Winston and starts peppering Marney with questions about Dominic: What's his apartment like, does he get along with his sister, is he close to his mother, how often does he see her? How long have his parents been married, are they still in love after all that time? "You can tell a lot about people from their families," she declares.

"Then Dominic should run for his life," Marney says, which makes Gwen laugh.

One night her mother asks, "What if he wants children?"

They are alone on the roof. Marney hugs her knees. The distance to the ground seems farther than it used to, even farther than when she jumped off the roof during the fire drill and broke her collarbone. Dusk mutes the yard below, the uncut grass and splintered sandbox, the flower beds overgrown with weeds. She's never imagined herself as a mother, a scheduler of music lessons and doctors' appointments, things she used to manage herself since Gwen always forgot. But what if she moves in with Dominic? What if they have a child? He's easy to picture as a father, repairing the sandbox without breaking a sweat. With him, maybe she could be different, someone who could have kids. Maybe her mother could be different too. Maybe she would toss her pot and cigarettes and greet her grandchild with focused eyes and outstretched arms. Maybe she would watch smiling as Marney pureed baby food or tested bathwater with her wrist.

"You're too particular," Gwen says. "Kids need flexibility."

"Says the woman who uses *flexibility* and *chaos* interchangeably."

Her mother inhales from the joint before offering it. "Sarcasm keeps you from getting close to people."

"So does self-delusion."

"We're alike that way."

Marney takes the joint and stubs it out on her shoe, careful to keep ash off the brittle shingles. "No," she says. "We're nothing alike."

Marney and Dominic start apartment hunting. On a quiet street in Tompkins Square Park, in a row of well-kept, prewar brownstones, they find a lower unit with two bedrooms, windows everywhere, high ceilings, hardwoods. Their footsteps echo in the empty space.

"It's too perfect, and a steal at this price," says the real estate agent, whose overbright lipstick and aggressive cheer normally would piss Marney off. But the agent is right, this is what they want.

The second bedroom is small but airy and faces a sunny court-yard. Dominic paces its length, then opens the closet. "Finally, some-place for my stuff. No more carrying back and forth. And your desk would fit, plus a bookshelf."

He starts pacing again, so energetic and determined. So dear. There could be a cradle in this room instead of shelves. She could rock it while working. Gwen would marvel at her efficiency. "Who knew?" she might say. "Parenthood suits you."

Marney closes the closet door. "Maybe we'll need this room for someone else," she says.

Dominic stops pacing. "I thought you were barely ready for a puppy."

"Puppy, kid. How different could they be?"

The agent claps like a chipper seal. "There's a preschool around the corner."

"Hold your applause. I'm not pregnant yet," Marney says and watches Dominic laugh.

❁

That night, while her mother and Dominic rearrange the study (it took her mother less than a week to put the dining room mural on hold), Winston emails that he wants to visit. "Fence-mending time, before she stops recognizing me."

Marney sits in the living room skimming the brownstone's lease application. Even the scattered paint cans and drop cloths haven't ruined her good mood. Her brother won't either.

"Gwen's herself lately," she emails back on her phone. "You don't have to come."

He answers immediately: "I want to. There's something I should have told you but couldn't figure out how. I'm gonna be a dad soon—"

"Everything okay?" she hears. Dominic stands beside her. With numb hands she slips her phone under the lease application.

Winston is going to be a father.

Her mother walks in. "Where's my helper?" Paint speckles her hair.

"You look a little sick," Dominic says to Marney. His forearms are blue streaked.

"Finish with Gwen. And clean your arms."

He studies her. "When we're done," he says before leaving with her mother.

Marney retrieves the phone and deletes her brother's emails.

Later that night at Dominic's, after Dominic is asleep, she sits on his couch with her laptop and imagines sharing her brother's news with Gwen, how excited she'll be, how confident that Winston will be the perfect father, despite his years of silence. How much more she's always believed in him than in Marney. Though maybe Gwen's right. Maybe he really will be a better parent. Maybe Marney won't be able to raise a child without following his lead, like always. But she's done being the worshipful follower.

She clicks open her email and starts typing.

"I've been hiding something too, ever since Dad died. Gwen's actually fine; she's even getting stoned less often. I have a job that I'm good at, people I love. I'm happy for you, really, but we don't need you. Don't come."

She deletes the email and sits watching the night fade.

The Tompkins Square apartment turns out to be too drafty, she decides. Another is pricey for the size. She won't move back to Jersey into Dominic's place. She already lives too close to her mother.

"Maybe we should consider one-bedrooms," she says loudly above the screech of subway wheels one Saturday afternoon. They just toured a rundown two-bedroom that she swore smelled like cat pee though there wasn't a cat in sight. It's been two weeks since Winston emailed. She hasn't answered him yet.

Dominic frowns, says something she can't hear. She leans closer until his breath is on her cheek.

"What about needing the extra bedroom?" he says into her ear.

This is where she should say, *I'm afraid to be a parent. I don't know how.*

"I changed my mind."

She sits back. He looks at her, unsmiling. They're silent all the way to her place in Chelsea. Later, as they're cleaning up after takeout (he claimed he was too tired to cook), he says, "You're the one who brought up kids."

She loads cartons into the trash. "I was just trying on the idea."

"Seemed to fit pretty good."

"It made me feel fat, like an old Italian momma." She hates how serious he looks, like this could be a deal breaker. *I'm afraid. Help me learn.* Say it. But he looks so young, so untested. He's only thirty, after all. He doesn't know any more than she does. Maybe less. "Are we back to making your mother happy?" she says, tying the trash bag. "Because you definitely need a better reason to knock me up."

"Think about it," he says. "That's all I'm asking."

Everything Dominic does starts driving her crazy: the way he jerks the car through traffic, stacks chewed toothpicks on the counter, ignores his mother's barely veiled complaints.

"You could at least defend me," Marney says one night as they're driving away from his family's market.

"From what?"

"Your mother. 'A little weight would fill out those wrinkles, dear.' It's insulting when you pretend nothing's wrong."

He grips the steering wheel. "The more you react, the worse she gets."

"Your father doesn't seem to worry about that."

"He's got nothing to lose these days."

"What's that mean?"

He stares out the windshield, his jaw working. "Drop it, okay?"

She bites back a retort, which could cause a real fight, their first. She's not ready for that.

Three weeks and she still hasn't answered Winston. She keeps writing responses and deleting them. Nothing fits her anger at the thought of a child cradled in his arms, making him smile, a child who will redeem him to their mother, prove that Gwen's right, he's better at this too, even though he and Marney had the same childhood, the same bad examples. A child who will follow him everywhere, even if it means a broken bone.

Other people fight with their parents when they come out. Vicious fights like yours with Dad after college, where awful things are said that can't be taken back. Last time I saw you, I asked you to forget all that ancient shit and just call him. For fuck's sake, Winston, he was dying. You got furious and said you couldn't pretend nothing happened the way I could, the way I had for years. How else could I still be speaking to him after what he'd said to you? How else could I ask you for the impossible? How could I betray you like that?

But I've never pretended that fight didn't happen. I remember everything he said. He called you beastly, diseased, a sin against nature. And worse. Gwen and I defended you to Dad, but we couldn't take sides. We wanted to keep being a family, even as fucked up as our family is. Was. We needed you for that. I needed you.

You're the one who left me alone to deal with them. You left me without a family and started your own.

You're the one who betrayed me.

Clattering in Dominic's kitchen jolts Marney out of her morning meditation. She's alone in his bedroom. He left for work hours ago, earlier than usual and without kissing her goodbye. Their almost-first-fight from last night still lingers between them.

More clattering from the kitchen. She grabs his bat from the bedroom closet where he stores his baseball gear, then creeps down the hall to find his mother hanging a skillet on the pot rack with her back to Marney.

Marney lowers the bat. "You startled me."

Rose screams and swings the skillet, whacking Marney's shoulder. Her chest heaves as she puts down the pan. "I almost had a heart attack."

Marney's shoulder throbs. She sucks in a breath as she rubs it. "Jesus, Rose. What're you doing here?"

"Dommy's always gone by now." She holds up a key and frowns, as if getting hit is Marney's own fault. "That needs ice." She herds Marney into a chair and fills a dish towel. "Use this," she commands, pressing the damp towel to her shoulder.

The espresso Rose makes in the old-fashioned stovetop pot tastes rich and strong. It usually tastes burned when Marney makes it. Rose clicks efficiently around the kitchen, wiping counters, unloading the dishwasher.

"I like to surprise Dommy," she says. "Clean, pick up laundry. Gabe says I spoil him, but you do for family." She takes the drippy ice pack and empties it in the sink. "This dish towel will take forever to dry. The new place will need a washer and dryer for all that extra laundry."

Marney nearly drops her cup. "Dominic told you?"

"I knew it. 'Marriage first would be better,' I said to Gabe just yesterday, 'but they probably should move in together before the baby comes.'"

"What? No. I'm not pregnant, Rose."

Dominic's mother leans against the counter. "At your age, it's now or never."

"That's not your decision."

"It'll be my grandchild."

Marney clenches the table's edge. No, it would be *her* child. To care for, to guide toward some semblance of a good life, a balanced life. But how do you do that, help a kid figure out who to be once she's grown? Who to emulate? Who to love? All Marney knows is how to fight with family, and screw things up. She can't face repeating history with someone she's given birth to.

"It's my life, and my body," she says.

Rose stares at her. "I guess you told me." She takes her coat and leaves.

"I haven't heard from you since my last email, where I told you I was going to be a dad. Maybe you didn't get the message. Skye thinks you're upset. She says it wasn't fair to email you, that you deserved to hear such important news in person.

"Skye, I should tell you, is my coparent. You must remember her, my closest friend from college. Maybe you also remember that Lou and I were talking about having a baby when he left. Actually, we had everything set with Skye, who's been chronically single for years. She and I used to joke in college that if we were still childless in middle-age we'd have a kid together.

"Well, we figured out we weren't joking. Having a baby with her and Lou felt natural, inevitable. Three parents and two households would be all our child knew. It would be normal.

"Lou seemed game until we found out his sperm weren't viable. Mine were, so I pushed him. I wanted us to be a family. I wanted the sense of purpose outside myself that comes from parenting. One morning we were talking about the nursery. I was planning a zoo theme: man-size stuffed elephants, ceiling-high giraffes. He worried that might scare the baby, but I told him he was being silly. 'Your way or the highway,' he said. I thought he was joking. Then he asked whether I'd told you yet. I'm ashamed to admit I said it wasn't your business. How long until the baby wasn't his business? he asked. Never, I told him. This would be our child. 'But only your blood relation,' he pointed out. 'Marney's your sister. She was your best friend. If you can cut her out, you could cut me out too.'

"I still wake myself up sometimes, reaching for him.

"Skye and I decided to go ahead anyway. Two in vitros and she was pregnant. She's due soon, with a girl. Last week we picked out a name: Lucy Pearl Copeland-Hills. That made her real, more real than any 3-D ultrasound. She's going to have her own opinions, likes, dislikes; she's going to want to know where her parents came from, who helped us become who we are. She's going to want to be loved across generations.

"It's been a long time getting to where I can completely forgive and ask you to forgive me. I know it won't happen overnight, but I want my daughter to have the family that she deserves. And we can still be a family. No matter how hard I've pushed you and Gwen away, the love is still there. At least on my end.

"Once Lucy is born, I'd like to bring her to meet you both. I don't want to confuse Gwen more than she already is, though, and I don't want to upset you. It's your choice. I'll wait for your reply."

After Winston's email, Marney avoids Dominic all week. She's nursing a cold, she tells him. "You sure it's not that sore shoulder from my mother?" he asks, which makes her laugh. Still, she puts off seeing him. She's not up for parenthood, she'll have to admit when she does. That frontier was claimed before she could stake it out, and she doesn't want to learn by example anymore. Childlessness is her frontier. Nobody needs to teach her how to do that.

When she arrives at her mother's house on Saturday evening, she discovers that Gwen has called Dominic and invited them both to his baseball game in Sinatra Park. He's picking them up momentarily. Her mother stands with a lipstick by a full-length mirror propped against the dining room's unfinished mural.

"Nice that someone can get you out of the house," Marney says.

"He said he hasn't seen you, that you said you were sick. I told him you've never liked anyone taking care of you, even as a kid." She speaks quickly and avoids Marney's eyes.

"Did it occur to you that I need a break from him?"

Her mother watches herself apply lipstick. "What occurred to me is that someone should stop you from screwing up a good thing."

"Says the queen of screwups."

"Dammit, Marney—"

The doorbell rings.

"That's him," her mother says and hurries into the foyer.

Marney kisses Dominic's cheek when he walks in but lets her mother do the talking. In the car, Gwen sits up front and exclaims about how well Dominic drives, how nice it is to be out on such a refreshingly chilly spring night. At Sinatra Park the baseball field is lit by floodlights and flanked by crowded bleachers. Her mother walks between them chattering until they reach the dugout, then goes to find seats. Dominic stands with Marney. "Gwen claimed this was your idea," he says.

"She's always had a questionable relationship with the truth."

He laces his fingers in the chain-link fence behind the dugout. "If you want to end things, at least have the guts to say so."

"That's not it." She takes a breath. "Let's talk after we drop off Cupid."

Marney joins her mother, who's sitting by an aisle. They watch Dominic trot to third base.

"Playing third takes quick reflexes," her mother says.

"Like you know anything about baseball."

Her mother leans forward, still watching the field. "Your father played when you kids were young. I loved when he hit. He'd smile at me, point at the back fence, and that's where the ball went."

"I don't remember you two enjoying anything together."

Gwen squints at the field. "Marriage, kids, they change you. He thought we had to get serious to raise a family. We could still live a little, I said. He wouldn't listen. So I did it without him." She whoops when Dominic catches a line drive. "I just want you to be happy. Live a little."

Marney allows herself to lean against her mother. "You mean well."

Gwen clasps Marney's hand. "Finally, we agree."

After a few innings, Marney notices Dominic's mother climbing the bleachers. Marney pulls her jacket tighter. An impromptu visit from Rose never bodes well.

Rose is slightly breathless when she reaches them. "Dommy mentioned you'd be here," she says to Gwen, who looks mystified.

"This is Rose, Dominic's mom," Marney explains and watches Gwen's face light with a polite smile.

Rose sits between them. "I keep telling Dommy to introduce us, but children always think they know better."

Marney looks at the field, where Dominic is jogging to the dugout. He stops when she waves, then gestures as if waving back. When she turns around, Rose is facing Gwen.

"We should talk about this situation," says Rose.

Gwen scoots a little farther from her. "Situation?"

Dominic waves again. "Ma, come here," Marney hears him call. His mother ignores him. He strides off the field.

"The age difference. I told Dommy, he wants things she can't give. Her eggs are drying up as we speak. But he won't listen, and now they're moving in together."

Gwen leans forward to look at Marney. "You are?"

"Nothing's definite."

"See, she can't even commit to living with my son, much less marrying him—"

"This isn't your business," Marney says, but Gwen drowns her out.

"How dare you interfere!"

"Sons don't think they need protecting, but they need it more than the girls. Not that you'd know."

"I have a son."

Rose smacks her knees. "Who can't stand to even talk to you, from what I hear." Immediately she covers her mouth, then touches Gwen's arm. "Wait, that wasn't—"

"Stop it, Ma!" Dominic is in the aisle beside their row.

Gwen stands, clutching her purse—"Excuse me," she says in a strangled voice—and hurries past him down the steps.

"What were you thinking?" Marney asks Rose.

She stares straight ahead, her face blotchy. "It came out wrong. But someone should be honest."

"That's always your excuse," Dominic says. His mother tries to answer, but he cuts her off. "You already chased off Savvy, and probably Pop. Keep it up, I'm next." He turns to Marney. "I'm sorry," he says, but she pushes past him to follow her mother.

She checks the restrooms and calls Gwen's cell phone, which goes straight to voicemail. Her mother could be anywhere. She could have gotten caught smoking and wound up stoned and disoriented in some police station. Marney is frantic by the time Dominic walks up.

"I sent my mother home," he says.

"Just help me find Gwen."

They roam around calling for her mother. Finally, they return to the emptying parking lot, where Gwen is leaning against Dominic's car. Marney runs over.

"You couldn't answer your cell?" she demands.

Gwen's makeup is tear streaked. She pulls a cigarette from her purse. "I was talking to your brother. Why didn't you tell me about the baby? And he treated me like I was senile, like I couldn't keep a thought in my head."

Marney stands there, staring.

"Admit it," Gwen says. "You lied to him, and me."

"I was protecting you."

"You were being a jealous brat."

"Dammit, stop pretending he's a saint. I'm the one who's put up with your bullshit all these years."

"Marney, don't," Dominic says behind her.

"You're taking her side?"

"I don't want you saying things you'll regret." His equipment bag is slung over his shoulder. Stubble is heavy on his cheeks. Hit this man with a brick and it wouldn't hurt him.

"What do you know about regrets? I'm your only blemish, according to your mother."

Marney turns and runs through the parking lot, the baseball field. He catches up to her at the path along the river. She tries to shake him off, but he holds her arms and then lifts her chin so she's looking at him.

"You think I've got it great." He lets out a short laugh. "I have another sister, Savvy, who you haven't met. She's about your age, actually. She just started talking to us again. It's been years. Sound familiar? Connie, the sister you met, her husband left her last month to become a Buddhist monk. I've been helping with their landscaping business so she can pay the mortgage, but she'll probably have to move in with my parents anyway. If there's room. My father's been living in my grandmother's old basement apartment for months. Which nobody's talking about. Ma claims he just likes the TV down there. And my mother. You've seen what she's like." He takes her hand. When she doesn't pull away, he hugs her close. "You work with what you've got." His voice vibrates gently against her forehead. "That's all you can do."

❊

Penn Station blares with voices and hurried footsteps. The 5:55 to Westfield leaves soon. Marney sits near the departure board. Gwen isn't expecting her. They haven't spoken in weeks, since the baseball game. Last Friday Gwen finally left a terse message ("Checking that you didn't die"), but Marney hasn't called her back yet. There's too much to say for a phone call, and she owes another answer first. She opens her laptop, tethers it to her phone for a hotspot. Then she opens her email and starts typing:

"Remember, Winston, when we used to bike to the creek by the horse farm, how the horses whinnied by the split-rail fence until we offered up the apples and cheese slices we'd brought for ourselves. Remember how icy the water felt streaming across our feet when we waded to where the rope swing hung from that old willow tree. Remember the slime on the rocks, how our toes disappeared in clouds of silt. The water under the swing barely reached my chest, and that bent plastic seat looked like it couldn't hold anybody. Try it, you used to tell me, go on. I did, once or twice, until the fire drill. After that, I was too scared. But you always swung out over the creek and leaped. You could have broken your neck in that shallow water, but you never got a scratch. I'm the only one who ever broke anything, the day we jumped off the roof. My collarbone hurt so bad, I thought I would faint. You held my hand and kept talking to me while the neighbors called an ambulance. At least you tried, you kept saying.

"But I was only trying to be you. I wasn't figuring out how to be me. Even when I tried to do something I thought you'd never do, I wasn't figuring out me.

"I'm trying now, Winston. Remember that when you get here."

Over the intercom she hears the initial boarding call for the 5:55 to Westfield. Once she clicks send, plans will move swiftly, beyond her control. Plane tickets bought, mountains of baby gifts ordered. Her fingers linger on the keyboard as she waits for the wince that usually accompanies such thoughts. It's there, but barely. Meeting the baby, seeing her brother for the first time in years, even witnessing the reunion between mother and prodigal son—none of that needs to wholly define her anymore.

One click and the email's on its way. Relief, and release. She closes her laptop, puts it and the phone in her messenger bag, alongside some listings for one-bedrooms. A new place still feels in order, even though it's just for her. Something that can accommodate a little clutter, maybe even a pot rack over a working stove. "I'll settle for some closet space," Dominic said last night when he kissed her goodbye at her door. "Baby steps." He's more cautious with her ever since she decided to keep living alone, but he's willing to let her jump into their future at her own pace.

Another announcement, almost lost in the station's noise: last call for the 5:55. She imagines boarding the train, riding miles through grimy cities and wetlands, suburbs of tightly packed townhouses giving way to larger, more widely spaced homes with shingled roofs to be conquered, trees to be climbed, creeks to be forded. She imagines the train slowing to a stop, herself stepping off and crossing the platform to the red-shuttered Westfield station. She will see through its windows the shiny cab by the curb. The faint scratch on the rear fender noticeable only to those who know to look.

Then she's running to the platform, her thighs pumping, her bag thumping against her back, the train getting closer, closer still.

Once Removed

Sylvie is late the first time she meets Kyle's son. An accident on Mulholland snarls traffic and she winds up rushing to the movie theater, impatient for Kyle to calm her nerves with an embrace, the quiet reverence of his touch. He's always finding reasons to touch her, to remind himself what she feels like, he sometimes says with a shy smile that leaves her giddy and flushed and goofy with love—everything she forgot she could feel until she met him.

From the parking lot she spots him standing by the theater with a teenage boy who must be Aiden. Damn that totaled Porsche. Some idiot speeds around a curve and now it probably seems like she's dragging her feet, reluctant to meet Kyle's son. But she's excited, mostly. At least he's sixteen. She's not great with younger kids. Still, she's not sure what to expect from this boy with a head injury. It must be hard to remember what day it is, much less whether his dad has a new girlfriend.

She hurries up in a flurry of apologies and barely registers Kyle's kiss hello, she's so intent on greeting Aiden. "Nice to finally meet you," she says.

Aiden keeps staring at the sidewalk. Should she wait for him to answer? Say hello again? Neither seems right. She steps back, expecting Kyle's reassuring hug. He grips his son's shoulder instead.

"Aiden, say hi to Sylvie."

The boy flinches. "Yeah, hi," he mutters. His eyes dart behind his thick-lensed glasses to the blazing marquee, the throng flowing into the theater—everywhere but to her.

"This is a little busy for him," Kyle explains. He clears his throat and jams his hands in his pockets, nervous gestures, like he's worried she'll flee, though he warned her his son could seem unwelcoming or even hostile. Aiden doesn't like new situations where people might stare at his shuffling gate. And his fear of being touched—common, his father says, in head-injury patients—makes him anxious in crowds.

She smiles and clenches her fists behind her back. It's hard to keep all this in mind. Aiden looks like any other clean-cut kid. He's tall like his father, with the same broad cheekbones. Comb tracks still show in his damp hair. He could be waiting for a pretty girl to lead inside. But there is his cane, and his set, angry mouth. She almost pats his arm—*We'll get along great, I promise*—but no. She's not supposed to touch.

"Once we're sitting, things will feel calmer," she says. "Let's get tickets."

Seeing Kyle's relief is like winning a prize. "Tickets. Right. Good idea," he says and pulls out his wallet. "Aiden, would you buy them?"

His son glares. "No way."

"It's okay. Here's forty dollars. Three adults, twelve dollars each. So how much change?"

Blushing, Aiden glances at her. He doesn't know. Now she's the one trying to find somewhere else to look, to save him some embarrassment.

"Tell me," he says to his dad.

The poor kid. She starts toward the theater—"I'll get them"—but Kyle stops her. "He's learning to be more independent," he says and helps Aiden through the calculations.

Aiden takes a deep breath. He looks at her. "You're coming?"

She nods.

"What's your name?" he says.

"I'm Sylvie." Smile, hands to herself. Smile some more.

He walks to the box office. Though he towers over most people, his halting steps make him seem fragile, as if he might topple over like a half-cut tree.

"I hate sending him alone," Kyle says. "But he can do this. We'll have a good time."

He shivers, as if shaking something off, then hugs her, finally. When she looks up, she finds him staring at his son.

❀

There has been a slew of births among Sylvie's friends, who are all in their late thirties like her. Time to shift focus from their careers, they agree. Sylvie is one of the few still working, at the plant nursery in West LA she's co-owned for years with her partner, Izzy, who's old enough to be her great-grandfather, he likes to joke, and who treats her like family. He's been after her to spruce up her tiny, spare apartment, which is the opposite of her old house in Venice Beach with its colorful walls and sprawling garden. Finn, Sylvie's ex-fiancé, bought her out last year, which seemed fair since she was the one who left.

Lately she'd rather spend time with Izzy than with her girlfriends. She doesn't have much to add to their conversations about colic and breastfeeding, things she has chosen to avoid. She's had one abortion—when she was twenty and too young to be pregnant—and one miscarriage last year, which turned out to be a relief. Not everyone wants kids, she tells her friends when they press her about whether she'll try again. What she wants to say is *Back off*, but they mean well.

After the movie, over dinner at a noisy family restaurant, she finds herself wondering what—or whether—to tell them about Aiden. He sits across from her and Kyle and traces his finger down his huge, laminated menu.

Aiden points at her. "Do you see pizza?" he says.

Kyle taps the menu. "Answer's right there, buddy." Quietly he says to her, "Reading's still tough, but he's up to the third-grade level."

Aiden leans in and whispers, "Find it for me, okay?" as if his father won't hear.

Sylvie looks from face to face. She wants Aiden to like her, and she would help any other child. But this is Kyle's son, and he isn't a child.

"If it's okay with your dad," she says and relishes the warmth of Kyle's hand on her back even as she pretends not to see Aiden's scowl.

After she helps him read the entire menu aloud—there's no pizza, they discover—Aiden chooses a burger and a milkshake. He rocks in his chair while she and Kyle order, and asks the waitress, over and over, "Bring my shake now, can you?"

The waitress shoots him quick glances. The injury knocked out his impulse control. He's still relearning to restrain himself. *He can be very persistent*, Sylvie imagines telling her friends. Her palms stick to the plastic tablecloth.

Once the waitress leaves, Kyle pulls a small notepad and pencil from his jacket pocket.

"So, Aiden, what was the movie about?"

His son frowns, rocks. "A guy with a kid," he finally says.

Kyle taps the notepad. "Guy with kid. Yup. Write it down, and the characters' names. Title, too. It has to do with the dad."

Aiden's expression clouds, then clears. "'Daddy O.'" He starts scribbling.

Kyle smiles. "Right. 'Daddy O.' Nice job." He turns to Sylvie and says quietly, "A memory exercise. We do it after every movie. It's a little monotonous, but his recall wasn't this good a few months ago."

He watches his son write. She clasps Kyle's hand under the table. His grip is steady, warm. This is a committed man, intensely loyal. During the six months she has known him, he's been preparing her for this meeting, describing how he's been helping to rebuild his son's body and memory since the accident eight years ago. "You think you're invincible until something like this happens," he told her once. "Then all you can do is devote yourself to making him whole." He works nights as a web designer so that he and his ex-wife, a landscape architect with her own business, can accommodate Aiden's schedule: physical therapy three times a week to help Aiden regain his balance, ophthalmology appointments for his double vision, reading classes, math classes, computer classes. There's a big, ancient dog Sylvie hasn't met yet who goes back and forth with Aiden from Kyle's house to his ex's. Kyle has shown Sylvie pictures of Aiden from before, given her books about brain injuries and the workings of memory—books that have seemed like dry theoretical musings until now. Still, she's read every page, determined to merit his trust. He rarely talks about the accident. Best to focus on moving forward, he says. Shortly after Kyle and his ex-wife separated, Aiden jumped from some bleachers on a dare. He hit his head on the pavement, spent months in a coma. His only other injury was a punctured lung.

Aiden points at Sylvie. "You. What's the son's name?"

"Be polite. She has a name, too," Kyle says.

"Oh yeah?"

Light glints off Aiden's glasses and obscures his eyes. She drops Kyle's hand so he can't feel her tense. Aiden really can't remember, though he's acting like a resentful child, pissed off about sharing his dad. Already she can anticipate the cues Kyle will offer, the agonizing wait while Aiden scowls and cajoles and tries to pry the answer from his father, her, the waitress, anyone who might save him from the tedious process of trying to recall information that once came effortlessly.

Aiden rocks.

Kyle says, "Think, buddy."

She leans forward. "Sylvie. My name's Sylvie."

"Sylvie," Aiden repeats and writes in his journal.

"He could have figured it out," his father says.

❁

The living room in her new apartment has a southern exposure. Though, really, it's not so new. She's lived there almost a year and picked it for that very room, which is bathed in light from dawn till dusk. Izzy, her business partner, keeps urging her to line the windowsill with plants.

"African violets would love it there," he says at the nursery, the day after her dinner with Aiden. Izzy sits on a bench in the shade house while she prunes a juniper bonsai. He is small and stout and full of advice. His wrinkled face is raised to the dim winter sky, obscured by the scrim overhead. She's never gotten him to commit to an age. Lately, though, on days like this one—damp and cloudy, bad arthritis weather, keeping him on the bench instead of wandering around picking brownish leaves off plants—he admits to a few degrees short of ancient.

He cups his knees with thick, rigid fingers. "A house isn't a home without something else living there."

She focuses on pruning the bonsai, close, delicate work, soothing in its precision. "I take care of enough plants here." A final tweak and the bonsai swoops through space, perfect.

He scoots off the bench. His gait is stiff-legged and painful to watch, like Aiden's. He shuffles among colorful perennials, ice plants dripping plump, waxy leaves. Staghorns, twisted and spiked like antlers, make the back wall look like a trophy case. She spends hours watering, pruning, fertilizing, organizing. Izzy taught her everything she knows about plants, common names as well as botanical, plants that thrive in full sun, those that covet shade. Plants are more predictable than people; follow a few simple rules and they're fine.

Izzy hands her a potted crown of thorns, its spiny stalks tipped by tiny white blossoms. "Here. A nice, easy succulent. Plop it in your living room, it'll care for itself."

It upsets him that she still hasn't taken his advice. Most of her belongings are in storage near her old house. Sometimes she drives by to see what's changed. Not much so far. Her ex even still varies the front beds with the seasons, the way they used to do together. A general contractor, he loves plants as much as Sylvie. Eventually there will be a second car beside his pickup, a play set peeking above the back gate. Finn thought life's progression should be easy, inevitable: find someone to love, have a family, grow old together. He was thrilled by her pregnancy, crushed by the miscarriage. Stunned she didn't feel the same way.

Inside the nursery, the front bell jingles.

"Back to work," Izzy says and shuffles into the store.

She waits a decent interval before following him. They pretend he's as independent as always, that she doesn't monitor his every move, worried he may stumble and break a bone.

Up front, Izzy is propping a ladder against a tall shelf. The customer, a nervous-looking blonde, watches with crossed arms.

"I have the perfect orchid pot up there," Izzy says.

"Can I help?" Sylvie asks.

The customer frowns. "I said I'd get it, but he insisted."

Izzy waves Sylvie away. "I'll be done in a blink."

They compromise. Up he goes, with her a few rungs behind. Below, the customer taps her foot. Sylvie focuses on Izzy making his slow, crablike way along the ladder.

Once the customer has paid and left, Sylvie leads Izzy outside to the bench with a cup of water.

"I'm all right," he says, but sweat beads his forehead as he sips his water. "So. You haven't told me about meeting the son last night."

She takes his hand and massages his knuckles. *He didn't like me,* she wants to say. *He can't keep a thought in his head.* But that sounds horrible. "He seems nice."

"You don't like him."

She drops his hand. "No. I don't know."

"You'll get used to each other."

"I'm not sure I want to."

There. She said it. Admitted that meeting Aiden has changed things. The reality of him is so different from what she imagined: a younger version of his father with slightly halting speech, maybe a hitch to his step, but otherwise almost whole again. And Kyle. He's someone different too. Despite what he's told her, she envisioned his role in his son's recovery as effortless, heroic, something separate and apart from the man she knows and loves. But taking care of his son colors every part of him, even the ones she so thoughtlessly claimed for herself.

"Things that I thought were mine," she says, careful to keep her eyes on the ground, "like how he's always touching me and repeats what I say to be sure he's heard me. They're just habits from helping Aiden."

She shifts on the bench, sneaks a look at Izzy, who regards her quietly before grasping her hand.

"Can't have the father without the son," he says.

Kyle takes her bowling the next time she sees him. "My highest score ever was a forty," she says, laughing as he backs her into the bowling alley even as he's kissing her, his lips tickling her cheeks, her ears, her neck. Aiden's not with them. It's his turn with his mom. Sylvie charmed him, Kyle says. "You're so patient," he tells her, "and you treated him like any other kid." Which makes her cringe.

At their lane Kyle sets up their scoring machine. "This'll be fun, I promise," he says as she slips on her stained rental shoes that smell faintly sour.

It's early and the place is almost empty, thank God. The fewer witnesses the better. Even so, she freezes at the foul line. The ball feels cool and hard under her chin as she gazes down the lane. All those pins. Odds are she won't hit even one.

"You okay?"

Kyle's voice behind her makes her jump. The ball crashes down, barely missing her foot, then bumps into the gutter. Briefly she covers her eyes. "This is a bad idea."

"It's a matter of confidence," he says and guides her to the ball return like he's trying to keep her from falling. She almost pulls away, but it's just his instinct, to help. Her ball spins out, a magenta swirl of color, lushly optimistic, like a dahlia in full bloom, inspiring her to succeed. But she's never been athletic and she doesn't feel like challenging that reality anymore.

Kyle grabs his own ball and demonstrates. He's a good teacher, clear and articulate, gestures slightly exaggerated to facilitate imitation:

ball up, elbows back, then several strides as his arm sweeps in a pendulum arc until he pushes off and releases the ball. It rumbles down the lane; pins scatter. Easy.

Not so easy for her. She hates the sensation of being watched as she tries to replicate Kyle's fluid grace. "I don't care if I suck," she says, but he's determined for her to improve. He examines her from every angle, makes suggestions about her stance, the timing of her release. Finally, she knocks over half the pins.

"I can't believe it," she says and hugs him.

He grins, hugs her back. "Now for some refining."

Her arms and shoulders start to ache. Fewer and fewer pins fall. And then she's had enough pointers and encouragement, enough oblivion to her frustration. She doesn't need fixing, dammit. Deliberately she gutters the ball.

"Even pros get a break," she says, laughing but emphatic.

He blinks, rakes back his hair. "A break. Of course, sorry. Let's sit."

The plastic bench feels cool against her back as she nestles under his arm. She would be happy never to see another bowling alley.

Next to her, he breathes deeply. "It's nice, doing this alone," he says.

She shifts to see his face. "What do you mean?"

"Aiden bowls." He glances at her, then away. "Every Saturday in a league. It's infuriating, sometimes, trying to get him to do things."

The shame on his face. She wants to kiss it away or joke him into smiling, but he stands up, his hands in his pockets, and stares down the lane like he's imagining his son striding to the foul line. She tries to imagine it too but can only conjure Aiden leaning on his cane as they left the restaurant, his dad urging him to stand up straight and swing his arms for balance. "You won't fall, buddy, you won't," Kyle reassured him, a mantra, a lullaby, a plea, but still Aiden hunched forward and muttered, "Yeah, I will."

She stands to stroke Kyle's back. "You're a good dad. The best."

He rubs his eyes before turning to her. "Aiden would like it if you came to his bowling league. Maybe next Saturday?"

The sting of being watched as she flings the ball, the embarrassment. "I don't want to make him uncomfortable."

Kyle entwines his fingers with hers. "You'll give him someone to show off for."

It was on their third date, before she knew about Aiden, when finally Kyle held her hand. He did it cautiously, as if fearful she might pull away, after an early dinner at a Korean taco place in Santa Monica, then a stroll down Main Street, the salty air ruffling her newly bobbed hair, his hands burrowed in the pockets of his frayed jeans. Later, on their sixth date, after they finally made love, their hips rocking, every pore sensitized, exquisitely so, his gaze fixed on her as if he were memorizing each movement to savor later, he would admit he'd been afraid. Afraid he'd forgotten how to touch, how to connect outside the confines of the ways he helped his son.

That night on Main Street, he veered down a narrow alley and walked beside her to the beach, where the sunset glinted off bits of mica in the sand and the surf sounded distant and calm.

He took his hands from his pockets and tucked them under his arms. "I love the beach at sunset," he said. "I never come here anymore."

She reached out to balance on his shoulder while she slipped off her sandals. "We can make out like teenagers on a lifeguard stand," she joked. When she looked up, he was blushing. This tall, slim man with his stern mouth and shock of bristly gray hair. Blushing. Something inside her unclenched, expanded, made her sigh aloud, then laugh. She kissed him then, a gentle pressing of her mouth against his. That's when he took her hand with fragile tenderness.

"I forgot," he said as he led her onto the sand.

Her dress swirled around her bare legs; his palm felt warm against hers. "Forgot what?" she asked, her words almost lost in the wind.

He stopped walking, roughly brushed his thumb against his own lips, then hers. "How soft skin can be."

When she arrives on Saturday, the bowling alley swarms with people in fluorescent bowling shirts. The thwack of balls against pins makes her teeth clench. She clutches a shopping bag with cartoon books for Aiden and searches for Kyle.

"The head-injury kids, right?" says the man at the snack bar when she asks for the Saint Mary's Hospital League. "They don't really play, but they try hard."

He directs her to the far lane, where she finds Kyle crouched down tying Aiden's bowling shoes. When Aiden sees her he pushes at his glasses with a stiff index finger.

Kyle kisses her, then does introductions. Sitting with Aiden is Donny, whose forearm crutch lies across the bench. Louise, with short white hair and tired eyes, is at the scoring desk. Beside her sits her son, Chuck, a thin, scruffy man scribbling on a magazine. He scribbles harder when Louise tries to get him to say hello.

Aiden points at Sylvie. "Who invited her?" he asks.

Donny giggles. She steps back. To walk out, be done with this kid. But Kyle is watching.

"Your dad said you did," she says.

"Really?"

"You told me, buddy, on the way to PT," Kyle says.

That's probably untrue, from the way his words rush out. Aiden picks at his pant leg before looking at her.

"Yeah. You can stay."

She passes him the bag. "These are for you."

He glances at Donny as he pulls out the books. "All these are mine?" His eyes search out his father, who's still watching Sylvie and Aiden's exchange.

She smooths her skirt. It didn't occur to her to ask about getting Aiden a gift.

"Is it okay?" she asks Kyle.

He nods, expressionless. "I like him to earn things, though. Reward him for trying something new." There's an edge to his voice she doesn't understand.

"He's getting to know me. That's new." She sits near Aiden and opens a book. "I've always liked *Calvin and Hobbes*. Calvin's so sarcastic."

Aiden opens another book. Kyle checks his watch.

"Time to play," he says.

Aiden doesn't look up. "Let Chuck go first."

She clasps her hands and fake-begs. "Come on, Dad. Please?"

Kyle hesitates before smiling. "Sure," he says.

Chuck starts scrawling on the desktop. His mother takes the pen. "Chuck, see the books Sylvie brought Aiden?"

Chuck stares at her. Louise sighs and helps him stand and walk to the ball return.

"Can I look?" Donny asks.

Aiden surprises Sylvie by tapping her leg. "Is it okay?" he asks. When she nods, he gives Donny a book. "It's not to keep, though," Aiden says. "Don't forget."

"I can't promise anything," Donny says.

The boys whoop with laughter.

She tries not to smile, but when she looks at Kyle, his lips are twitching. Soon they're all laughing, except Chuck, who watches his bowling ball nip a single pin. He stomps past his mother and stops close to Sylvie and the boys.

Kyle takes Aiden's book. "Your turn."

"That's mine," Aiden says, but he stands, his face blotchy. His arms hang awkwardly, slightly bent. He picks up his cane.

Kyle takes it away. "The therapist said to practice without it." Slowly, he walks Aiden to the ball return. The weight of the ball, the awkward dance to the foul line. Sylvie looks away, wincing.

There's movement beside her. Chuck stands close to her knees. He stares at the ground and points at her book.

"He likes the pictures," Louise says.

Sylvie gives him the book; he scurries back to his mother. Together they page through, Louise quietly reading the cartoon bubbles and touching each picture, sometimes guiding Chuck's fingers across the images. He wears the same empty expression he's worn since Sylvie arrived, but he hunches so that his nose almost touches the page. Louise strokes his bangs from his eyes. Sylvie's own mother mourned her decision to move to Los Angeles after college. "How will you find an apartment or buy a car?" she said when Sylvie called to tell her. "You'll be so far away." Her mother's grief flooded through the phone like water from a burst pipe. *Who will help you feed yourself, comb your hair, find pleasure in a picture book, when I'm gone?* Maybe that's what Louise thinks when she watches Chuck asleep in the room she once planned to convert into a study or a sewing room after her son ventured into the world, eager to shed his need of her.

"Good job, buddy," Sylvie hears Kyle say. "Sylvie, did you see that?"

Down the alley, six pins have fallen. "Woo-hoo!" she says and claps, giddy with relief.

"You're getting good, Aiden," Louise says. She goes to help Donny stand for his turn.

"Beat that, Donny," Aiden says. He notices Chuck scribbling in the book. "Hey, give it back!"

It happens so fast. Aiden tries to snatch the book. Chuck keeps scribbling. The page tears. Aiden shoves Chuck, who falls, keening, to the floor. Louise scrambles from Donny to Chuck. Kyle grabs Donny before he falls too.

Aiden takes a few shuffling steps toward Chuck. "You ruined it!"

Sylvie stands and grabs him. "Aiden, no!"

"Don't touch me!" He towers over her, his fists clenched. The sour smell of rage; his breath on her face in short, hot bursts. He could hurt her.

"That's enough!" Kyle pushes between them and grabs Aiden, who tries to jerk away. Kyle staggers but holds firm. "Calm down, buddy." His anger has a scent, like his son's: acrid, overwhelming. "Jesus, Sylvie."

"I was trying to help," she snaps. A hammer to her chest, his words. She crouches beside Louise and Chuck.

"A little turf battle," Louise says. "That's all."

"Aiden's sorry," Kyle says. "He'll tell you himself soon."

He leads Aiden to where Donny sits watching. Aiden's hands are still curled into tight fists. Kyle sits beside him, murmuring. Sylvie stays crouched on the floor, breathless.

A week later, early morning, she finds Izzy lying near the bench under the nursery's scrim. The sky is dusky. She rushes over, hesitates before touching him. Not yet. No. His cheek is clammy. He opens his eyes.

"Sylvie," he says slowly. "I had a fall."

A series of small heart attacks, the doctor tells her after she's checked Izzy into the hospital and jotted down phone numbers that Izzy recited from memory: his cousin in Laguna Woods, the lawyer who does his estate planning, the doctor who arranged for a private room in the cardiac unit and now explains Izzy's condition. He will be bedridden, who knows for how long, and will require round-the-clock care. As the doctor speaks, she strokes Izzy's forearm and focuses on the parchment feel of his skin.

"He's exaggerating," Izzy says after the doctor leaves. His words are thick with effort, though he smiles with half-closed eyes. "I'm fine."

"You will be," she says, but he's already drifted off. She presses her stinging eyes against his blanket. *Fine. He'll be fine. Please, let him be fine.*

Izzy's cousin arrives late in the day. Her name is Althea and she's even smaller than Izzy, her slender fingers tipped by the same blunt, squared nails as his. She looks almost as ancient, her skin pleated with wrinkles, her scalp shiny through a thin netting of white curls. She kisses his cheek, leaving a blurry lipstick splotch, before beckoning Sylvie into the hallway.

"The other ones were never this serious," Althea says. "Years ago, he had two, who knows how many since. He stopped telling me, I fussed so much."

Sylvie hugs herself, suddenly cold. "He hasn't had any since I've known him."

Althea shuffles back inside the room to Izzy's bedside. "Secretive bastard wouldn't have told you," she says and smooths his blanket. "You're an old man, Isadore. No more denying it. I've got a room all ready for you."

"Don't call me old." He opens his eyes and frowns, then sees Sylvie. "There you are," he says in a whispery facsimile of his normal voice.

"We'll keep each other company," Althea says. "I'm all alone in Laguna Woods these days. We'll even build you a little greenhouse. Better than a nursing home, hmm, Cousin Iz?" She nods at Sylvie. "Tell him, dear, how he'll be better off in Laguna Woods."

On a good day Laguna Woods is an hour's drive. He wouldn't be better there. He would do better here in West LA with her. A hospital bed cranked to sitting in her tiny living room; every surface lined with pill bottles, trailing vines, crowns of thorns, and other succulents. The growing translucence of his skin each morning as she sponges his arms and back, more intimate than a kiss. She watches Althea stroke Izzy's hair with those blunt-tipped fingers. It's not Sylvie's place to care for him. She's not really family, not even once removed.

"Promise," Izzy says and takes Sylvie's hand. "Promise to get some dahlias."

She returns to the apartment later that evening and sits on the couch, cradling her cell phone. Everything has been settled. Izzy will move to Laguna Woods after his release. She'll visit when she can. She'll run the nursery, same as always. Nothing will change.

Everything has changed. There's no one to call. She hasn't returned Kyle's message from a few days ago. He sounded like himself, no hint of their strained goodbye at the bowling alley last week. She walked herself out after he brushed his lips against her cheek. She didn't mind; she kept her arms crossed as she hurried away.

The apartment presses around her, tight and dark with night. She leaves to go for a drive, entering and exiting freeways until she's across town at her old house. In the driveway is her ex's pickup filled with bags of potting soil. She parks far enough away so he won't see her if he emerges. He might not recognize her anyway, with her new car—a hybrid hatchback instead of the gas-guzzling SUV—and new hairstyle, cropped into a bob the way he didn't like. She tucks her hair behind her ears. What would he do if she got out and started emptying the pickup as if she'd been gone only hours?

Five years together. Finn wanted a baby so badly; she convinced herself she wanted one too. Midway through her first trimester, they threw themselves an engagement party. Friends filled their backyard around the shaggy avocado tree that shed fruit the size of walnuts. The garden, which they'd just replanted together, overflowed: cone flowers, gardenias, artfully disarrayed Mexican sage. Near the party's end, she found Finn in the far bed planting a sapling fig tree. Her grandfather had planted one for every grandchild in his own back-yard. "Here comes Mama Sylvie," Finn called before she shushed him with a kiss. They were waiting to tell anyone. His flush—from beer (she tasted the yeasty sweetness on his tongue) and pride—changed his hazel eyes to amber. The way he looked at her: Mama Sylvie. The thrill of it rushed through her.

A week after the party, she started spotting, faint and brown, then small reddish clots, then a long, aching cramp followed by one huge clot, like a broken egg with a brilliant, crimson yolk, its metallic stench still lodged in memory.

Finn's grief was as predictable and rhythmic as a waltz, a pure, uncomplicated cleansing. Her own sorrow was marbled with relief. They had their garden, their businesses, the comfort of shared inter-ests and friends. Their life together felt complete. This loss was actu-ally a reprieve.

Something must be wrong with her to feel that way, Finn said, but his anger didn't sway her. Parenthood—its unpredictability and sacrifices—wasn't a natural progression but a choice, one that she decided not to make.

The driveway gate swings open. Slowly, then more quickly, she pulls away from the curb. She could stop, roll down her window. *I miss us sometimes*, she could say. She tries to picture his reaction (anger, sadness, surprise?) but can't. As she whizzes by, a man walks past the pickup to the street. In the rearview, she sees him lift his hand. To wave? Probably not, probably to shade his eyes for a better glimpse of the bobbed brunette, vaguely familiar, speeding away in a Prius.

The nursery feels vast, empty, even when she's hurrying from customer to customer. Shadows tease her peripheral vision. If she just turns quickly enough, she'll see Izzy resting on the bench, or holding out plants to her. Outside of work she avoids her girlfriends and their babies. It's unsettling to spend time with them without Izzy around to remind her what she values about this life she's made, this family she has—had—in him. He phones often, stronger and joking—"I'm fit as a fiddle with a busted string or two"—but it's not the same as having him there.

Kyle catches her off guard one evening when he comes by the nursery shortly before closing. It's been weeks since his voicemail. He's waiting at the counter when she walks in from the shade house. She startles and stops a few feet away, one hand over her thudding heart. He smiles, but his face stays guarded, like when they first met, before he told her about Aiden. Before he trusted her.

The store is empty except for them. She walks over and kisses him lightly. His lips feel rough, like he's been biting them. He touches her shoulder before leaning against the counter.

"We've missed you," he says. "Aiden and I."

She rubs her hands against her apron. "I was about to close," she says.

"It's my two weeks with Aiden. I thought you could come visit tomorrow." When she starts shaking her head, he adds, "Just for a while."

But she doesn't belong there with them, not really. This is where she belongs, in this nursery with its shade house and bench, the plants with their glossy leaves, the bonsai. Everything in its place, organized, understood. This is home. Or it was, when there was someone else to share it with.

"Please," he says.

She looks at him, at his serious, unsmiling mouth, the skin taut around his eyes.

"Just for a while," she says.

❀

When she pulls up the next day, Kyle is sitting on the porch checking his watch. There's a huge black dog lying beside him. She grips the steering wheel. Drive away, drive until the house is a blip in the rearview. Instead she parks and walks up with a bakery box, brownies for Aiden. A mea culpa. *I don't want you. Forgive me.*

The dog stands with effort and barks when she approaches. His raised hackles are streaked with gray, as is his muzzle, but his booming bark stops her. Kyle says something to the dog, who lies down obediently, his grizzled muzzle resting on his paws, his eyes fixed on Sylvie's approach. Cautiously, she climbs the porch steps and sits beside Kyle. He smiles tentatively but doesn't move. In his lap is a manila folder.

"Okay, Butchie," he says.

The dog drags himself to his feet and ambles over to her, resting his head in her lap. He examines her as she rubs his floppy ears, then settles at her feet.

She hands Kyle the box of brownies. "For Aiden," she says. When he sighs, she holds up her hand. "I know he's supposed to earn things, but you could make an exception."

"He'll never have a normal life if I keep making exceptions." His voice is tight with impatience, as if she should know this.

She takes back the brownies. "That makes perfect sense to you, but I wouldn't have guessed on my own. I don't understand kids. I don't know that I want to." The admission hollows her out, leaving her strangely peaceful.

He offers her the folder. "I thought you should see these."

"You're not listening," she says but takes it.

Inside are pictures. Some Kyle has already shown her: Aiden as a toddler, a quarter pressed to one eye like a monocle; a taller, skinnier Aiden squirting a jet black Butchie with a hose; Aiden standing on the beach with a boogie board under one arm. In each picture his eyes are Kyle's, sharp, inquisitive, insistent on knowing everything.

Kyle takes a photo from the bottom: Aiden strapped in a wheelchair. He lists to one side, his arms as slender as broomsticks. At the base of his throat is an angry red scar. Kyle touches the spot. "From the trach tube."

"I didn't know," she says.

"See how far he's come," he says. "See what my boy's done."

He's still so far from who he was. He might not go any farther. When she draws a ragged breath, Kyle takes the folder. Sadness is useless to him. There can be no thought of imperfection; he must rejoice in each small gain. A gift and a curse, his refusal to envision any future other than one in which his child—forever damaged, no matter what the progress—is whole. This is what commitment means to him, this optimism that spurns failure. She's not sure she has it in her.

He squeezes her hand. "Please try," he says as if he hears her thoughts. "Please hang in there." Then he stands and opens the door. The dog stands too. "We're going for a boat ride. Want to come?"

She hesitates, then picks up the brownies and follows them inside.

The parking lot swarms with people, cars, trucks towing power boats and jet skis. Beyond is the lake, vast and smooth and glittering, a man-made jewel nestled in the dusty hills. Kyle helps Aiden out of the car. Sweat dampens Aiden's forehead. There's a trickle down Sylvie's own back. He hasn't acknowledged her yet, even when Kyle prodded him. Maybe someone without a memory can still hold a grudge.

Kyle opens the trunk to grab a bag of food including the brownies. Aiden steadies himself against the car.

"Dad, my cane," he says.

Kyle shuts the trunk. "You don't need it, buddy. I'll go see about a boat." He hugs her and whispers, "Just keep reassuring him," then strides toward the lake with the food.

She starts after him—"Kyle, wait!"—but he picks up speed and doesn't look back. Damn him. The parking lot yawns around her and Aiden, the cracks and potholes all sudden, ready threats. Please don't let it be her fault if this boy gets hurt again.

She walks back to the car and stands beside Aiden. "We should go," she says. His lips snarl; he clutches the car roof and ignores her. No way this pissed-off teen is going to listen to her, but she's got to try. "Aiden, your dad's waiting for us."

He takes an unsteady breath. "I'm gonna fall, I know it."

He's afraid, not angry. Afraid. She's not sure how to comfort him. Finally, she taps her own shoulder.

"You could balance on me," she says.

He hangs on to the roof without looking at her. Then, scowling, he stands behind her and puts his hands on her shoulders. The clammy heat of his palms radiates through her thin sweater. She walks slowly, keeping time with the awkward cadence of his gait.

He trails her like a kite tail as she navigates through the parking lot to the crowded pier. A little girl points them out to her mother. Sylvie turns Aiden away to look at some jet skis flying across the lake.

"They must get wet, really, really wet," he says and stares, as if wishing he could be as soaked and wild and free.

By the time they reach the boat shack, his steps are more assured, though her shoulders are damp with his sweat. He doesn't protest when his father hugs him.

"I knew you could do it," Kyle says and grins at Sylvie with such happiness that all she can do is smile back. He points to several bobbing, weathered rowboats, engines attached in back. "Ours is the first one," he says.

She plants her hands on her hips. She expected a ferry encased in guard rails.

"Can you handle one of those?" she asks.

Aiden pushes at his glasses. "Dad?"

"Don't scare him," Kyle whispers. "This'll be great," he says to his son and guides him along.

The floating dock quakes beneath her feet. Water laps the edges. She can't help if Aiden falls here, but there's no going back. With every step through the parking lot, she committed herself to seeing this day through.

Kyle and a dock worker help her and Aiden into the teetering boat and coax Aiden into a life vest. Each move is a negotiation, marked by muttered protests. The splintery plank seat digs into Sylvie's palms. Finally, Kyle starts the motor.

The spray kicked up by the boat chills her. She perches on the middle seat, Kyle steering behind her, the food at his feet, Aiden in front facing her, his back to the view. Whenever the boat jerks, she jerks with it, certain Aiden will fall overboard. His face is bunched with frustration. "Can we stop? Are we done yet?" he keeps asking. Over the motor's buzz his father calls, "You're fine, this is fun," like some lullaby Sylvie has yet to learn. She wants to add her own chorus: *I've had enough, this is too much.* The boat moves farther from shore.

"Hey!" Aiden's voice startles her. He taps her knee and points at a nearby power boat trailing a water skier.

"He must be getting wet," she says and hesitates.

Aiden finishes: "Really, really wet."

Her laughter bursts out. There's a faint grin on Aiden's face. Sylvie looks at Kyle, who focuses on their path through the water, more relaxed than she's ever seen him. He could be right. They could be some sort of family, if she can find it in herself to carry the responsibility of this boy who may always be a child, to choose to lead him through life instead of just herself. To love him most, like Kyle does. For an instant she envisions what might happen later, after they've dropped anchor somewhere shady to consume the food, the brownies eaten first at her and Aiden's insistence; after they've chugged near shore so Aiden can get a closer look at a swooping hawk or maybe a girl sunning herself on a pebbly beach; after they've returned to the dock and Kyle has looked at Sylvie and said, "Walk him to the pier, okay?" She will jump out and wait while Kyle helps Aiden from the boat, and she will drape Aiden's arm across her shoulders in anticipation of his stumble. Just out of sight is the vision of Aiden solidly supported against her as she whispers something soothing that erases his fear and makes him smile.

Elephant Teeth

Elephants have six sets of molars, I learned the summer that I made Eugene move downstairs. They use the front set to eat. When those wear down, the back molars push forward, ejecting the dull ones and leaving fresh ones for chewing. Once the final set wears down, elephants die.

That summer, I related these facts to my daughter, Lucy, whenever I brushed her teeth. She was seven years old, but our dentist claimed children aren't dexterous enough to do it themselves until they're at least eight. Brushing her teeth had been her dad Winston's job before he moved out of our duplex's lower unit to make room for Eugene, whose insistence on an open relationship prompted my request that he live downstairs. What I couldn't see up close wouldn't hurt as much, was my reasoning.

Before then, Eugene and I had lived upstairs with the kids for two years, since the birth of our son, Tate. Winston and I had a much longer history, dating back to college. He was my dearest friend, my confidant. After he and his husband divorced, we decided to have Lucy, fulfilling our freshman-year pact to have a baby together if we were still single and childless as middle age loomed. We bought the duplex so we could coparent while maintaining separate lives. Which we could still do. Lucy would adjust to Winston living a few blocks away. I would adjust to Eugene sleeping around. We would survive.

The first time I brushed Lucy's teeth was the morning she started camp at the Los Angeles Zoo. I was alone with the kids. Eugene had been downstairs a week, and Winston had just left for Vancouver to produce a movie. Winston always made brushing Lucy's teeth fun, singing silly songs or sharing animal facts to keep her attention. She was crazy about animals. "We're lucky you're not a chinchilla or water would make your fur mold. I'd have to use volcanic ash instead," I heard him say sometimes while I changed Tate's diaper in the kids' room. "Teeth don't have fur," she'd giggle.

I sat Lucy on the tub's edge and started brushing while I recited what I knew about elephant teeth. I had to yell over Tate, who stood beside me babbling an off-key lullaby and grabbing for the toothbrush. Lucy squirmed, her lips frothy with toothpaste, and glared at him. The tiny bathroom felt sweaty, close. I strained to hear noises from downstairs, but there was nothing, no flushing toilets or clearing throats like I heard sometimes when I was up late trying to write. Eugene was probably still asleep. Alone, I hoped, though I couldn't object if he wasn't. We had agreed: no asking about visitors; no spying on backyard activities; no policing the other's comings and goings. To successfully navigate an open relationship, we had to respect each other's privacy.

Tate hugged my knees, making me sway. "Go asleep, sweet noodle," he sang and yanked the toothbrush out of Lucy's mouth.

"Ow!" She poked him hard. "You're so annoying."

He shrieked, hit her.

"Dammit, enough!" I yelled. Immediate silence. Then, scowling, he started singing again. She stayed put, watching me. I took back the toothbrush and kept brushing. "Teeth are important," I said brightly, as if this were so much fun. "We can't eat without them. If we can't eat we die. So brush, brush, brush to keep on living."

Lucy stood to rinse, then pushed at her glasses with one small finger tipped by chipped blue nail polish. "I'm not supposed to sit on the tub," she said. "I could fall and hit my head."

I dropped the toothbrush into the sink. "Why didn't you tell me?"

"Why didn't you know?" She stomped out.

Tate grabbed the toothbrush and sucked on it. I leaned against the counter, too tired to move.

That first week of camp, we were late every day, racing Tate's stroller through the massive parking lot to camp headquarters near the zoo's entrance. Lucy and I were always so breathless and frustrated that we barely said goodbye. Afterward, Tate and I would wait for the zoo to officially open, Tate napping in his stroller while I pulled out my iPad and pretended to work on my overdue novel. Better to pretend there than in my campus office, where colleagues might catch me surfing the web. Some mornings, I could hear the elephants trumpeting to each other from their faraway hilltop habitat. Occasionally, my phone buzzed with texts from students, or, more often, from Eugene: *Shirts still at cleaners?* or *No milk in downstairs fridge.* I longed to reply, *What's your point?* or, better yet, *You're Vivian's problem now,* but I was trying to be civil.

The second week of camp, Lucy decided to set the alarm clock Winston gave her when he moved. It was a little, wheeled, oblong robot that rolled around if the alarm stayed on too long. I didn't hear it go off the first morning. Tate and I were sprawled on my bed, finally asleep after hours of toddler nightmares. Suddenly, a blaring thing crawled across me. I screamed and swept it away from Tate, who giggled sleepily. It crashed against the wall.

"Mo-mmy, my clock," Lucy wailed as she scooted from beside the bed to the robot's now-silent pieces. Tate kept giggling, his curly hair sticking up like a fright wig. Lucy shook the pieces at him. "It's not funny. Make him stop!"

She was already dressed in typical Lucy fashion: a polka-dotted sundress worn over purple leggings despite the heat, along with mismatched Crocs (one orange, one yellow) on her feet. Her long, straight hair veiled her eyes. "It's not fair, Skye. You broke my clock and now you're letting him be mean. Winston wouldn't do that!" Her little back rigid, she marched into the bathroom.

"It's 'Mommy' not 'Skye,' smart mouth," I called after her.

She was seated on the closed toilet holding her toothbrush when I rushed in with Tate, who wore only his diaper. I was barely dressed myself.

"Hurry up," she said. "I'll miss the condor hunt."

"I overslept. It happens."

I sat Tate by the door and snatched the toothbrush from her. He yelled, "Mine!" and held out his hand.

She folded her arms across her narrow, polka-dotted chest. "We'd never be late if Winston still lived here."

I rummaged in the vanity for the toothpaste. "He's gone all summer anyway, and I need Eugene around to babysit when I teach."

A poor excuse for our new living arrangement, especially since I was only teaching Intro Fiction that summer. I was barely even writing. My productivity had slowed to a trickle since I'd discovered Vivian's thong wedged between our pillows the previous month. "Just send some chapters," my agent kept emailing me, "to show the publisher you're close." Lately I could only focus at night while everyone else slept. Even then, I often found my fingers poised over the keyboard as I listened, breathless, for some bump or sigh from below, signaling what Eugene was doing; who he was with.

Lucy picked at her nail polish. "I want Winston to babysit."

I crouched so we were face-to-face. "When he gets home. And you'll have two weeks together every month."

"It's not the same as having him here."

I stood, impatience rising like bile. "Should we argue or get to camp?"

She pointed at Tate, half-naked by the door. "If he takes off his diaper, we're screwed."

"Lucy Pearl Copeland-Hills, unlearn that language. Monkey see does not mean monkey do."

Arms outstretched Tate stood and toddled toward Lucy. I smiled before turning for the toothpaste. It happened so fast I barely saw her grab his chubby arm and chomp down.

"What the hell, Lucy?" I yelled as I gathered up Tate, who sobbed, "Mama, Sissy bite!"

"He deserved it," she said. "He's always in the way."

The other campers were just finishing their sharing circle when we ran in, red faced and huffing. Tate kept rubbing his crescent-shaped bruise with its gap from Lucy's missing front tooth. Lucy stepped away from me when her favorite counselor, Rune, a slim, freckled redhead with a can-do smile, waved to us. Rune was somewhere in her twenties and had a boy about Lucy's age who also attended the camp. He sat with Rune now, just outside the sharing circle. I had noticed him before, his shaggy reddish hair and round, blank face, his habit of humming in a corner, his eyes averted from everyone else. According to Lucy, he never spoke, though sometimes he came up to her and stood close, humming and shuffling his feet.

Rune whispered to her son before she stood and walked over to greet us. "I heard the 110 is nuts," she said to me before turning to Lucy. "Fender's excited to see you," she said, gesturing to her son, who glanced over at us before staring at the carpet. "And you're just in time for the condor hunt."

Lucy was tall and slender like Winston but had my wide, full mouth that lent itself to scowling. "Tate broke my clock and made us late," she told Rune.

"That's not what happened," I said and glared at Lucy, who glared right back.

Rune touched Lucy's shoulder. "What matters is you're here." She waved at me and Tate—"Enjoy the day!" she said, annoyingly chipper—then led Lucy to the sharing circle. "Later there's a bird show," I heard her say. "You'll meet their trainers too."

Lucy looked adoringly at Rune, the way she used to at me. Fender stared as they approached him. I picked up Tate, who curled against me, and watched them walk away.

Tate was an oops baby. Eugene wasn't interested in children or monogamy. Which hadn't bothered me when I'd met him, a law school dean twenty years my senior recently retired to California after a long, distinguished career back east. His piercing intelligence had gutted me when he'd asked a question at one of my readings that showed he understood the subtleties of my latest novel. Lucy was plenty for me, I decided when he made his views known, and I had come to prefer casual relationships. Why open myself to the hurt and tumult that love inevitably bred, especially when I had a daughter to take care of? Then, three months in with Eugene, I got pregnant despite two forms of birth control, and suddenly monogamy mattered a lot. Not because I cared about him having sex with other women—of course I didn't, ours was a casual relationship, emphasis on *casual*, I reminded myself often—but because I hated the time those women stole from our family, time Eugene could have spent helping me with the kids, or at least with Tate.

A knock at the front door made me hurry with my lipstick. I stood by my bedroom mirror. It was a few days after the biting incident and my night to teach, the night that Eugene came upstairs to watch the kids. Since his move downstairs, I'd taken to wearing makeup and flowy dresses that hid the little paunch that defined my midsection after two pregnancies. But I only dressed up to go to school. Only to teach. Only for the few minutes before I left the house, when I instructed him how to take care of the kids and prayed he'd notice me again and decide he missed me more than he wanted Vivian or anyone else.

"Mommy, Eugene's here," Lucy called from the living room. She sounded mad, but that had become her norm, especially around him.

When I walked in, he was sprawled on the rug tickling Tate's belly while Lucy frowned from her burrow on the couch. Eugene and Tate looked up, their smiles so similar that I let out a little gasp.

Eugene gestured for me to help him stand. "I'm getting creakier every second," he joked. I resisted smiling with him, but his hand felt comfortable in mine as I pulled him to his feet. He picked up Tate and took a deep sniff of his head. "Fountain of youth right there," he said and looked at Lucy. "Right, Lucy? Take a whiff of this guy."

She held a throw pillow close. "No thank you."

I slung my computer bag over my shoulder. "Dinner's in the oven. Make sure they're in bed on time." I lingered by the door, waiting for him to notice my carefully made-up face, the sarong dress he liked.

He sniffed Tate's head again and finally looked at me. "How's the novel?"

I leaned against the doorjamb. "Still struggling with revisions."

He stayed quiet a moment. "Push forward, Skye. It's too good to let go."

Not good enough to keep your interest, I almost said. Instead I took a breath. "With all these changes at home, there's not much time for anything besides the kids."

"Lucy's in camp, and we can afford some daycare for Tate. You're happier when you're writing. More yourself."

His smile held such understanding; his rich, dark eyes were tender, transfixed. I found myself moving closer, touching his chest. He knew me.

He kissed my palm and stepped back.

"By the way," he said, tickling Tate again, "I thought Vivian could help babysit sometimes, so Tate gets to know her. You too, Lucy," he said, his gaze finding her on the couch.

My hope drained out in a sickening rush. That woman. In my house. All I knew about her was that she was in her midforties like me and a lawyer like him, though a practicing corporate lawyer, not an academic. That she was divorced, no kids. I'd resisted the urge to google her picture. Sometimes I heard her downstairs. Her voice sounded husky but distinctly feminine, and her footsteps were light and springy, which made me imagine her as petite with sculpted arms and legs from exercising in all her child-free time. That must have been what attracted him to someone my age instead of a dewy young thing; Vivian must be fit, athletic, childless, able to devote herself to him in a way that I couldn't, and didn't want to. At least there was that.

"I'm surprised she's still around," I said, trying for a bantering tone. "I thought you wanted variety."

Eugene regarded me steadily. "Let's not do this now."

"Then when, dammit?" I clutched my bag. "After she meets my kids?"

"There's that nastiness that puts people off."

It took all my reserves not to hit him.

Lucy stood, the pillow shielding her. "Is Vivian who visits downstairs? I don't want her here."

Eugene raised his bushy eyebrows, gently removing Tate's fist from his cheek. "You don't run this household, young lady." He turned to me. "If you can't handle this, Skye, we need to make some changes."

"No," I said, my hand on my tense throat. "Lucy, you may as well get used to her."

"You can't make me, you can't!" she shouted and threw her pillow at Eugene. It barely grazed him.

His lips drew back as if he'd smelled something rotten. "Control your daughter," he said and stalked from the room carrying Tate, whose small face looked flushed and confused.

I whirled to face Lucy. "Dammit, be quiet, for once!"

She plopped back down on the couch, her eyes wide, her mouth bunched with—what? Anger, frustration, fear. I should have apologized. How could I not have apologized? I should have said everything would be okay. But I couldn't tell her what I didn't believe.

※

Tate liked the chimp exhibit best with its grassy hills and huge rock structures where the chimps showed off their climbing skills. Sometimes they ambled over to us and bared their teeth in ghoulish ape-grins or squished their puckered, hairless asses against the exhibit glass while Tate pointed and yelled, "Mama, poop hole!" He would spend hours watching them if I let him.

Monday morning, the third week of camp, I only stopped there briefly to indulge him on our trek to the elephant exhibit: six acres of prime real estate centered with an enormous, bright red barn that housed Billy, a magnificent, six-ton specimen who'd been the zoo's sole elephant for most of his life; Tina, with a fringe of dark bangs hanging in her eyes like a shy teenager; and Jewel, named for the jewel-shaped tuft at the end of her tail. According to my internet research, the girls were more recent editions, former circus animals who were too old to breed and therefore good companions for Billy, who'd been alone so long that it was too dangerous to introduce him to a young, mating-age female. The sides of his head were usually streaked with an oversecretion of hormones caused by his proximity to females for the first time in decades. He was kept separate so he didn't become violent. He and the girls trumpeted to each other, and they were allowed to touch trunks through a metal gate with bars as thick as my torso, but that was the extent of their contact. Deprived of companionship and left to his own devices, he'd forgotten how to behave himself, resorting to brute shows of strength as his only means of self-expression.

The observation platforms surrounding the exhibit were expansive with good viewing angles. I chose the one centered by a shallow fountain, closest to Jewel and Tina. A few people were scattered about. Holding Tate, I leaned against the railing. It soothed me to watch the girls' slow, confident steps, the gentle way their trunks grazed each other's flanks, linked together, then curled down to the hay strewn at their feet.

Tate pointed at them. "Sisses," he said before snuggling against my shoulder and rubbing the spot where Lucy had bitten him.

That's how they should act, I wanted to say. Instead I kissed his hair and agreed, "Yup, sisters."

My cell phone rang inside the diaper bag. I almost didn't answer. It might be Eugene, wanting something. That weekend while I'd been up late working, I'd heard voices murmuring in the bedroom

below, Eugene's mellow drone, a woman's husky chuckle, then muffled yelps of pleasure, headboard smacking wall in short, sharp
bursts. Those taut thighs spread beneath him. "Stop it," I found
myself whispering. "Stop." I started surfing the net. Elephants eat
three hundred pounds of food a day; their skin so sensitive, they
can feel a fly landing; their herds almost solely female, mothers,
sisters, cousins; males implant sperm, wander on. Chuckle, yelp,
smack, spread. Stop it. Stop. Stop.

It was Winston on the phone.

"Lucy just called," he said when I answered. "She claimed she was
sick and wanted me to pick her up, but she knows I'm away. What's
up?"

I put down Tate, who toddled to the fountain. "Nothing," I lied.
"I'll get her."

"She decided she felt better when I said I couldn't come."

"That figures."

Rustling on his end, like he was shuffling papers, biding his time. I
pictured his long, lean face, so serious and calm, measuring how best
to say something he knew I didn't want to hear. "I've been meaning
to tell you. Before I left, she asked to live with me, just until you figure things out with Eugene."

I inhaled sharply. It hadn't occurred to me that she would want to
leave. "Why didn't you say anything?"

"She asked me not to. She's afraid to hurt your feelings."

Tate splashed in the fountain. I hurried over and held his waist
so he wouldn't fall in. He was small yet sturdy, a determined, cheer-
ful child, so different from Lucy. Even as a baby she'd been more
inclined to scream than smile. She'd been a biter at Tate's age, though
usually as a way of experiencing the world's tastes and textures. Still,
whenever she bit my shoulder as if sampling a peach, I could barely
keep from biting back.

"It's not the worst idea," Winston said. "If she lived with me, you
could focus on resolving this Eugene stuff." He said Eugene's name
as if it left a bad taste.

"You've never liked him."

"No newsflash there." More rustling papers. My body clenched,
waiting. Finally, he said, "You've been distracted lately. Lucy feels it."

"Are you saying I've been a bad parent?"

"I'm saying let's think about what's best for her."

I sat on the fountain's lip. My chest felt tight and hot. "I know. I'm sorry," I said, one hand on Tate as he splashed. "Why does everything have to be so hard with her?"

"She's seven. She's looking for attention."

"Well, she's getting it."

Tate tried to dive into the fountain. I pulled him away, but he kept struggling, emitting little grunts of effort.

"Please don't let on I told you," I heard Winston say, but I was too busy with Tate to pay much attention.

Lucy seemed peaceful when we picked her up that day. In the car, she even offered Tate a few of the animal stickers that the camp gave out for contests and good behavior. Kids could use them like money at the zoo gift shop. Lucy was saving for a stuffed elephant. She'd never given Tate a sticker.

I glanced at her in the rearview mirror while weaving through dense traffic. She turned to the window.

"Good sharing, honey," I said, braking for a minivan.

"Rune says I should try harder to be nice. Nobody at camp likes me."

My gaze flew to the rearview. Lucy kept staring outside.

"Of course they do," I said.

"I don't like them either, except Rune. And Fender, a little. Nobody likes him either." Her tone was matter-of-fact. "I like the animals, though. Rune says if I feed them and talk quietly and don't move around too fast, they'll like me too."

I gripped the steering wheel, focused on Tate's sandals toeing my seatback. Friends were overrated, I wanted to tell her. All you needed were a trusted few like Winston. Better to be guarded than to risk disappointment's bitter fallout, like I had with Eugene. I glanced at Lucy again. That stubborn, wide mouth so much like mine, now set in a grimace. Her eyes looked shiny. My difficult child, my little anarchist, always searching for something to resist.

I maneuvered past a slow truck, waited until my throat unclenched. "I'm glad you've got the animals," I said.

Later, after the kids were in bed, I emailed Rune. Did Lucy really have no friends? Rune's prompt response was carefully worded. It was only the third week. Lucy was shy with kids but great with animals. "She so intuitive, particularly with the babies," she wrote. "And she's always nice to Fender. I'll bet she's a fab older sister."

A lot she knew. "Keep me posted," I wrote back. Then, I snuck into the kids' room and sat beside Lucy's bed listening to her breathe.

❀

The rest of the third week, I set my own alarm so we'd be extra early for camp. Maybe Lucy would settle in if she got there before everyone else. Instead of fleeing to try and write while Tate napped, I hung out to watch the other kids arrive. Camp headquarters was in the California Condor Rescue Zone, an expansive discovery center that helped kids experience the world from the viewpoint of a California condor, an endangered vulture species. In one room were fake rock formations, caves, and other re-creations of condors' preferred terrains. Kids could climb the rocks before camp or play in another room set up like a veterinary hospital, complete with plastic scalpels and stethoscopes and several stuffed condors whose lace-up bellies contained removable organs. Lucy liked to don a stethoscope and examine the condors on the metal exam tables. Fender usually stood close by watching quietly. Sometimes he passed her a scalpel or pointed at the stuffed organs she lined up on the exam table. They seemed happy in their silent game.

As soon as other kids showed up, though, Lucy left Fender at the exam tables and retreated alone to a darkened cave, making sure her feet—encased in their mismatched Crocs—stuck out. The other kids stayed away when they saw her shoes, which made me think she was right about their not liking her. Still, she always left camp with a slew of new animal stickers, which she solemnly counted while we drove home, saving some for Tate.

One morning, she walked up to where I was helping Tate climb a fake rock. "Time to go, Mommy," she said.

I glanced at her. "You just got here."

"The other mommies left already."

She took my hand and led me out. Tate trailed us whining, "Wanna stay!" Fender followed us too, though he stopped when Lucy turned and shook her head at him. He nodded and smiled at her, an open, lovely smile that made me yearn for him to talk, to laugh with my daughter, just once.

At the door she waved—"Bye-bye, Mommy"—and then marched back inside, where I imagined her playing in the vet clinic while Fender watched, or sitting by herself in a cave dreaming up stories about the animals or the friends she didn't have. Maybe if I went back and talked to her about making an effort, convinced her she didn't need to be alone. That she could make friends who could actually talk to her. Then again, I was no expert at keeping people close. I stood holding Tate's hand and stared at the empty doorway.

Friday was so blisteringly hot that, instead of cooking, I decided to brave a restaurant dinner by myself with two small kids. Lucy trailed me down the front stairs while I lugged Tate and the diaper bag. My hair stuck to the sweat trickling past my ears.

Eugene's front door opened as we reached the bottom. There was no avoiding him and the woman who emerged. He smiled, squinting in the early evening light.

"How's my boy?" he said and walked over to kiss Tate.

I barely paid attention. I was too busy staring at the woman. According to Google, she was my age, but she looked older, with frizzy gray hair loped off at the chin, a gentle face nested with wrinkles. Her loose dress didn't hide her generous curves. She looked more like someone's mother than I did.

Behind me, Lucy said, "Mommy, are you okay?" Her small hand slipped into mine.

Eugene saw me staring. He massaged his jaw, then said, "Skye, meet Vivian."

She stepped forward; her kind smile revealed wide-gapped teeth. "What beautiful children," she said.

It wasn't that he wanted someone more fit, more free. He just didn't want me.

"You bastard," I said to Eugene.

"Jesus, Skye, don't make a big deal."

"Get out. Get the fuck out."

As I fled down the walkway, I hugged Tate so tightly he started crying. Dimly I heard footsteps tapping as Lucy ran behind me calling, "Mommy, Mommy, wait!"

❀

Tate and I had just reached the elephants on Monday morning, the fourth week of camp, when Rune called my cell phone. I needed to come immediately, she stated in a clipped voice. Lucy had bitten another camper.

Rune and Lucy were waiting outside. Rune's freckled face looked uncharacteristically stern. Lucy stood turned away from her, which otherwise might have secretly pleased me. I trotted up pushing Tate's stroller, heedless of the uneven pavement.

Biting was one of the most serious offenses, Rune explained. Lucy needed to write an apology to the boy in order to return, and even then she'd be on probation. Another incident would get her expelled. "We talked," Rune said, "and Lucy knows how serious this is. Biters don't get stickers, right?"

Lucy stared stubbornly into the distance.

"Answer her," I said and turned her chin toward me. She was scowling but her eyes were shiny with unshed tears, which made me want to hug her.

"He deserved it," she said. "He stole some of my stickers."

I gripped her chin harder. "I don't care what he did. You. Don't. Bite."

"So you don't care about me," she said and jerked away.

At home she wrote her apology at the kitchen table while I made her a snack. Every now and then, I checked the front windows to see whether Eugene was walking up with Vivian. I hadn't heard anything from below all weekend, not even when I sat up late typing and deleting sentences, paragraphs, pages. Maybe they were staying at her place, which I pictured as dimly lit and filled with heavily carved Indonesian relics and colorful wall hangings, cluttered with books instead of toys.

I had let myself love him, and he didn't want me.

By the time I brought Lucy some cheese and apple slices, she'd drawn a sturdy set of fangs surrounded by zoo sticker drawings, below which she'd written, "I bit you."

I clanked down the plate. "You were supposed to write 'Sorry I bit you.'"

She pushed at her glasses. "But that's lying."

"Do you want to stay in camp?" Slowly she nodded. I took away her note. "Then lie."

Lucy started carrying her stickers in a pouch around her neck, and she stopped sharing with Tate. When I dropped her at camp, she sat alone by the door. If Fender tried to join her, Rune guided him away to another part of the room, where, humming loudly, he retreated to a corner. The kid Lucy had bitten—an aggressively snub-nosed boy named Michael—sometimes pointed her out to his friends when we arrived, usually late. I stopped setting my alarm clock after Eugene emailed me, the evening of the camp biting. He would find me a babysitter, come by to pack. Let's keep things amicable, he wrote.

Whenever we picked up Lucy, she climbed in the car and ignored Tate, who chattered away. She only spoke if I asked about the animals. Then, she became animated, authoritative. Late one afternoon, a week after biting the boy at camp, she sat on her bed counting stickers and told me about some Komodo dragon babies in the zoo nursery who'd been taken from the mother right after hatching since Komodos often ate their young. "That's why the babies live in trees, so their mommies can't kill them."

"How awful." I sat on the floor handing Tate stuffed animals. He threw them at his crib and belly-laughed when one landed inside.

Lucy kept counting stickers. "It's true. Maybe I'll buy a stuffed baby Komodo instead of an elephant. I got more stickers, so there's enough." She glanced up. "Who was that lady with Eugene?"

I'd braced myself for this question, but it still winded me. "A friend."

She peered at me from the shelter of her hair. "Do you hate her?"

Tate batted Lucy with a tiger. Quickly I pulled it away. "I was just surprised to meet her," I said.

Lucy considered this before returning to her stickers. "Maybe I *will* get an elephant. The gift store has one bigger than me. We could keep him in a window downstairs to scare away burglars until Winston moves back in."

I gripped the stuffed tiger. "I'm not sure what will happen."

"But you told Eugene to leave. He can live with that lady you hate."

I clutched the tiger tight, tighter, until Tate grabbed it from me.

"It's complicated, Lucy," I said. Though it wasn't. Eugene didn't love me. He had to go. He was already gone.

"I thought—" She considered her stickers. Her trembling lips formed a frown. She looked at Tate. "There are three missing," she said.

"Maybe you dropped them at camp."

She hopped off her bed and stuck out her hand to Tate. "Give them back."

Giggling he batted her with the tiger. A primal growl rose from her; she shoved him so hard he toppled backward, hit his head on the crib. He started screaming. Blood dripped from a gash above his eye.

Into the bathroom, him kicking, howling; I wet a washcloth, wiped the blood, pressed the cut hard, cradled my crying boy. "It's okay," I murmured again, again. He nestled close; his sobs slowed to hiccups. There was a lump, but the gash was actually small and shallow. Still. He could have lost an eye.

"Mommy, I'm sorry," I heard Lucy say, but I didn't turn around. His eye. His beautiful, dark brown eye.

"I've had it, Lucy," I said. "You want to live with Winston? Go ahead."

Something thumped behind me. When I looked, she was sitting in the hall, her legs splayed.

"He told you?" she said in a hollow voice that made my throat catch.

I wasn't supposed to know, I remembered. I beckoned to her. "Forget it, okay? I didn't mean it."

"You don't want me," she said. "Only Eugene and Tate." She stood and trudged to her room.

The next morning, Lucy rose early, got dressed, even brushed her own teeth. She barely spoke to me, even when I crouched down and whispered, "I won't ever let you go."

She hesitated before briefly hugging me back. "We're late," she said.

At camp, I asked Rune about replacing Lucy's lost stickers. "I'll pay for them," I said, raising my voice above the din of children racing around the discovery center.

She tugged at her fiery hair before shaking her head. "Then we'd have to let everyone."

I rocked Tate's stroller, considered my words. "Look. I think that boy Michael might still be taking her stickers."

"'Still'?"

"That's why she bit him, remember? Maybe you can keep an eye out, make sure he leaves her alone."

Her bright smile tightened into place. She looked away from me to Fender, who sat by himself in the sharing circle, his eyes fixed on Lucy's Crocs sticking out of a cave. "I'll try," Rune finally said, "but Lucy needs to control herself, no matter what other kids do. I hope you understand." Then she walked over to sit with Fender.

I strode out, thrusting the stroller ahead of me. Someone had to cut Lucy a break. Someone. Me.

I headed straight for the elephants, ignoring Tate's pleas to stop at the chimps. Once there, I let him play in the fountain while I watched the animals. Within minutes, he was soaked, but I didn't care. There was Billy across the way, solo still, the girls in their separate habitat bordered by those thick metal bars that kept them safe from him. The girls walked slowly to a hay bale, their flanks touching. The dependability, the comfort of each other's presence. What I should have been offering Lucy instead of focusing on dismantling the barrier between me and Eugene. My dogged, difficult girl who kept trying to be strong for me. I needed to tell her how sorry I was, that she was my darling, she and Tate. Nobody else.

When I called camp headquarters, a counselor said the kids were watching Billy's feeding on the observation platform across from me. I strapped Tate's wet, squirmy body into the stroller and trotted along the fence skirting the elephants, down the hill past the gorillas, then uphill again to the other side of the elephant exhibit, the map of the zoo ingrained in me.

As I got close, I saw kids wearing camp shirts on the platform overlooking Billy's habitat. I paused when I spotted Lucy standing alone at the far corner. In her arms was a stuffed condor from the vet room. She whispered to it and pointed at Billy, who pawed the ground near the fence. His head was streaky with fluid. He trumpeted to the trainer who stood in a long concrete trench cut into the habitat and fenced by massive steel bars. The trainer was emptying crates of cabbages and yams into Billy's side of the enclosure. Billy snuffled around eagerly with his agile trunk, searching out the yams. Lucy kept whispering to the stuffed condor, maybe describing the scene. *The trainer has to feed Billy from a safe place*, I imagined her saying. *Billy doesn't want to hurt anybody, but he's so big he might by accident. Or maybe he doesn't know how else to show what he wants.*

My sad, smart girl.

That's when I noticed some kids pointing at her. Michael, the boy she'd bitten, broke off from the group, walked over, and grabbed the stuffed condor. She snatched it back. Soon, they were both tugging. "Leave her alone!" I yelled and started running, shoving the stroller forward.

Tate twisted to look at me. "Mama, Sissy mad."

In my periphery I saw a flash of red hair, heard Rune call, "Lucy, Michael, that's not okay!" Rune would smooth things over without solving anything; maybe she'd even make this Lucy's fault. I had to get there first.

"Hold on, sweetie!" I yelled, running faster, almost there.

Lucy looked over. Michael ripped away the condor and waved it overhead. I jerked to a stop, almost hitting Michael with the stroller. Michael stared at me, shocked, and held tight when I grabbed the condor. I felt another small body beside me and then Fender was there too, tugging with me. Dimly I heard Rune shout, "Fender, Skye, please!" and Tate's little voice, "Mama, Mama, toy!" Michael gave a sudden shove that broke my grasp and sent Fender flying.

"Leave him alone!" Lucy shrieked and lunged at Michael. They toppled down; the condor sailed out of Michael's hands and into the elephant exhibit, hitting Billy in his large, rough ass. Fender ran to the fence, leaned over, reaching, crying. Behind me I heard Michael scream—"Ow!"—and I knew, even as I focused on Billy's dulling molars steadily chewing yams.

I turned around as Rune reached us. "Strike three, Lucy," she said, huffing and red-faced as she dragged Fender away from the fence, then helped Michael up.

I took Lucy in my arms, held her shaking little body tight. It didn't matter what she'd done or whether I longed for her to be easier, happier, less like me. She was mine, no matter what.

"Good girl, honey," I said, loud enough for everyone to hear. "Good girl."

Malocchio

The morning I started kindergarten, my grandmother was the only person I wanted to see. This was way back in 1948. I woke up early to a dark sky, my stomach jittery at the thought of walking with the neighborhood kids to the elementary school a few blocks away. The apartment was quiet, as usual. My father died in an accident during basic training for World War II when Mama was pregnant with me; so it was just her and me in the middle apartment of my grandmother's triple-decker row house, with my grandmother's apartment below us and my uncle Louie's above. Mama was already downstairs in Nonna's kitchen cooking breakfast before she left for work. Nonna was in the barn milking the cows while Uncle Louie filled bottles with milk and loaded them into Nonna's cart. She would leave for her deliveries soon. She might already be gone.

I hurried to my bedroom window and strained to see across the large, dusky yard. The milk cart tilted, horseless, in front of the barn. Nonna was still milking. I could catch her and get her opinion about how to make friends at school. I hadn't had much success in our neighborhood, even though it swarmed with a ragtag bunch of Irish and Italian kids who spent hours jumping rope and kicking cans and filling the air with shouts and laughter. I hardly ever ventured beyond the cinder block wall surrounding our property, a deep corner lot that spanned half a city block in Fairview, New Jersey. The few times I worked up the nerve to join the other kids, they ignored me, even when I asked to play the way I practiced with Nonna. Although practicing with her wasn't my best idea. She didn't much like children, except for me, her only grandchild, her *cucciola mia*—her little puppy. Whenever kids played handball against our wall, she pretended to throw the evil eye at them. "You scare my cows and make sour the milk," she would yell as they ran away shrieking. Mama told me not to bother with them when I came home crying one day. They were low class little grunts, not our kind of people. Nonna overheard and said, "I no contessa no more, Carmella. We no better than nobody." But she didn't encourage me to leave the yard either. She and Mama both felt safer with me at home. They viewed the world with suspicion ever since a flu pandemic took seven of Nonna's children. Mama, the middle child, and Uncle Louie, the youngest, were the only ones who survived.

Standing by my window, I saw my uncle outside leading the horse out of the barn. Quickly I pulled on the lace-collared blouse and yellow pinafore Mama made for my first day. The starched outfit itched all over, but if I changed into my regular cotton shirt and dungarees, Mama would yell and I'd never catch Nonna. I buckled my dress shoes and raced downstairs to Nonna's walkout basement apartment where we ate all our meals.

At the kitchen stove, Mama dropped batter-coated apple slices into a sizzling pan. Polenta bubbled in a pot on another burner. An apron protected her tailored shirtdress from splatter.

She glanced at me. "That pinafore fits nice."

"It's itchy," I said. "I want my dungarees."

"Girls don't wear slacks to school." She pointed at her high heels. "I stand in these things all day even though they make my feet ache. You know why? Because to move up in management, you need to dress like management."

I scuffed my shoes against each other. I didn't understand who "management" was or how dressing like one would help me, though I knew my mother worked in a factory down the hill where she bossed around forty women sewing children's snowsuit pieces. She reminded me often about how she'd worked there since she was thirteen, when Nonna decided they needed extra money more than my mother needed to learn geometry or the history of the Roman Empire.

"School's not a factory," I said.

Mama stirred the polenta. "Same rules. You want respect, you have to act like you deserve it."

But I wanted to be liked, not respected. I wanted to make friends, something I couldn't figure out how to do, even on my own block. Nonna would understand, or at least listen.

The refrigerator door squeaked as I opened it to grab a carrot for my favorite cow, small, brown-spotted Sophia, who lowed whenever she saw me. Mama stopped stirring and pointed her spoon at me. "No barn this morning," she said.

I planted my fist on my hip, the carrot poking me in the waist. "Nonna's there. Uncle Louie too. I'm allowed." That was the rule: I could only go in the barn with an adult. Mama said the barn was an accident waiting to happen. Too many sharp tools waiting to gash me; too many animals waiting to bite me—though Nonna taught me: if I treated the animals right, they would treat me right too. "I need to talk to Nonna."

Mama frowned. "You can talk to me, Rosie."

I looked at the carrot, the linoleum, anywhere but at my mother. Navigating between her and my grandmother was tricky. But this morning was important. My grandmother loved me best. She knew me best.

Finally, I looked at my mother. "I need Nonna," I said.

Mama shook her spoon at me; drops of polenta sprayed across the linoleum. "You're wearing school clothes. The barn's filthy."

"I'll stay clean," I said and raced out of the kitchen, through Nonna's tiny bedroom, to the back door.

"Rose Concetta Morroni, get back here," my mother yelled, but I ran out into the dusky morning anyway, intent on seeing my grandmother.

Our two-acre lot was the only one of its size in the area, even in 1948, when the city of Fairview wasn't nearly as congested as it is now. Back then, if I stood by the barn at the bottom of the sloped yard, I could barely hear the street noise. I could pretend I was in another world with just our family, our animals, our home.

That's what I wanted to pretend the morning I started kindergarten. Sunlight had barely licked the sky as I trotted across the yard, past the rope swing strung by my grandfather between the black-barked cherry trees for my mother, Uncle Louie, and the other children. Mama and Nonna hardly ever talked about them or my grandfather, who died soon after the children. My uncle was so young at the time, he didn't remember much about any of them.

I saw Uncle Louie as I neared the barn. He stood on the wide dirt driveway hitching the horse to Nonna's unheated, enclosed cart with "Dottino's Milk and Cream" painted on the sides in large swirling letters. I loved playing on the cart after my grandmother finished her route, sliding the doors open and closed as I made imaginary deliveries, or standing on a milk carton at the narrow front window so I could pretend to steer the horse. Mama wanted Nonna to get a truck instead. "You'll catch your death in that rickety thing," she kept telling my grandmother, who would frown and answer, "I built like the ox. You too soft, not me."

When I stopped to kiss my uncle's stubbled cheek, he flashed his most charming grin.

"Lookit you, all gussied up," he said.

I tugged my lace collar. "Mama made me, for school."

"Your ma would make me wear tails and a top hat to muck the stalls if she could." He straightened the horse's bridle. "What am I gonna do without my sidekick today?"

My uncle babysat me every morning until Nonna got home from delivering milk. Barely out of his teens, he'd been my babysitter and my grandmother's sole employee for a few years, ever since my mother and grandmother made him stop running numbers for a local bookie, which he'd taken up after dropping out of high school when my father died. While Nonna made deliveries, he and I would play cards or dig in the garden, though just as often he'd sit me by the radio to draw while he napped. That morning, his thick-lashed eyes looked tired and his curly black hair was still slicked back with pomade, like he hadn't slept on it yet, which meant he'd had another late night playing cards.

"I come home at lunch," I reminded him and ran for the barn.

"Make us proud, Rosie girl," he called behind me.

When I reached the barn door, I stopped and peered inside. Nonna sat on a stool beside a cow, her forehead planted against the cow's flank, her hands in their fingerless gloves busily jerking teats. The stool seemed small beneath her bulk. Usually, she pretended not to notice when I snuck in with Sophia's carrot; then, just as I held out my hand, palm flat like she taught me with the carrot displayed for Sophia's eager lips, a stream of milk would hit me—in the eye or the nose, sometimes the ear. I'd spin around and Nonna would be smiling, her hand on the cow's dripping teat. "Again, *cucciola mia*," she would say. "Every time, I get you."

That morning, though, she looked up as soon as I slipped through the door. "So pretty for school," she said. "Maybe go back inside so you no get dirty. Mama, she be mad at us both then."

"She said okay."

I couldn't look at Nonna as I walked to Sophia's stall and fed her the carrot, her bristly whiskers tickling my palm. When I turned around, my grandmother was considering me as she tucked a stray hair into her gray, tightly tamed bun. We both knew I never made it to the barn without Mama protesting.

Nonna sighed, then gestured me onto her ample lap. Once I was settled, she guided my hands to help me jerk the cow's slippery teats. I breathed in my grandmother's familiar, fragrant scent of the lemon balm leaves she chewed, with a whiff of salty-sour cow thrown in. It was so peaceful there, her large, soft chest pillowing me, the only sound the cows chewing cud and the milk hitting the metal pail in a clickety stream. The thought of school seemed scary by comparison, with all those kids who didn't know me, or already seemed to dislike me.

Still, they didn't have cows and a horse like I did, or a watch-dog penned by the barn or hens clucking in the coop with its eye-watering stink or even the feral cats that nested in the hay bales. And I got to help with the animals and plant the garden with my uncle and swing beneath the cherry trees whenever I wanted. I loved to climb on the swing's wooden seat, worn smooth by years and weather, and imagine my aunts and uncles who sat there before me, how we would push each other on the swing and search out four-leaf clovers unclaimed by the grazing cows. I imagined all seven children looked like Mama and Uncle Louie, who shared the same slim build, black curls, and hazel eyes that turned moss green when they got angry. Or maybe some of the sisters and brothers were built like Nonna, thick and tall and strong but with reddish hair inherited from my grandfather. Maybe Nonna had pushed my aunts and uncles on the swing the way she sometimes pushed me, though usually she just watched me swing while she worked in the yard. The few times I found her sitting there, she shooed me away, her mouth tight and set. She must have been wishing for those children, mourning them.

Now that I was going to kindergarten, I wouldn't have nearly as much time to help her with the cows or daydream about my aunts and uncles. I would spend my mornings being taught reading and writing and math, even though I could already read from reading nightly bedtime stories with Mama or Nonna, and I knew basic arithmetic from playing gin rummy and blackjack with Uncle Louie. But maybe I could learn different things. Maybe I could learn to play with the other kids the way I pretended to do with my imaginary aunts and uncles. Maybe it would be easier at school than at home. Though maybe not. My stomach started tingling again.

"Is school fun?" I asked my grandmother.

She shifted behind me, used one rough fingertip to tilt up my chin so I could see her dark eyes nested in her sun-spotted, furrowed skin. "*Non lo so, cucciola mia.* In Italia, tutors come to the villa to teach me, and I study French and Latin and maps—"

"Ma, you know I don't want her in here today."

My mother stood by the barn door. Her arms were crossed under her breasts like she was cold, even though it was a mild September morning. She looked out of place in her work clothes and carefully made-up face. The shadows thrown by the barn's sole lightbulb didn't mask her stormy expression.

"She neat like the pin," said Nonna. "We careful."

My mother stepped forward, hugging herself tight. "Come inside, Rose, or you'll stink like the barn on your first day."

"You mean she stink like her *nonna*." My grandmother's face looked grim and a little sad, as if she wanted something from my mother she knew she'd never get. "You worry about all the wrong things, Carmella." She kissed my forehead. "This one, she smell like the rose where she get her name, huh, *cucciola mia*?"

My mother frowned. "You spoil her rotten."

"She a baby. She need spoiling."

My mother snorted. "Like you ever spoiled us."

I stood up, between my mother and grandmother, and pretended not to take sides, even though I knew whose side I was on. Nonna's. Always Nonna's. Which my mother also knew and held against us both.

"I'm helping," I said.

Mama glared. "Get in the house now or I promise you will spend all afternoon in your room." She spun around and marched back outside.

Nonna stood and stroked my hair. "Always jealous, that one." She showed me her hand, which she'd made into a fist with the index and pinky fingers carefully pointed at the ground—the *mano cornuto*, to ward off the evil eye. "She bring *il malocchio* and be my death if she no careful."

I fashioned my hand into the same horned fist and shook it at the ground, just like my grandmother.

Mama wanted to walk me to school on that first morning. "It's on my way to the factory," she said. "I'll barely be late. Plus, I can take an early lunch and pick you up afterward, to be safe."

We were standing on the front stoop. Her pocketbook hung from one shoulder and she wore a tense, determined smile. It was unsettling, her willingness to break her routine. Consistency paved the path to success, she insisted her whole life. Yet there she was, ready to change her entire schedule just to walk me to and from school. It made me think there was something to fear. It made me want to walk without her.

Across the street, several neighborhood kids had gathered. There were a few other mothers, the ones who stayed home all day instead of working like my mother; the ones who stared at Mama when she grocery shopped in her carefully tailored work clothes and barely nodded at her after church. These mothers wore loose, flowery housedresses and slipperlike shoes. Some had scarves wrapped around the curlers in their hair. They looked the way mothers were supposed to look. I couldn't imagine Mama walking with those women, her ignoring them, them ignoring her; the kids following their mothers' example and ignoring me.

I shook my head so hard my ears rang. "I don't need you to come," I said.

My mother hesitated like she might give in before she held out her hand to me. "You're five. I decide what you need."

The kids and mothers started walking.

"Stay here," I said and raced across the street with my snack bag clutched in one hand. I looked back and saw Mama standing there, openmouthed, her hand still outstretched, as if she were too shocked to be mad—yet.

As I trailed the kids to school, I noticed her trailing me. She ducked behind a car or a tree whenever I looked back. Once, I whirled around and hissed, "Go away!" but she just stepped into a storefront entryway until I kept walking, the kids and mothers now half a block ahead. I had to hurry to catch up. Finally, when I reached the squat, brick schoolhouse, Mama turned and headed down the street. She didn't even wave. I paused to watch her go, her back rigid. Probably she was furious at me, which seemed less scary than what awaited me inside. I almost chased after her. Instead, I forced myself to walk into the school.

In the kindergarten classroom, the girls all wore dresses or pinafores, like me, and the boys wore button-down shirts and church slacks. The teacher, Miss Falucci—who was younger than Mama and not nearly as pretty—droned on and on about the rules, like what we were and weren't supposed to touch in the classroom and the importance of using proper manners with lots of pleases and thank yous and elbows off tables. Eventually, she read us a story about newborn kittens who talked to each other and lapped milk out of bowls. This was something I knew about. I raised my hand to explain that newborn kittens didn't lap milk.

"They nurse from their mamas' teats," I said, which made Miss Falucci frown and the other kids giggle. One boy with a scalped-looking crewcut blushed the color of cooked beets to the tips of his jug ears. He said his name was Nazzy when we introduced ourselves, but Miss Falucci insisted on using his full name, Ignazio—"Nicknames aren't appropriate for school," she told him, which also made him blush.

"It's a story, Rose," she said after I finished explaining about kittens. "Use your imagination."

The other kids' curious gazes burned into me.

At snack time, I chose a seat at the end of the table and listened to my classmates chatter about what they would do after school together: play hopscotch and mother, may I, run in the woods behind our barn, where I never bothered going. There was so much to see and do in my own yard. "I have a horse and three cows and a dog and kittens, and a rope swing too," I said, but quietly, in case they didn't believe me.

Nazzy looked up from his Fig Newton. "Wow. A horse," he said. "Does it eat apples?"

A girl sitting nearby put down her crustless sandwich and looked at Nazzy as if he were a bug. Her name was June. She lived in a row house across from ours. Her auburn pigtails were still tidy, even after our hour on the nap mats, and her shoes still looked newly polished, unlike mine, which were covered with fresh scuffs.

"Of course it eats apples, Ig-*nei-ei-eigh*-shus," she said, braying the middle syllable like she couldn't believe anyone had such a silly name. "All horsies like apples."

"That's not my name," Nazzy said, but she had already turned to me.

"Your grammy delivers our milk," she said and smiled like she was happy to remember who I was. Maybe she was actually nice. Maybe she made fun of Nazzy because she was scared, like me. I could invite her over to feed Sophia, or we could push each other on the swing. "Mommy says your yard smells like poop," she told me, "and your grammy shouldn't have farm animals in the city."

My face felt as hot and red as Nazzy's ears. "It doesn't either smell."

The girl sitting beside June giggled. With her heart-shaped face and frizzy curls, the girl could have topped a Christmas tree, but her giggle sounded nasty.

June took a bite of her sandwich. "Your grammy's a cailleach. Mommy says."

I must have looked confused because Nazzy said, "That's Irish for *strega*."

Strega. Witch. My biscotti crumbled, dry and tasteless, in my mouth. "She's a contessa, not a witch!"

"What's that?" asked June.

"Like a princess."

She shook her head. "Uh-uh. Princesses aren't tall and fat and wrinkly like her."

Something dark and mean rose up inside me. "You're just jealous," I said. "You're gonna bring the evil eye."

She dropped her sandwich. "That's not real."

"Is too. It'll eat you up. My *nonna* says." I made a fist with horns and shook it sideways like Nonna did at kids playing handball. "Now it's gonna get you." I said, even though I knew it didn't work that way. Casting *il malocchio* required shaking my horned fist upright at the sky. "Never for real you throw *il malocchio*," Nonna had warned me. "People, they get hurt."

June's lower lip trembled. She started crying like a baby. The girl with the frizzy curls—Bella, I remembered from circle time—started crying too. I dropped my hand. The dark, mean thing inside me shrank to almost nothing.

Miss Falucci hurried over. "What's going on?" she asked and hugged the sobbing girls.

I wound up banished to the coatroom for the rest of snack time.

After kindergarten ended, I trailed the other kids and a few mothers on the walk home. I was too angry to talk to anyone, and nobody talked to me, though Nazzy waved when I crossed the street to my triplex.

Mama had come home for lunch and was waiting at our gate. Her smile faded as I silently trudged past her.

"How was your first day?" she called.

I gripped my half-full snack bag and kept walking down the hill to the patio and the back entrance of my grandmother's walkout basement, through her bedroom, and into the kitchen. She sat at the table reading a newspaper. Across from her sat my uncle chewing a toothpick and playing solitaire. He took the toothpick out of his mouth when he saw me.

"Who died, kiddo?" he said.

"Hush, Louie," said my grandmother. "Rosie, come to Nonna."

She opened her arms wide. I nestled my head against her chest as her arms encircled me.

"I hate school," I said. My eyes stung, dry and angry.

Mama's heels clicked on the linoleum behind me. "Rose, what happened?" Her hand stroked my hair, a gentle touch she usually saved for when I fell off the swing or stepped on a bee.

"The kids are meanies," I said, my voice muffled against my grandmother's chest. I breathed in her lemony, loamy scent—plus that whiff of cow. Maybe I smelled like cow too. "And the teacher's a dummy."

My mother's hand dropped from my hair. "Don't be disrespectful."

"She's being honest," I heard my uncle say.

"Like you know anything about honesty, Mr. Card Shark—"

"*Basta così!*" my grandmother said, her voice rumbling in her chest against my cheek.

I nestled closer. "I'm not going back."

My mother's sigh was long and loud. "For pity's sake, it's only the first day."

"You too hard on her," my grandmother said. "She no work for you like those factory ladies. Poor *cucciola mia*. Let her be home longer. What they teach her she no learn here already?"

My mother's footsteps crossed the room; there was a rush of water as she turned on the faucet. "You may not have thought school was important for me, but it's important for Rose. She's going."

I lifted my head from my grandmother's chest. My uncle winked at me and went back to playing solitaire. At the sink, my mother was scrubbing pots, her back a stiff, stubborn line that made me determined to resist, like it would for decades.

"You can't make me," I said. "I'll hide so you can't find me."

Her shoulders tensed. "Don't test me, Rose," she said without turning. "You're lucky it's your first day of school or I'd have tanned your bottom by now."

I threw myself in a chair beside Nonna. All I wanted to do was cry, but I wasn't going to let my mother know. Nonna sighed and patted my knee before picking up her newspaper. My uncle gathered up the cards, shuffled them, and dealt a hand of blackjack.

"Penny a point," he said.

After a moment, I picked up my cards and started playing.

Nonna hadn't always delivered milk. That was my grandfather's job until he drank himself into an early grave within a year of the children's deaths. My grandmother—disowned when she was sixteen for running away to America with my grandfather, the family's gardener—was left with Mama and Uncle Louie to feed and nothing to her name but the property and the cows. My mother was nine years old, my uncle four. So Nonna took over my grandfather's delivery route and brought my mother and uncle with her to help. On icy winter mornings, they wrapped straw around their shoes with burlap strips and padded their coats with newspapers for warmth.

Mama claimed Louie had it easier growing up because Nonna babied him. Really, though, the family started doing better. By the time my uncle turned thirteen, my mother had married my father, a construction foreman. Between him, Mama, and Nonna, they started saving some money, so Uncle Louie got to stay in school. Mama never forgave him for using my father's death as an excuse to drop out freshman year and run numbers instead. She was determined I wouldn't squander my chance at an education the way Uncle Louie had. I would do better, have more, than them both.

When I started school, though, all I knew was that my first day made me want to climb under my covers and stay there.

Mama and I read an extra story that night before she tucked me in. Instead of turning off the light and leaving, as usual, she stayed seated beside me on the bed.

"You'll make friends, I promise," she said and took my hand.

I spun her wedding ring around her finger. "Who taught you to make friends?"

"I don't know, Rosie. I just knew."

I imagined her brothers and sisters standing in a row from youngest to oldest, their dark curls unruly, their eyes fringed with thick lashes, my uncle at the very end, my mother somewhere near the middle. The way they must have teased each other and played together; the way they must have watched out for each other.

"Did your brothers and sisters teach you?"

Her hand stiffened in mine. "I barely remember them. You know that." It made her mad when I asked about the others. Maybe it made her think about how her life might have been different if she hadn't lost so much so early. Probably.

I sat up and considered her tense face. "But how do I get kids to like me?"

"I work all day, Rosie. I try to get ahead. Whether people like me isn't important anymore." She sighed, a little impatiently. "You'll figure it out. You're a smart girl."

"Then why do I need school? Nonna didn't go, and you only went a little."

"Nonna got more of an education than I did." She sounded stern, like herself again. "Believe me, you don't want to be out in the world with just a sixth-grade education. Nothing comes easy then." A quick kiss and she stood to cross the room. "Tomorrow will be better." At the door, she paused. "Remember," she said, "if you want respect, act like you deserve it." Then she turned off the light and closed the door behind her.

Later, when I was almost asleep, my grandmother slipped in to see me. She looked tall and powerful in the glow of my nightlight, her thick, dark eyebrows a slash across her forehead.

"Shh," she said, her finger to her lips. She knelt beside my bed, closed my hand around something smooth and cool attached to a slender chain. "*Il cornicello*. It keep you safe from *il malocchio* at school," she whispered. "It help you stay strong. Don't let nobody push you around." She chucked me under my chin. "No tell Mama, you hear? She no believe, like we do."

After she left, I opened my hand. In it was a red coral horn strung on a gold chain. I slipped the chain around my neck and clutched the horn until I fell asleep.

Every day that first week of school, I wore my red *cornicello* around my neck under my dress, making sure my collar covered the chain. June and Bella stayed away from me, and I managed to escape Miss Falucci's notice until Friday, when she caught me reading on my sleep mat. I was supposed to be napping like everyone else.

"Rose, dear," she whispered with a wide smile, which by then I knew was as fake the "dear." We didn't like each other one bit. "It's time to rest, not look at books."

On a nearby mat, June slowly brushed hair from her eyes. She was watching us.

I turned back to Miss Falucci. "My mama lets me read to get sleepy."

"Imagine pictures in your head," Miss Falucci said. "That should do the trick."

She took my book, which made June smile. The mean, hard thing inside me lurched awake.

"I'm reading," I said. "It's not the same."

I reached for my book, but Miss Falucci hugged it close.

"Go to sleep, Rose," she hissed in a tone that made June's eyes widen. The teacher stalked past June, who quickly pretended to sleep.

I could feel June watching me the rest of the morning. Later, as I trailed everyone home from school, she spun around to glare at me. "You can't read," she declared.

I touched the *cornicello* nestled against my chest. "Can too. My mama and *nonna* taught me."

The other kids gathered closer, Nazzy among them. June put her hands on her hips. "My mommy says your grammy can hardly speak English."

My throat got tight. I wrapped my fingers around the horn. "That's a lie."

She stomped her foot. "I'm not lying, you are." I made a horned fist, but before I could shake it, she turned and skipped down the street chanting, "Liar, liar, pants on fire!"

Nazzy hung back while everyone else followed June and chanted along with her.

"I believe you," he said, "but maybe don't do the evil eye. It's scary."

Then he followed June and the others. I unclenched my fist and watched them go.

All of Saturday, I stayed far away from our wall, but I could still hear kids calling to each other on the street, the squeal of bike tires, the thwack and whoosh of jump ropes. A few times, I saw kids peering over our cinder block wall. I was almost certain June's smug face was among them, which probably meant Bella was there too. I found myself hoping Nazzy had stayed away, that he wouldn't be as mean as the others. "Liar, liar," I heard the kids call once, so quietly I thought I'd imagined it until Nonna walked over to where I was helping Uncle Louie in the garden and shook her horned fist sideways at the wall. The kids ducked back down, but their giggles lingered. I stared at the cows grazing by the barn and blinked hard to keep myself from crying.

Beside me, my uncle overturned dirt in neat piles with a shovel. "Little brats," he muttered.

My grandmother put her hand on my head. "They no special," she said. "Pretend they no there." Then she walked to the grazing cows and led them inside the barn.

My uncle pulled a kerchief from his pocket and mopped his forehead. His hazel eyes had darkened to a mossy green. "Hold the stake while I tie up this vine," he said.

He picked up a thin wooden pole and dug it into the ground. I grabbed the pole, which felt smooth and bendy; the wet, dark smell of newly turned dirt comforted me.

He glanced at me as he tied the vine to the pole. "Do you remember what I taught you about bluffing in cards? Don't let on what you've got, good or bad. Play like you're the boss and make 'em pay for whatever they take from you. Do that with those brats," he jerked his head at the wall, "they won't know what hit them."

I shook my head. "I can't hit them, Uncle Louie. Mama would be mad."

He finished tying the vine. "All I mean is, stand your ground."

So, for the rest of the afternoon, I settled on the swing and tried to stand my ground. Whenever I heard giggles or whispers, I made the *mano cornuto* with one hand and shook it in my lap, where only I could see it.

The next day was church. Nonna never came with us. She stopped going after the children and my grandfather died. "I no waste time in God's house if he no waste time in mine," I heard her tell Mama sometimes. I knew better than to ask to stay home with Nonna, even though the last thing I wanted to do was go to church. June would be there with the rest of the neighborhood. It would be hard to avoid her after Mass, when the adults gathered in the small vestibule to shake hands with the priest and visit with each other.

That morning, after the priest said the final blessing and processed down the aisle trailed by altar boys swinging incense, I followed Mama and Uncle Louie into the vestibule and stood cocooned in a circle of chatting adults, mostly women from Mama's factory talking shop, as always. Whenever I peeked past my mother's skirt, I saw June lingering close by with Bella. Finally, they approached, their hands folded behind them.

"Hi, Rose," June said when she and Bella reached our group.

I grabbed my uncle's hand and rested my cheek on his hip, his wool pants scratchy against my skin and smelling faintly of cigarette smoke. He squeezed my hand but kept talking to one of the factory women his age.

Of course, my mother heard June. "Rose," she said, "these girls are talking to you." She smiled at them. "Are you in Rose's class?"

June nodded. "Can she come play?"

I tugged my mother's skirt and whispered, "I don't want to," but she stepped aside and nudged me out of the circle of adults.

"It's okay, Rosie, go make friends. Just stay where I can see you."

Uncle Louie leaned down and whispered to me, "Don't forget, make 'em pay."

There was nothing to do but walk off with June and Bella.

They stopped across the vestibule, out of my mother and uncle's earshot.

"Where do the animals sleep?" June demanded. "In the house with you?"

I stared at her, convinced she was making fun of me again. Neither she nor Bella laughed. They stood waiting for my answer.

"In the barn," I said. "Only the dog sleeps outside in his pen to protect us."

Bella frowned. "When it snows too?"

"He likes snow, and he has a doghouse, and he gets extra furry in winter."

"What about the horsey?" June asked.

"He sleeps in the barn. He's too big for the house. Like the cows." Their questions confused me. Didn't they know anything about animals? Plus, they'd been calling me a liar, but now they were treating me like an expert. "Why?"

June straightened the bows on her pigtails. "My mommy says you don't really have cows. She says your grammy gets milk from a farm in Kearny."

I stared at her. "But your mama thinks they smell bad. And you saw them yesterday when you spied on us."

June considered me, her hands on her hips. "I bet your grammy casts spells so people only think they see cows."

I grabbed the *cornicello* around my neck, not caring who saw it. Maybe if I held it long enough, June and Bella would disappear in a poof of smoke, their own evilness deflected back onto them by my horn. The girls kept smiling, their eyes narrow and mean.

"My *nonna* milks them every morning," I said. "I help her sometimes."

"You lied about reading," June said. "You're lying about the cows."

I marched to a table piled with church bulletins and snatched one. "I can too read," I said and recited an ad from the bulletin.

June startled, then frowned. "You still lied about the cows."

"They're real!"

"Show us up close."

Her smile was triumphant, like she knew she'd tricked me into a corner. I couldn't show them the cows. Mama barely wanted me in the barn; she definitely wouldn't want me bringing kids there, with or without an adult. But if I didn't let June see the cows, she'd keep taunting me and pretending my life with Nonna wasn't real.

I crumpled the bulletin with both hands. That meanness—the evil eye, maybe—reared up inside me, along with an idea. I would take Uncle Louie's advice. I would call June's bluff and make her pay while doing it. I'd risk Mama's rage and sneak June and Bella into the barn to show them the cows—for a price. Quickly, I calculated in my head. Two pennies would buy a bag of Mary Jane caramels with the peanut butter centers at the five-and-dime. Another two and I could also buy an egg cream.

I put the crumpled bulletin back on the table. "Two pennies each."

The other girls huddled together whispering. Finally, June turned around. "We get to see the horsey too."

I stuck out my hand the way I'd seen Uncle Louie do with his friends when they agreed on something. "Deal," I said.

We shook.

I was five years old with no real plan except to sneak in June and Bella while Mama and Nonna were cooking Sunday dinner and Uncle Louie was upstairs in his apartment listening to the dog races on the radio. Late that afternoon, when Nonna patted my head and said, "I make *pasta e fagioli, cucciola mia,*" I smiled and waited until she shut the back door to her apartment and then I raced up the driveway to the gate where June and Bella had agreed to wait. Mama and Nonna would be busy at the stove and kitchen counter with their backs to the narrow basement windows overlooking the yard. If one of them saw me leading the girls down the driveway, I would say we were going to play on the swing. Mama told me to make friends; that was what I was trying to do, I would claim.

I patted my dungaree pockets filled with carrots before easing open the gate. June stood with Bella and Nazzy, whose jug ears flared when he saw me. Sneaking two kids into the barn was one thing. But three—someone was sure to see.

"You can't all come," I said.

Nazzy ducked his head. "Sorry. June said it was okay."

Which made me feel bad. He was the only one who'd been nice to me. I found myself wanting to slam the gate on the other two and lead him down the driveway for free.

June nudged his ribs. "Told you she's a scaredy-cat," she said.

"Pay first," I said and held out my hand for their pennies, which felt cool and satisfying against my palm. After depositing the coins in my pocket, I put a finger to my lips and said, "Be quiet or you'll scare them and they'll stomp you dead." I gripped my *cornicello* to deflect the evil eye from my lie.

As we snuck down the hill, I kept watch over the kitchen windows. No sign of Nonna or my mother. My gaze traveled up our triplex to find my uncle standing by his bedroom window. I couldn't make out his expression, but when he gave me a thumbs up, my racing heart slowed. He was on my side. Still, when the last kid entered the barn, I shut the door behind us with relief.

I didn't dare turn on the light, but my eyes adjusted quickly to the dimness. "Sophia, I'm here," I called quietly. She answered with a welcoming moo. Animal stink made the air dense and close. The other two cows shuffled in their stalls. Outside, the dog let out a yip. I put my finger to my lips again and gestured for the kids to follow me to her stall. "Watch out for cow patties," I said, even though Uncle Louie had just mucked the stalls. The lie was worth the way June wrinkled her nose and tiptoed behind me.

Sophia was already at the stall door when we reached her. Her hide smelled musky, her breath sweet with hay. She lipped my outstretched palm for the carrot I had ready for her. "Good girl," I whispered.

"What did you give it?" asked Nazzy.

I turned around to find the other kids hanging back, warily examining Sophia like she might eat them.

"A carrot," I said. I fished one from my pocket and held it out to Nazzy. "Wanna feed her?"

"Sure," he said and reached for the carrot.

I snatched it back. "Gimme another penny."

"No fair," June whispered.

She sounded furious. But Nazzy already had dug a coin from his pocket. We traded, then he stepped up to Sophia and held out the carrot on his flat palm, the way I showed him.

His eyes widened. "I felt the teeth," he said. He held his hand high so the girls could see. "And she spit on me," he said, as proud as if he'd hit a home run. "You're so lucky, Rose."

I stood a little taller, my chest tight and full. This was what it felt like to make a friend.

Bella was more hesitant than Nazzy on her turn, but she managed to stroke Sophia's nose before snatching away her hand when Sophia snorted.

June shook her head when I offered her a carrot. "No more pennies," she said, but I could tell she was afraid.

The mean, hard thing bloomed.

"For free," I said and grabbed her hand. She tried to pull away, but I dragged her to the stall, where the cow stood expectantly, eager for more carrots.

"I don't want to," June insisted as she struggled.

I let her go so suddenly she staggered. "Okay," I said. "If you're a scaredy-cat."

She straightened her dress. "Gimme," she said and snatched the carrot from me. Before I could show her what to do—clearly she hadn't watched the other kids—she held out her fist to Sophia, who grabbed for the carrot top peeking out.

June let out a piercing shriek and stumbled backward. "It bit me," she wailed, then burst out sobbing.

Sophia snorted and stepped away from the stall door as she chewed her carrot. I grabbed June's hand, which didn't have a mark.

"She didn't," I said, but she kept wailing.

The barn door slid open, flooding the space with daylight. Mama, Nonna, and Uncle Louie raced inside.

Mama reached me first. "We heard screaming. Rosie, are you okay?"

She checked all my limbs before she noticed the other kids. Bella and Nazzy stood there, silent and still. June had been startled into silence too, though her face was tear streaked and she held her hand against her chest like it was broken.

My mother looked at me. "What are you all doing in here?"

"Showing them the cows—"

"We gave her two pennies to see them and one more to feed them," June said and pointed at Sophia. "That nasty one bit me."

"Not really," Nazzy offered. "Maybe on accident."

My grandmother shook her finger at June. "Sophia no bite unless you do something bad."

June stomped her foot. "She did so!"

"Maybe I bite you too," Nonna said.

"Ma, stop," my mother hissed, then frowned at me. "I didn't raise you to be a con artist like your uncle, Rose Concetta Morroni." She pointed at June, Bella, and Nazzy, who were all staring, open-mouthed. "Give back their money. Now."

Uncle Louie jammed his hands in his pants pockets. His smile lacked its usual dazzle. There was something cold and hard about it. "Leave her alone, Carm. Whatever she did, those two deserved it." He jerked his chin at June and Bella.

My mother planted her fists on her hips. "This was your idea, wasn't it? You helped her plan this."

"I didn't plan anything. But somebody has to teach her to look out for herself. You treat her like she's gonna break, Carm."

"Well, you treat her like a poker buddy and now she's cheating people. No wonder nobody likes her!"

The words knocked the breath out of me. I looked at Nazzy, who gazed around the barn, everywhere except at me.

"Carmella, *basta così!*" my grandmother said. Her arms were crossed, her face stern. "Always the nasty words that cut right through. That's not how I teach you."

"That's exactly what you taught me," my mother said. Her face was pale, her eyes dark. "How do you think you talked to me? You were nicer to the damned cows than you were to us."

My grandmother's voice rose. "Those cows, they keep us alive." She smoothed her apron, breathed deeply, then said in a quieter voice, "Past is past. This is about Rosie. Nothing wrong with her to make a little money."

"There is if I say so."

I could feel my face flush, my fists clench. Nonna was right. Mama always got in the way. She never tried to understand. She cared more about being angry at Nonna than she did about loving me. "Nonna says it's mine."

My mother turned to me. "Enough, Rose! I'm your mother, not her."

The meanness bubbled over. It made me act before I thought, the first of many times in my life. I grabbed my *cornicello* with one hand, made a horned fist with the other, held it up to the sky—I should have pointed it at the ground, why didn't I point it at the ground?—and shook it at my mother. "You're jealous," I said. "The evil eye gets all the jealous people! It'll make you dead!"

Mama's face froze. Even Uncle Louie looked shaken. Before my mother could start yelling, I turned and ran from the barn.

Dinner was silent that night. My mother wouldn't look at me as she and my grandmother hurried around the kitchen, putting out plates of food. When my grandmother sat down to eat, my mother kept herself busy wiping counters and washing dishes. Uncle Louie took his cue from the rest of us and ate quietly, his eyes traveling between Mama and Nonna.

Finally, Nonna pushed away her plate. "Carmella, eat. You stay mad is no good for nobody."

My mother threw her dishtowel on the counter. "It's not like I have anything to be mad about. Just because my own kid calls me jealous and wants me dead. I can't imagine where she learned any of that. Can you, Ma?"

My grandmother tossed her napkin on her plate. "Always so dramatic. You make a big deal where there is nothing. She say sorry. Yes, Rosie?"

I sank lower in my chair and stared at the table. Mama's harsh laugh made me look up.

"You two deserve each other," she said. Suddenly she shook her own fist with two extended fingers—the wrong ones—at my grandmother. "There. You get the evil eye too, Ma. How does it feel, for your own kid to wish you were dead?"

She marched out of the kitchen; her footsteps pounded up the stairs.

When I looked at my grandmother, she was staring after my mother. I held out the *cornicello* from my neck, to ward off the evil eye.

"I won't let her get you, Nonna."

My grandmother extended her hand. "*Il cornicello*. Give me. She right. I fill your head with nonsense. You no respect Mama. That no good."

"But, Nonna—"

"*Basta*, Rose!"

She wore the harsh, closed look she usually saved for fighting with my mother. I never dreamed she would use it on me, her *cucciola mia*. I looked at my uncle for support, but he just pushed away his plate and reached for a deck of cards. I took off the necklace and handed it to her. She closed her fist around it, touched it to her chest, then pointed at the ceiling.

"To your room," she said. "Think what you did bad. Then say sorry to Mama."

Frowning, she watched me until I stood and stomped upstairs.

I hid in my room for what felt like forever. My mother's door stayed closed. There was no way I was going to say I was sorry. But the longer I sat on my bed, the more vividly I imagined my grandmother's stern, disappointed face.

The sun had dropped lower in the sky by the time I looked outside to check for her in the yard, where she sat on the swing with her back to the triplex. She leaned against one rope as if she were too sad to move, the way she sat sometimes when I imagined she was thinking about my grandfather and her dead children. That day, though, her sadness was my fault. Mama's too, I kept reminding myself. She never should have tried to throw the evil eye at Nonna. Even so, it felt like my burden. I had never upset my grandmother. My chest hurt deep inside, like something was twisting my heart.

I crept from my room, past Mama's closed bedroom door, out of the apartment, and down the shared hallway to the triplex's front door. Outside, I crossed the yard to Nonna, who was still seated on the swing with her back to me.

"Nonna, I'm sorry," I called, but she didn't move. She must be so, so angry, I remember thinking. I kept walking. "I won't use *il malocchio* ever again."

When, finally, I faced her, I saw her eyes were closed. One hand clasped the rope; the other rested in her lap.

"Nonna," I said, but she didn't answer. Her lips were parted, as if to let out a sigh. I touched her shoulder, shook her arm. She slumped. "Nonna, get up."

I shook her harder. She pitched forward; her chest hit the ground, her head bent at an odd angle in the grass, her bottom still planted on the swing. There was a sound, not exactly a sigh, more like an expulsion, air rushing from a pricked balloon.

I grabbed her hand. It felt cold, unnatural. I dropped it. The thumping in my throat made me gag. I should have done the sign before I touched her. I should have done a better job warding off *il malocchio* when my mother tried to cast it. But I hadn't, and it had come to rest inside my grandmother. *Il malocchio* had killed her. I had let it kill her.

I heard the back door to my grandmother's apartment creak. "Rose, I want to talk to you," my mother called.

Her heels clicked on the back patio. Soon she would round the corner of the triplex and see my grandmother planted face-forward in the grass, hair trailing from her bun, her arms spread like Jesus on the cross. And I would be standing there, my face as guilty as if I'd stolen a pocketful of Mary Janes from the five-and-dime. My mother's eyes would widen and she would shriek, "What have you done?" Even though it was her fault too. Her fault, not mine. Oh, how I wanted it to be anyone else's fault but mine.

I raced across the yard, past her. She tried to catch me—"Rosie, come back," she called—but I kept running, slammed my grandmother's back door, raced through her kitchen, upstairs to our apartment and into my mother's room, where I slipped under the bed. One sneeze, another, as I gulped dusty air. It was warm under there, warmer than outside. But I was safe. No one would find me; blame me.

Through the open window I heard my mother call to my grandmother, followed by her shout, "Louie, come quick," then my uncle's voice: "She's gone." Sobbing. Then quiet.

Soon, I heard distant footsteps, our apartment's front door opening, louder footsteps down the hall, heaving breaths, rustling, thumping, before the footsteps entered the room. I peered from beneath the bed skirt. My mother's heels, her slender ankles, hurried past me toward the window; a whoosh as she shut it; snap, the blind pulled down. A man's boots, mud caking the soles, walked backward—a neighbor? Uncle Louie's boots followed, a body's length away. Both men grunted, low and labored.

"Jesus Lord, all those stairs," I heard my uncle groan. "Her own bed would've been fine."

"Too small," was my mother's tense response. "Make sure her head's on the pillow."

"It's not like she's gonna know, Carm."

Nonna. They were putting Nonna on the bed above me.

There was another whoosh as the soft, feather mattress sank over me. Weight settled on my back. I tried to wriggle forward, backward, but I was pinned. *Call to Mama, she'll save me*—but then she would find me, punish me. For something she did—or mostly did. I hated her. Hated her, hated her, hated her. Really, what I felt was shame, the weight of the jealousies and misunderstandings between the three of us settling as heavily on my five-year-old brain as the weight of Nonna's body on my back. I had pushed her off the swing. I hadn't warded off *il malocchio*. I was just as much to blame as Mama. More, because Nonna loved me most.

All three sets of shoes marched out of the room. I heard my mother say, "I'll call the funeral home," before the door clicked shut behind them, leaving me trapped beneath my grandmother.

I fell asleep, lulled by the closeness of the space, the warmth. When I woke up, my eyes were crusty, my nose stuffy from the dust. I forgot where I was until I tried to roll over. Nonna's weight kept me stuck on my stomach. I lifted the bed skirt. The room was almost dark. By the door was the dim outline of my mother's dresser. Off to the left I could make out a sliver of the vanity. No one breathed except me. I wasn't sure how much time had passed. Not much, or my mother would have been calling my name, frantic to find me. Or she might be too angry to look.

Muffled footsteps sounded in the hallway. The door opened. There were my mother's house shoes with their flat, rubber soles. Her shoes stopped as soon as they crossed the threshold. I could hear her breathing, deep, quick breaths. She *was* still angry. If she found me she would swat my bottom and send me to bed without supper and make me milk the cows in the morning by myself. Maybe she would banish me. Probably.

I couldn't get myself to make a sound. Instead, I raised one fisted hand, extended my index and pinky fingers and shook them at the floor. *Evil, evil, go away, come again some other day*, rang in my head. *Make Mama know where I am. Make her love me again.* No. I hated her. Her love shouldn't matter. But it did. It always would, no matter how much I wanted it not to.

I was pregnant with my son when she died. He was conceived by accident, when I thought I was finished with the changes and couldn't get pregnant anymore. My two daughters were almost teens, already pulling away from me and my temper that kept besting my heart. Mama was in hospice when I told her about the baby. I hadn't told anybody yet, not even my husband. Her skin was as sallow as candle wax from the kidney disease that would kill her. We had never learned to forgive each other, or at least admit our roles in the distance between us. But I could give her this. I could tell her about her newest grandchild before anyone else. She stared at me afterward, her eyes blinking rapidly, her jaundiced hands picking at the blanket. Then she frowned. "Do better with this one, Rosie," she said.

In my mother's bedroom where I lay trapped beneath my grandmother's body, Mama's house shoes stepped closer. Her breaths got louder, harsher. Then one long, shuddered breath, and she sighed. Was she crying? She couldn't be. She never cried. Her feet backed up, then stepped to the left. I heard her drop onto the bench in front of the vanity.

I managed to inch forward on my belly. Above me, I could feel Nonna's body shift along with me. *Careful*, I remember thinking, *be careful.* But I needed to know whether Mama was really crying. From my new position, I could see the length of her thin ankle, the curve of one shapely calf extended in front of her. A quick, strangled gulp of air almost made me shift backward. Then her voice: "Nothing's ever easy with you, Ma, not even this. You had to just drop dead, no warning, nothing."

Snuffling sounds, a nose blowing. "I'm selling the cows, Ma, and the horse. The cart and milk bottles. I'm selling it all. People can buy their milk at the goddamn grocery store. I don't want your life. Not for me or Rose. And I won't just kiss her when she's sleeping. She'll know I love her no matter what."

My mother's leg disappeared from view. I heard rustling as she stood, then her house shoes walked to the doorway and turned to face the bed. I heard her blow her nose again. I imagined her dabbing her eyes—darkened from hazel to green—and that harsh frown she got when she was angry. But she loved me; she'd said so. She wouldn't hate me, no matter what I'd done to Nonna. She would love me the way Nonna had; she would love me best.

I struggled as hard as I could, writhing forward. My mother's feet turned to march out of the room. I gave one mighty tug; the weight of my grandmother lifted then thumped back down lower, onto my butt. "Don't go!" I shouted.

"Holy God!" my mother screamed.

There was a clatter as Mama fell, her body sprawled beside the bed skirt, her eyes closed, her breaths so shallow I thought she'd stopped breathing altogether. Later she would tell me that Nonna's body had jumped in the air just as I'd yelled, convincing her that my grandmother had risen from the dead, sufficiently chastised by her angry daughter to beg forgiveness. Whenever she told the story over the years, there was a yearning in her eyes, a sadness, quickly dispelled before she smiled grimly and finished the story. "I should have known," she always said. "Your grandmother never apologized for anything, and you, Rose, are just like your grandmother."

Which I am. But I'm like my mother too. God help me, I'm like them both.

La Cuesta Encantada

The last thing Althea needed with Owen missing was Irene nosing around. Yet there she was, pacing outside the store, her wrinkled cheeks ruddy from the early morning chill. Althea hid inside in the dark, behind a shelf of stuffed seals, willing her friend to leave. Owen might be wandering along the freeway, traffic swift with impatient commuters. He might need her. She gripped the shelf. No. He was a grown man, her husband of almost fifty years. He could still take care of himself.

Irene stopped pacing and rapped on the window. "I know you're there, Althea," she called. "It's 8:00 a.m. I've got news."

Althea sighed and flipped on the lights before unlocking the door. "Can't it wait? I'm getting ready to open." She walked to the cash register and started dusting.

Irene followed her. "Our whole lives, you've never been too busy to gossip. Where's Owen? I haven't seen him in forever."

"Upstairs," Althea lied. "He overslept."

Owen had sneaked out before dawn while she was showering. No note, nothing. But that wasn't anybody's business. He always came back eventually, sometimes his normal self, sometimes not. On Friday he had been gone all afternoon. When he finally returned, there were twigs in his thick white hair, and he let out a whoop before dancing her up and down the aisles, right in front of the customers. Then he had barged out of the store and upstairs to their apartment, where he had slept straight through until morning.

Irene plopped her gloves on the counter. "Wait till you hear. Someone wants to buy the hardware store from me and open a Starbucks."

"Oh, please. You'll never get around the ordinance."

Twenty years before, in the early eighties, when Althea had still been on city council, she had helped draft an ordinance banning franchises. No cookie-cutter chains would besmirch their town. Althea's own store typified Cambria hominess, a two-story clapboard brimming with postcards, coffee mugs, and sweatshirts bearing images of the region's beloved elephant seals, plus replicas of Hearst Castle's glassware and china.

"Rules are written on paper, not stone," Irene said as the bells on the front door jingled.

Owen, at last.

Instead, Beatrice walked in, blowing on her knobby, reddened hands, her long white braid trailing down her back. Althea made herself kiss her hello just like any other day.

"Lucky I was driving by," Beatrice said. "It's been too long since we coffee-klatched. What's our topic?"

"Selling the hardware store and retiring," Irene said.

Beatrice snorted. "Oh please. You wouldn't know what to do with yourself."

"I'd move someplace social," Irene said. "Some of us don't have husbands for company."

She pulled a brochure from her coat pocket. It showed detached stucco townhouses, elderly couples strolling beneath graceful arbors. Laguna Woods Leisure World, down south near Los Angeles. Althea touched a glossy page. She and Owen walking hand in hand along a sunlit path. Or maybe he would gallop her past the other residents in a frenetic foxtrot.

"Women outnumber men three to one in those places," Althea said.

"Better odds than here." Irene took off her knit cap, fluffed her wispy hair. At seventy-one she remained lovely despite the wrinkles and bluish veins roping her hands and neck. A person couldn't help being drawn to her face with those eyes like bright slices of sky. She had always known how to use them to her advantage, even when they were all children. "There hasn't been a decent single man around here in decades." She paused. "Not since Hank."

Althea tossed her dust cloth on the counter. Even after so much time, just hearing that name infuriated her. But she couldn't let on. She had promised herself. "You've dated plenty since him."

Irene folded her cap, then looked up smiling. "He's still my gold standard."

Beatrice spun the greeting card rack. "Owen sleeping in again?" she asked, her eyes on the rack. "He should get checked for that chronic fatigue."

Althea couldn't look at Beatrice and busied herself with the coffee maker behind the register. "He's fine. Touch of flu, maybe."

The front bells jingled; this time Owen walked in. Finally. Althea suppressed the urge to scold; instead, she hurried over and stood on tiptoe to kiss his cold, rough face. At least he'd remembered a coat. He looked like himself, so handsome still and imposingly tall with large capable-looking hands, watchful eyes that normally drank her in, even after so many years of knowing her.

"There you are, sleepyhead," she said, loud enough for Irene and Beatrice to hear, then whispered, "Where've you been?"

Frowning, he considered her question. Did he even know?

"Around," he said. "I left a note, like always."

"You didn't. I checked everywhere."

He regarded her absently, then kissed her, a full-on smooch that he usually saved for private.

"And you complain Owen's not romantic."

He looked up at the sound of Irene's voice. Althea patted his arm. *Focus, hon*, she wanted to say. But not with the others there.

"Irene and Beatrice stopped by," she said.

"Take it down a decibel. My hearing's fine. I can see, too." He let Irene and Beatrice each peck his cheek, then walked to the coffee maker, where he picked up the pot and wiggled it at the women. "Offer you some?"

Beatrice declined—"Gives me heartburn lately"—but Irene nodded. He poured a cup and brought it over.

Irene propped her elbows on the counter and took a sip. "Owen, what do you think about selling our stores and moving to Laguna Woods? Bea, you and Stuart could sell the bed and breakfast lickety-split, it's in such a prime location. Imagine, buying side-by-side condos and barbecuing every evening. No more foggy cold. Just balmy days and nights."

Owen stared at Irene, then down at the counter, which he started wiping with Althea's abandoned dust cloth.

"Stop talking craziness," Althea said. "We're staying put."

Irene thumped down her coffee mug. "There was a time you couldn't wait to leave. You packed up faster than a man running from a jilted fiancée that time you two moved to Los Angeles."

Irene was right. That *had* been Althea's dream, once. She watched Owen's slack face. "We were children back then. This is home. We know this place. Right, hon?"

"Just because we've lived here forever," Irene said, "doesn't mean we have to die here." She smiled at Owen. "Talk to her, O. If we work together, we can get that ordinance overturned in a blink and sell to the highest bidder. Then Laguna Woods, here we come."

He shrugged, a quick quiver, as if shaking off a trance.

"If Althea's not interested, I'm not either." He picked up the coffee pot, wiggled it at Beatrice. "Offer you some?"

Beatrice hesitated, then tapped her chest. "Heartburn, remember?"

Althea forced herself to turn away as Owen paused, then said, "Of course. What was I thinking?"

Within a week Irene started a petition to overturn the franchise ban.

"She's planning to knock on every door within a twenty-mile radius," Beatrice shouted to Althea above the elephant seals' baying. They stood on the bluffs overlooking the Piedras Blancas haul-out beach, which writhed with activity: elephant seal pups jostled mothers for milk; bulls bellowed their ardor to cows. It was twilight, the end of Beatrice and Althea's docent shift for the elephant seal conservancy. Each held bullhorns and wore badges with red letters—"Ask Me Anything!"—visible even in the incessant fog that blanketed the area during winter.

Althea adjusted her badge. "She won't get much support. Everyone loves this town as is."

"The petition's already as thick as my thumb."

On the beach below, a woman watched a boy poke driftwood through the tall chain-link fence at a pup who mouthed the wood. Docents were supposed to keep visitors from bothering the seals. The huge two-ton bulls with their long, meaty snouts could be dangerous now, during mating season, when they sometimes battled over cows. Amazing how often Althea had to warn people who reached through the fence, even climbed it, wanting to touch the animals.

The boy kept poking the pup. Althea aimed her bullhorn. "Please don't tease the seals." Her words echoed in the cove. The boy whirled around, searching for his admonisher. "You'd think parents would teach children more sense," she said.

"Sense runs off when people really want something." Beatrice cradled her own bullhorn as she regarded Althea. "Irene's lonely, Thea. She's been talking about Hank again like he was here just yesterday. Only way she thinks she'll find somebody is by selling and moving. So she'll keep getting signatures."

Althea stared down at the seals. Again with that man. Lately Irene acted as if losing him had swept away all her options, as if she hadn't had a lifetime full of opportunities. Which wasn't true, not a bit. Irene had always been popular, always had dates and boyfriends, even now. There was no reason for Althea to feel guilty. "She won't get my signature," she said, keeping her eyes on the beach. "How's Stuart?"

Beside her, she sensed Beatrice shifting quietly, as if deciding whether to let Althea change the subject.

"He's frustrated," Beatrice said. "A guest woke us after midnight insisting we fix her cable TV or give her a rebate. The ninny. As if we could do anything at that hour." She paused. "We're getting too old to run a B and B."

The skin under Beatrice's eyes was puffy. She was Althea's age, seventy, but seemed frail wrapped in her quilted coat. Her long braid was thin and scraggly. How had she aged so much without Althea noticing?

"Hire a manager," Althea said.

"That's one option."

"You haven't signed—"

"No. Although admit it, selling to a franchise, the money would be nice. That dry heat in Laguna Woods would be better for Stuart's gout than this constant fog."

"Excuses, excuses. The weather's not so different and you know it."

"Don't get snippy. I'm only thinking out loud." She paused, then said, "What about Owen? Has he changed his mind about all this?"

There it was, the guarded tone Beatrice used lately whenever she asked about Owen. She suspected something was amiss, which was why Althea had been turning down invitations that included Owen, sending him into the stock room if Beatrice or Irene stopped in (though they had caught her off guard last week by arriving so early). If they knew about Owen's diagnosis, they would try to cajole Althea into action. Irene would bring her brochures for in-home aid and full-care facilities. Beatrice would hold her hand and say in her blunt, practical way that the most difficult path was usually the right one.

Not in this case. The thing to do was to enjoy the times when Owen was himself. Which mostly he was. Occasionally he even left her silly notes in random places, the way he used to. For the other times, there was the young man from San Simeon whom Althea had hired to help around the store. He had Owen's measured way of doing things, was good at getting him to hang around by asking how to fix something or where to put a new shipment of seal magnets or sweatshirts. For now, that's what Owen needed, a young man to show the ropes, someone to focus him on the familiar, ground him in routine, like the doctor had advised. And this place, with its shops and lifelong friends and proximity to the Castle, was ingrained in them, as routine and familiar as their own mottled, aging skin. She had been here so long, so much longer than she had ever intended.

"Owen still agrees we should stay," she said, then squeezed Beatrice's hand. "Just like you do."

Beatrice put an arm around her. Althea hugged her close. Together they watched the seals on the beach below.

The summer of 1946 was the hottest on record along California's central coast. Sweat stuck Althea's clothes to her skin even in the early hours. Every day she helped her mother in the store, though business was slow. No one wanted to be out midday. The sun's pounding glare made everything—the town, the store, their daily rhythms—even more tedious, screamingly so.

Althea sat behind the register plucking her new dress with its grown-up, belted waist away from her damp skin. It was probably ninety degrees already and only 10:00 a.m. Oh, to be somewhere else, like the castle on the hill a few miles away, owned by William Randolph Hearst, the newspaper magnate. La Cuesta Encantada, he called it. The Enchanted Hill. There were rumored to be two huge swimming pools, one indoor, one outdoor. Probably a servant stood by the outdoor pool with big, fluffy towels so guests emerging from the water didn't catch cold. Althea fanned herself with her hand. As if catching cold were even possible right now. Someday she would leave here, someday soon.

A lone customer, scruff-faced and lanky, kept glancing over from a nearby shelf. His fingernails were black crescents, his armpits sweat-stained.

"I'll take a pint," he said.

"I don't know what you mean." She smoothed her belt and tried to look stern, older than fifteen. You never knew when Mr. Hearst might send a snitch, her mother said.

The man regarded her with narrowed eyes. "Kay around?"

"Mama," she called without standing, "someone's asking for you."

Behind her there were footsteps, quick insistent clicks on the floorboards. Her mother ducked around the curtain shielding the back. Her high-cheeked face looked stern as she assessed the man's creased clothes and dusty boots. Even in heels, she barely reached his shoulder, but he cowered a little under her gaze.

"Who sent you?" she asked.

"Donny. He said you'd know—"

"Not here."

She turned and pushed past the curtain, the man trailing her. Althea cringed when she noticed his eyes fixed on her mother's shapely bottom.

They kept liquor in the back, in pint-size bottles that were easier to hide, though prohibition had been dead for over a decade. Mr. Hearst had strict rules about alcohol at La Cuesta. One cocktail a night per guest, limited wine at dinner. Merchants weren't supposed to sell to people on their way there. Mr. Hearst had his guests' bags searched upon arrival. Better to be discreet, Mama said, than to risk being run out of business like Carmichael's, whose owner had dared to keep whiskey on display.

Bells jingled up front. A bird squawked. Althea looked up to see Irene wearing a wide-brimmed hat and hurrying down the main aisle. Beatrice followed close behind. On her shoulder was her cockatiel, Cecil, clutching the tip of her long dark braid in his claws. He screeched as he swiveled his head and eyed the shelves.

"Irene did something stupid again," Beatrice sang out. She looked tiny and solid next to Irene's willowy figure. "To help her meet boys."

"Oh, Bea, hush," said Irene. "You have Stuart, you don't need to worry. Thea, wait till you see." She swept off her hat. "What do you think?"

Her hair, normally auburn, was bleached platinum like Jean Harlow's. The color made her eyes bluer than the tiny cornflowers dotting her shirtfront dress. Althea's own new dress looked dowdy by comparison.

"Does your grandma know?" she asked.

"I'm sixteen. It's my hair. Besides, her vision is so bad these days she can barely see."

Behind Althea, her mother pushed aside the curtain. The man followed, slipping a bottle into his back pocket. Irene craned her neck to watch, smiling slightly when the man grinned at her as he left the store. Sometimes she was positively shameless.

Irene touched her hair. "Hi, Mrs. Hamilton. Notice anything different?"

Althea's mother glanced over as she shut the register. "Someone stumbled into the bleach."

Irene flushed. Beatrice snorted and scratched Cecil's neck. He arched his crest, trilled. Althea's mother wheeled a dolly to the dry goods and started loading flour sacks.

"Althea," she said over her shoulder, "next backroom customer, get me right away. Don't wait to be asked."

"How am I supposed to know if they don't ask?"

"Use your instincts. You need to learn to read people if you're gonna take over this business."

The back door opened. In walked the new stock boy, Reggie. He'd only worked for them a week, and he wasn't a boy, he was eighteen. Wavy black hair, gray eyes. Usually Althea wouldn't bother looking at someone like him, who wouldn't notice a girl like her: small, fussy, persistent, like a sparrow seeking crumbs, Irene sometimes teased. Reggie had traveled some before settling in Cambria with relatives. Althea imagined where he'd been: San Francisco, Los Angeles, maybe even Chicago. Big cities where no one would know anything about her, where glamour and excitement didn't reside solely at the top of a hill that offered no invitation. Cities where she wanted to go.

She straightened her belt and sucked her teeth before smiling. "Reggie, how're things?"

He waved—"Hey, kiddo"—then turned to her mother, who wheeled the dolly of flour sacks over to him.

"Rush delivery for the Castle," she said. "Big party tonight and they've got weevils."

"Sure thing." He eyed Irene. "You girls keeping outta this heat?"

"I must not be working you hard enough," Althea's mother said, "if you've got time for chitchat." She strode out the back door.

He grinned as he wheeled the dolly after her. Althea watched him go.

Irene twirled a brittle strand of hair. "You didn't say there was a new boy."

"He's nobody." Althea found a cloth and started dusting the spotless register, but not before she caught Beatrice's sympathetic look.

Beatrice offered Cecil a palmful of seeds. "He just moved here, Irene. He's probably not looking to leave first chance he gets."

"Turn a boy's head, he'll take you anywhere." Irene stared thoughtfully at them. "Let's get him to bring us to the Castle."

Althea pictured Irene flipping her hair, the way Reggie's eyes would linger. "Mama would fire him."

"We'll flag him down around the block. She'll never know."

Althea's mother walked back inside wiping her forehead with her apron. "Must be the hottest day of the year."

Irene clasped her hands behind her. "Mrs. Hamilton, can Althea come for ice cream?"

Her mother walked to the windows and lowered the blinds. "Might as well. We won't have many customers until evening."

"Mama, there's still inventory—"

Irene tugged Althea closer. "Don't you want to see the Castle?" she whispered.

Hearst Castle. La Cuesta Encantada. They had all dreamed about it, the ever-expanding mansion looming on its nearby hilltop estate. Mr. Hearst had set up a telescope on the San Simeon pier for locals to catch a glimpse. The one time Althea used it, she saw a car chugging up a dusty road, graceful, scaffolded domes evoking a Spanish cathedral. There were rumors—confirmed by Beatrice, whose father was the local vet—that Mr. Hearst kept all kinds of exotic animals, though many of them had been sold over the years. Althea imagined droopy-humped camels, tigers with bristling stripes. She especially loved big cats. Plastered on her bedroom walls were posters of panthers, lions, leopards, along with their fearless trainers. Sometimes she pictured herself in a pen surrounded by white tigers, her whip raised confidently as she took the cats through their paces. She wouldn't be afraid, even when the biggest one flattened his ears and hissed. She would flick the whip, growl instructions; he would growl back but obey. She would be in charge, the kind of girl that boys like Reggie would look at.

"Let's go," she said.

Irene was already halfway to the door, her hat abandoned on the counter. Beatrice shrugged at Althea. Together they followed their friend outside into the heat.

Althea stood by the rumpled bed and clipped on her docent badge. Her coat pockets were stuffed with seal magnets for the children too shy or scared to leave the cliff. She always offered to watch them while their parents and more adventurous siblings trekked down the narrow path to the beach. She understood the children's hesitation, the safety in the familiar.

Just this past week, two bulls had battled by the shoreline, the slapping of their skin echoing in the cove. Nearby a pup wailed, frightened but clearly too weak to move. Althea had noticed him wailing earlier as bigger pups pushed him off the teats of different cows. She radioed the conservancy for rangers, who arrived in their pickup with tranquilizer guns and first aid supplies. By then, the bulls had moved on and the pup lay motionless. The children, awed and silent, clustered around Althea on the cliff as they watched two rangers maneuver the pup into an animal carrier, lift it into the truck bed, then speed down the beach to the conservancy's seal shelter. Althea had gathered the children close, told them everyone would be fine. Their powdery scent and the feel of their small, shifting bodies still lingered.

Docent badge in place, she went looking for her bullhorn. It wasn't where she kept it in the closet with her handbags. She searched under the bed (cluttered with dusty shoeboxes full of Owen's old notes), in drawers, the living room, the second bedroom that had been her mother's. In the kitchen, she found Owen seated at the table reading the local newspaper, a sandwich by his elbow. He was supposed to be downstairs at the store. Thank goodness for the new boy, Greer.

He was big like Owen, quiet and capable. He wouldn't spread rumors or offer advice. Three afternoons a week, he ran the store and kept an eye on things while she volunteered at the haul-out beach. Three afternoons a week, she could breathe easily, away from Owen.

She started opening cabinets. Owen kept reading.

"Have you seen my bullhorn?"

"Can't say I have."

It was tucked behind the oatmeal canister and some cans of creamed corn. There were also three rolls of quarters and a package of fishhooks. No notes though. She took out everything that didn't belong.

"How'd these get there?" she asked.

He looked up. "I must have rushed putting groceries away."

"That must've been it," she agreed. "I'll be a little late tonight. We're bottle feeding that pup we just saved."

He spread out the newspaper. There was Irene's picture below the headline, "The Path to Wealth Is Paved with Lattes." Two weeks of petitioning and already she was front-page news.

"She's making progress," he said.

"A million articles won't convince the planning board."

"This ordinance gets overturned, we could make a mint, go anywhere."

Laguna Woods' manicured hills, the warm breeze as they read by the pool. Owen would angle the umbrella to keep the sun off her face and make frothy drinks for them all, Althea, Beatrice, Stuart, and Irene applauding him from their wicker lounges.

He would get worse, perhaps suddenly, though it would only seem sudden. The symptoms likely had gone unnoticed for some time. Last month, in an office lined with medical degrees, a tired-looking specialist suggested they consider alternative care options. Owen had gripped his chair arms, breathed slowly. "Better to know now," he said once they were home. "We can plan for the future before I forget about it." He got her to smile with that one, even as she cried, curled on their neatly made bed. The bed he had made every day of their marriage until recently. These days, the sheets were often rumpled, the pillows in a heap. His notes—those silly, random, lovely things—were intermittent now, and rambling, digressing to long-ago events. "I walked by Beatrice and Stuart's old place, where they lived all those years they were trying to have a baby," he wrote in one she'd recently discovered underneath her bedside lamp. "Remember how Irene would bring Hank there for cocktails? Your mother was still alive. Hank thought guard dogs would've been a better bet to breed than cats. Kind of a know-it-all, used to puff himself up like a peacock. Although maybe he had a point about the dogs. I always tried to be friendly, for your sake, and Irene's. He didn't make it easy though."

Hank—the blowhard, the cur best forgotten; she'd done the right thing about him, though she could never tell anyone. Hank, Owen remembered. Where the fishhooks belonged, where he went in the mornings and afternoons when he left her, that he forgot. There was no way of knowing which memories would fade first or which would be the last to go. But the most recent memories, the basics of daily life, could be among the earliest casualties, the doctor had warned. What would happen when Owen started forgetting to eat? Forgetting who he was? Who she was. They would wait and see. They wouldn't change anything. Better not to risk a disorienting change.

Owen smoothed out Irene's picture, then picked up the packet of fishhooks. "Irene's got the right idea. We could afford a house near wherever I wind up. Near Irene and Beatrice and Stuart, if they're willing. You could travel like you've always wanted, then come back and tell me about where you've been. Or pretend I went too. I won't know any better eventually."

"We're both staying put."

He slammed down the fishhooks, making her jump. "Stop being pigheaded. If we don't sell now, we never will. And then you'll be here all by yourself." His face was flushed and angry. "I need to know you're safe. That you'll be okay without me."

Carefully, she took the hooks, folded the newspaper to hide Irene. She rubbed his back as his breathing slowed. "It's not time to worry about that yet," she said and rested her cheek against his coarse, white hair.

Althea and Owen's move to Los Angeles that one time so long ago occasioned his very first note. He was twenty, with a couple inches yet to grow, all ears and wrists and gulping Adam's apple, a slight heart murmur enough for a 4-F when he registered for the draft. She was twenty-two, still sparrowlike in her darting motions, with billows of curly black hair. Together their belongings fit in a trunk and one large suitcase.

They had met three months before at a Cambria Presbyterian dance. He'd driven into town from his family's apricot orchard in Morro Bay. She wore a bottle-green, cinch-waist sheath she'd sewn from a Vogue mail-order pattern. He towered over the other boys in his ill-fitted jacket and leaned in close for Althea to hear his quiet voice above the polka band. "There's more to life than Morro Bay," he'd told her, his steady gaze drinking her in.

They had married within weeks.

The day they moved to Los Angeles, where Althea had a distant cousin, everyone gathered at the train station to see them off. "Make sure to call Cousin Izzy for advice. Or I could always lend a hand," her mother kept saying as they waited on the platform, until Althea stopped bothering to respond. Nearby, Irene, Beatrice, and Stuart talked with Owen. Beatrice—long braid already graying, eyes gazing absently—stood quietly clutching her belly, as if she sensed this pregnancy would fail like the others. Stuart, with his round face and droopy cocker-spaniel eyes, looped one arm protectively around her waist as he smiled and nodded at Irene, who held Owen's elbow and chattered away. She hadn't yet met Hank. Her lips seemed perpetually pursed, as if she couldn't believe the turn her life had taken.

"Just you wait," she told Owen. "Once our boys are home from Korea, I'll find someone to move me right next door."

His head was tilted attentively, but he winked when he caught Althea watching, then gestured for her to check her coat pocket. Inside was a slip of paper. "Los Angeles, here we come!" When she looked up, he was smiling at her, only her.

So many notes followed, written in his careful print on ruled notebook paper and tucked behind the cash register, underneath dinner plates, in cabinets between canned goods, to be found when she least expected them. "Counting the minutes till I see you again" or "Odds are you're stuck with me forever" or some other gushy thing that he would never say aloud but knew would make her laugh. She kept them all, folded neatly in boxes under the bed.

Once in Los Angeles, they rented a storefront and started a pet store a few doors down from her cousin's flower shop by the Fairfax Farmers Market, where there was ample foot traffic. The risk, the adventure, of selling things people wanted but didn't need. Teacup terriers and Siamese cats sold best. Eventually, she and Owen would breed the cats themselves. Blue tips, they decided. At night on the bed squished into the stockroom, they schemed about how they would find an apartment once they were established, how they'd open another store in Beverly Hills, buy a house, have a baby. "Let's call her Velma," said a note under a bag of pet food. "Luke if it's a boy," said another behind the mop. The time they spent, talking about a baby, trying to make one. The surprising, yearning, lovely ache of trying.

Her mother called like clockwork at month's end to say hello, she claimed, but really to gauge how close they were to failure. Fish or reptiles were cheaper upkeep, she suggested. Or sell something practical, like hardware. Althea always said goodbye quickly.

After a year, her mother called midmonth. It was probably nothing, but she kept falling. It was difficult to swallow. Her hands wouldn't work right. Owen wanted to move her to Los Angeles, where they could help out and still keep their store going. Althea said no. Her mother would want to run things. Before long, they'd stock more pet food than pets. Better for Althea to return to Cambria, nurse her mother back to health, then rejoin him in Los Angeles.

"Don't go," said the note she discovered in her handbag upon arriving in Cambria. She threw it in a dustbin near the train station exit.

Owen had a string of good days after their argument about Irene's petition. Instead of wandering, he kept to the store, sweeping, unpacking seal magnets and T-shirts, avoiding customers' questions with a smile, like always. When Greer was working, he followed in Owen's wake, a steady, watchful presence. If Althea kept her distance, she could pretend that Owen was instructing the young man about how she liked the shelves arranged or where to put this or that, which, sometimes, he was.

Then one night she woke to find the bed empty beside her. Her heart pulsed in her throat. He'd never left at night before. Moonlight cast a sulky glow as she pulled on a robe and checked the apartment. Of course he wasn't there. The stairs creaked beneath her slippered feet as she hurried down to the store. That's where he'd be. Please, let him be there.

Outside, a biting wind tugged at her robe and the fog, thick and viscous, clung to her hair and lashes. The sidewalk was empty. She peered through the store windows. It was dark inside except for one dim light. She unlocked the door, crept to where Owen sat by the register, jotting in a notebook beside a hurricane lamp.

He smiled when he saw her, a wide, inviting smile that washed over her. They would go upstairs. She would make tea. They would sleep, wake up refreshed, renewed.

"Hon," she said. "Why're you down here?"

He glanced down at his notebook, then back to her. "Can I help you?" he asked. "We've got some fine Siamese blue points. Pretty little things. Although now we're breeding puppies—big guys, guard dogs who'll know their way around. They're the better bet."

He watched her, lips taut, eyebrows raised, waiting for an answer. She stood there, barely able to breathe. This was their future. This. This.

Hank started courting Irene near the end of Althea's mother's illness. Owen and Althea had been back for three years already. Hank seemed too good to be true, a wealthy San Jose banker who met Irene during a weekend at Beatrice and Stuart's bed-and-breakfast. Ten years older than Irene, he was short and stocky, with slightly bulging blue eyes so pale they appeared almost colorless. He was exceedingly well groomed—manicured nails, dark suits custom fitted to his thick arms and long torso—but his skin was coarse and his voice, loud and cigarette-roughened, asserted his opinions for everyone to hear.

He claimed to be a World War II hero, a bombardier who'd shot down countless enemy planes. "You two are lucky you've never been called to serve," he'd say to Owen and Stuart as he puffed a cigarette. "The horrors. Those Jap planes were the worst. If they couldn't shoot us out of the sky, they'd try colliding with us. Fight until death. That's their culture, you know." Or he'd grin at a blushing Irene and announce how, once he had a family, he'd need something grander than his San Jose townhouse, and a vacation home too. "I've got my eye on some property near La Cuesta," he told them a few weeks after meeting Irene, over drinks at Beatrice and Stuart's fixer-upper cottage they'd bought the previous year when Beatrice had carried a pregnancy almost to term. "I'll build a summer place on it. Nothing on the scale of La Cuesta, of course, but with a pool and servants' quarters. Only the best for my family. That's the ticket."

Irene clasped Hank's hand. Tiny creases already gathered around her lovely eyes, and her hair had taken on a strawlike consistency. Her voice, though, was still girlish with hope. "Just think," she said, "a maid serving us poolside, almost like a Hearst guest."

"Wouldn't that be something," Beatrice said and placed a restraining hand on Althea, who smiled tightly and pinched the meat of her own palm to keep herself from saying something she couldn't take back. Irene cared about this Hank. It wasn't Althea's place to judge. And even she had to admit, as she watched Irene stand to refill her drink, that Hank seemed smitten, his pale eyes following Irene as she crossed the cozy living room; his lips parted in a slight smile as if he couldn't believe his luck.

The first time Irene brought him to the apartment above the store, he spent much of the evening darting glances at Althea's mother, who had Althea strap her to her wheelchair that night so she could sit upright to inspect Irene's new fellow. She rarely met new people since getting sick. Amyotrophic lateral sclerosis, made famous by Lou Gehrig. Her formerly precise, decisive speech was garbled at best. Most days she required feeding, turning to avoid bedsores, diapering and changing like a baby. Soon there would be an iron lung to help her breathe; she would barely be able to blink.

Near evening's end, she turned to Hank and pointed a shaky finger at her own chin. "Foo ... on ... ma ... face?"

The room went silent. Althea watched Irene look around, Owen and Stuart by the bar cart, freshening their drinks, Beatrice frozen with her hands in her lap. Althea's mother kept looking at Hank, as if daring him to do anything except apologize. He considered her, then turned his soft palms upward as he shrugged.

"Actually," he said, "I've been noticing how beautiful you are for a woman of any age."

It was the only time Althea ever saw her mother blush. Everyone laughed, including Althea. Owen stirred his drink and watched her. Let him. Let him see what she looked like happy, a rarity since their return to Cambria. There was no room, no time, for happiness or playful notes. They communicated mostly through terse instructions and slept on the outer edges of the double bed in Althea's childhood room. Owen still reached for her occasionally, but often all she could muster were a few distracted kisses before surrendering to exhaustion. Running the store consumed her, as did caring for her mother, who turned her face away at every ministration. "So . . . sorry," she'd said the first time she'd wet the bed. The middle of the night, her mother's bedside bell ringing insistently. Her mother was heavy, and Althea struggled to move her limp body and change the soaked sheets, the pungent stink strong enough to taste.

"Thea, do you need me?" she heard whispered behind her. There by the door stood Owen, his pajama bottoms askew, his long, lean chest and muscled arms bare in the moonlight. Ready to help.

Oh, to lie her head against the comfort of that chest. But her mother's set grimace, the tears sliding past her temples. This was a woman who had been left a teenage widow with an infant and a heavily mortgaged store, who had sold liquor in defiance of the great William Randolph Hearst to make a life for herself, for Althea. A woman who had never asked anyone for help yet still managed to achieve her own small measure of success. Althea gently set down her mother and walked to Owen.

"I've got her," she said. "I can do this."

A sharp intake of breath, then he cupped her cheek. "I know," he said and padded back down the hallway.

She returned to the bed and wrestled the sheets free, her mother's breathing quick and labored in her ears.

Irene had been seeing Hank for several months when he cornered Owen one night while the women played cards in Althea's mother's room. Her mother had been in bed all day, too weak to move. Althea propped her mother's cards on a music stand, then sat so she could see her blink: one blink for yes, two for no, multiple blinks when she got frustrated by not making herself understood.

From the living room Althea could hear the men's voices, Hank's blaring with cheer, Owen's a quiet, wordless drone, Stuart's sweet tenor weaving in and out. Althea could imagine them sitting where she'd left them earlier: Hank's cigarette smoke swirling around their heads, Stuart and Owen on the worn couch, Hank in the armchair, tumblers of bourbon sweating on the coffee table, alongside an overflowing ashtray. "A business loan would be just the ticket," she heard Hank say, his voice louder than usual. "It's a chance to get out from under this place."

Irene, Beatrice, even Althea's mother looked up.

"Leaving . . . again?" she asked, one hand trembling as she tried to raise it from the blanket.

"Of course not, Mama."

Her mother managed to raise her hand enough to make a shooing gesture. "Better . . . leaving."

Althea couldn't look at her, couldn't let her see the longing that flared.

Across the bed in her folding chair, Irene leaned forward, splaying out her cards for anyone to see. "Hank and I want to help however we can, Thea. There are convalescence homes, or nurses. We could—"

"That's awfully kind," Althea said briskly, though the room suddenly felt stifling. "But I'll manage. Bea, collect that trick before Mama and I grab it." Her face burned. She pointed at her mother's cards. "This one, Mama?"

Her mother blinked rapidly. Althea threw the card, and they started playing again. She strained to hear, but the men's voices had dropped back down to a murmur, Stuart's tenor reentering the mix. "That's not the way we do things," she imagined Owen saying as he spread his large hands decisively over his knees.

Once everyone had gone, her mother was asleep, and she and Owen were cleaning up, him washing dishes while she dried, their rhythm studied and peaceful, she said, "That Hank is a piece of work."

Owen put a wet saucer in the dish rack. "No worse than Irene's others." When she snorted, he glanced over with his old, sly smile. "Although if he puffed himself up any more, he could float in the Macy's parade."

"She deserves better. I'd tell her so, but she wouldn't listen." Althea dried the saucer. "I heard him offer you money. As if we'd take a handout, especially from him."

He turned off the faucet. "It'd be a loan, not a handout. I said we'd think about it."

She should have embraced the idea, a means of paying the medical bills that would keep them tied to this circumscribed life long after her mother died. A means of having the pet store, the house, the baby she'd craved before coming to dread the sound of someone calling her name, needing something. At the very least she should have noted the hope on Owen's face, the steady determination underlying that hope, the love. But all she could picture was the San

Jose mansion that Hank would buy Irene, the vacation cottage in the shadow of Hearst Castle. Gathering by the pool for drinks handed around by a maid who would even clean up afterward. Maybe Irene would lie back on her chaise, a flowing beach robe partially covering her expensive bathing suit, and ask, "How's business? Hank says you're doing so well." As if Althea and Owen's success had been conferred on them by Hank and, by extension, Irene. As if Althea were still the yearning, homespun girl living in the shadow of her platinum-haired friend.

"We'll need something of our own," Owen said, "once your mother's gone."

She placed her dish towel on the counter. "I will not be beholden to that man."

⚛

Owen started sneaking out to follow Irene.

Althea found out when Irene brought him back just before closing one cold, brittle evening. He'd been gone since before dawn. Althea had searched all the regular places, as had Greer. She'd been about to call the police.

When Irene and Owen entered the store, they wore scarves, hats, and gloves and carried clipboards. They'd been collecting signatures, Irene explained, ever since Owen had appeared on her doorstep early that morning.

"We covered twice the streets I do alone," she told Althea. "I'm glad you changed your minds. We'll be able to sell before long, and I'll finally have the life I've always wanted."

She kissed Owen's cheek, then gestured for Althea to follow her. Greer tried to lead him to the storage room, but Owen jerked away and stood watching Irene and Althea.

"I wanted to mention," Irene said quietly, her back to the men. "Owen seems a little off. Said a couple times there'd be a new litter soon. 'Litter of what?' I asked, but he just shrugged. Is everything all right?"

Her hand felt warm on Althea's arm. Althea closed her eyes and pressed her palms to her cheeks. Two weeks since she'd found him at the register. Since he hadn't recognized her. Since he'd started sneaking out again. She couldn't take much more. Not alone.

When she looked up, Owen was staring at Irene.

"I haven't changed my mind," Althea said. "Owen, what were you thinking?"

"We need this overturned as much as anybody," he said. "More, even. You know I'm right."

"Listen to him, Thea," Irene said. "We can all start fresh—"

"Stop it," Althea said to her. "Just because you want to start over doesn't mean everybody does. You've only ever thought about yourself, our whole lives. Don't bother coming around if you don't like my decision." She pushed past Irene and her startled expression.

The next day, Althea hired Greer full time to watch Owen. On the afternoons she volunteered at the conservancy, Greer's younger brother worked the register so Greer could focus on Owen. The extra help was expensive, but they had the money saved. She couldn't stop volunteering. She needed the time away.

If Owen realized he now had a babysitter, he didn't acknowledge it. During the day while he worked alongside Greer, he became talkative, almost garrulous, chatting with customers as he never had before, telling anyone who would listen about Althea's mother, how she had been Cambria's first successful businesswoman. He even bragged about Althea, how she had given up everything to nurse her mother and then decided to stay on, to keep her mother's memory alive in the store. "That's devotion," he would say and shake his head as if awed. Devotion, not defeat, which was how she had always thought of it.

He still managed to sneak away, usually when she was out volunteering and Greer was helping a customer with a question his brother couldn't answer. Sometimes Owen was at Irene's hardware store, picking through nuts and bolts, or he was pacing the street in front of Irene's house. Irene hadn't brought him back again. So far, Greer had found him before it came to that.

Still, whenever Greer brought Owen home, Althea couldn't help think that maybe the universe was paying her back for what happened with Hank. But that was nonsense. Besides, there was no score to settle; there had been no malice in her actions. She had protected Irene. Done the right thing.

Nights with Owen were the worst. After the store was tidy and Althea and Owen had locked up and climbed the stairs to their apartment, he sat staring silently at the TV's flickering images. He'd grunt when she suggested shows to watch, nod at her questions. It was as if he were marking time, waiting for her to fall asleep so he could make his escape.

When she put bells on the apartment door, he took them down. She set the alarm clock to go off every few hours, but by the second time, he was usually gone. She would dress, drive to Irene's, where he stood by the curb, watching the dark windows, maybe thinking this was his home and the woman inside was the one he'd spent a lifetime with. Still, he never resisted when Althea guided him to the truck, although once he shook her off so hard she fell, her tailbone whacking the asphalt. He kept staring at the house. Only when she started crying—"Dammit, I'm right here!"—did he look over, his eyes suddenly sharp with recognition. "Thea. Oh, Thea. I've got to help get this done." He pulled her up, wiped her face with his bare, cold hand. Then he led her to the car and drove them home.

The truck bounced along the narrow road winding up the mountain toward La Cuesta. Cecil stalked the dashboard, his talons pricking the vinyl. Althea's head bumped against the ceiling.

"Ouch!" She rubbed the sore spot. Maybe this wasn't a good idea, no matter how many tigers she might see. But to glimpse them, just once. To peek into that other world, the other life that might be hers someday. She straightened her spine and shifted in Beatrice's lap, where she sat sideways with her shoulder blades pressed against the passenger window. Her new dress—hopelessly wrinkled—clung to her clammy back. Perspiration beaded Beatrice's upper lip, and Althea's own face felt oily, her hairline sweaty. Only Irene looked fresh and unflustered. She sat in the middle, close to Reggie. Working her way into his affections.

Beatrice bounced her knees underneath Althea. "Stop squirming."

Reggie glanced over. "Everything okay?"

Althea's smile ached. "A little cramped is all."

He stretched his right arm across the seat back. "This should make some room."

Irene shifted closer to him. Beatrice raised her eyebrows at Althea, who looked out the windshield and said, "They say Mr. Hearst lets the animals roam free."

Irene shuddered. "I hope not."

Reggie laughed. "An antelope was the most dangerous thing I saw on my last delivery."

"Daddy told me and Stuart that most of the dangerous ones have been sold, and the ones left, like the tigers and bears, are penned up," Beatrice said. "The rest roam around." She pointed out Reggie's window. "Look down there. Zebras."

Irene craned her neck to look past his driving arm. "They're gorgeous," she breathed.

All Althea could see was Irene's fair hair and Reggie glancing from Irene to the road. She was practically in his lap.

Althea poked Irene's shoulder. "For pity's sake, stop hogging the view."

"Thea, that hurt!"

Beatrice glanced between them. "It's hot. We'll get out soon and stretch."

"You'd better not," Reggie said. "I don't think they'd like me bringing girls."

All this discomfort for nothing. Althea felt Irene watching her. Stubbornly she stared out the windshield. A cool, dry hand clutched her own.

"Maybe we could find the pens," Irene said, "and park far away. I'll bet we can still see them. No one would know."

Irene's hand squeezed Althea's. She couldn't help squeezing back. That was the thing about Irene. Just when you couldn't believe how self-centered she was, how she'd take any opportunity for herself, she did something to change your mind.

Reggie shifted his arm from the seat to Irene's shoulders. "Your wish is my command."

Beatrice poked Althea. *Oh, please,* she mouthed. Althea forced a smile. What she would give to be the one Reggie was talking to.

The conservancy's elephant seal shelter was peaceful, its outdoor pens and tanks empty except for where Althea stood bottle-feeding the rescued pup on the concrete deck surrounding his tank, where he'd lived for over a month already. She stroked his head as he gulped greedily, his long throat pulsing, his damp body leaned heavily against her shins. A runt, he was still nearly half her size. His black fur was soft and plush, with silvery hints of his future coarse coat.

Beached bulls were so huge after months feeding at sea that they could last all mating season ashore without food. This pup was far too small to go without or to compete with the other, bigger pups for the cows' milk. Lucky that Althea had noticed him, or he would have starved.

The pup nudged the empty bottle. Althea looked through the chain-link fence to the parking lot. Beatrice was walking toward the conservancy. Althea put down the bottle and patted the pup's head. As he dove into the tank, she hurried down the deck stairs and slipped out of the gate, behind the cab of a flatbed truck. Beatrice would see her if she headed to her car. Since Owen had started shadowing Irene, Althea hadn't been able to face either of her friends. She'd even changed her docent schedule to avoid volunteering with Beatrice. Irene had probably mentioned Owen's odd behavior, Althea's anger. Beatrice would want an explanation. *Time to own up*, she would tell Althea. *Let's fix whatever's wrong.* Althea turned to walk back to the conservancy.

"Thea, wait," she heard behind her. She turned back around to see Beatrice hurrying over.

Althea's arms felt awkward hanging at her sides. "I didn't think you were working today," she said.

"I came to see you. Getting hold of you lately is like trying to pin a cloud."

Althea watched a gull dive-bomb the shore. Last night she'd found Owen sitting by the register again. Guard dogs were the ticket, he kept insisting. "They'll keep us going, Thea." At least he'd known her name this time. But what about next time? And the next?

Beatrice said, "Irene and I have been talking."

"Actually, I'm glad. I've been wanting to tell you, but I didn't know how—"

"Thea, Stuart and I found a buyer for the bed-and-breakfast."

"But the ordinance—"

"We both know it'll be overturned soon enough." Beatrice took a breath. "It's Owen, isn't it? Whatever's going on with him, that's what's keeping you from selling too."

Althea stepped back. Owen would wander to the beach, to the gas station down the 101, to where the hardware store used to be. She would find him, bring him home. The next day, he would disappear again, going farther afield, determined to find whomever had left. But if everyone stayed, if everything stayed the same, he might remember a while longer.

"You don't understand. If we move, he'll get worse so much faster."

"Not necessarily. And eventually he's going to need more care than you can give him. What'll you do then, live here without him or us? Think long-term, about what's best for both of you."

"So I should abandon him, like you're abandoning us. That's your solution."

"You know that's not what I mean," Beatrice said.

"I would never betray you or Irene like this. Never."

Her words sounded wrong, even as she said them. Betrayals came in all sorts and sizes. Hide something you've done that caused a friend pain, even if it was for her own good, and it would surely haunt you. Hank. She had forced his hand, given him an ultimatum that had torn Irene apart. Now Althea was the one who would lose everything. It was only fair. She shook her head, a quick jerk that shuddered through her. Such nonsense. But the thought gripped her hard and wouldn't let go.

"Althea, listen—" Beatrice said, but Althea had already started walking, then jogging, then running across the beach, her lungs blazing, unaccustomed to the challenge.

The day Althea made the long, hot drive to San Jose to confront Hank about his loan offer to Owen, she told everyone she was going to see about changing the store's title into her and Owen's name, something her mother had been after her to do. Her mother was relieved. She beckoned Althea over to her wheelchair by the living room window, where she liked to look down on Main Street at the people strolling the dusty sidewalks. Her forearms lay frail and wasted on the wheelchair's sturdy armrests. Her limp hand felt hot in Althea's.

"Owen nee . . . you," her mother said. "Be goo . . . ea . . . other. I . . . gone . . . befo . . . long."

"There's time left in you yet," Althea said and kissed her mother's flaccid cheek.

Irene often mentioned the bank—San Jose Savings and Loan— though she'd never been there or even to San Jose. "Ladies shouldn't travel with men before marrying," Irene said. "This time, I'm doing it right. Besides, Hank says I'd be bored, with him always working."

Althea was impressed despite herself when she pushed through the bank's brass-edged revolving door into the massive lobby with its vaulted ceiling and heavily veined marble floor. Neat rows of desks sat to one side of the velvet-roped lanes leading to teller cages. Beyond the desks along the bank's perimeter were several offices. One would be Hank's, where he talked on the telephone, met with important men to discuss the pressing matters of the day. Hank was ambitious. He was going places, would take Irene places that Althea would hear about but never see. Still. A handout was unthinkable. She drew off her gloves and placed them carefully in her purse. That's what she would explain to Hank, how insulting his offer had been, no matter how well-intentioned. She would put him in his place.

She approached a man at one of the desks. "Bank Clerk" said the placard near his phone. His chin receded into his neck and dandruff flecked the shoulders of his navy suit. "May I help you?" he asked in a hushed voice.

Althea shifted her handbag higher up her arm. "I'm looking for Hank Ashcroft."

"He'll be back shortly. You're welcome to wait."

The man stood and walked her to the desk nearest the offices. He pulled out a guest chair, gestured for her to sit. On the desk was another "Bank Clerk" placard. She ran her fingers over the letters. Nearby was an ashtray overflowing with Hank's brand of cigarette butts. A thought blossomed.

"Is this his secretary's desk?" she asked.

The man looked at her curiously. "It's *his* desk," he said before walking away.

She sat, purse in lap, the words thrumming inside her—his desk, his desk, *his*—with a faintly triumphant beat. But no. This was no triumph, this discovery. This was a betrayal, Hank's betrayal of Irene. Althea had to do something. She had to protect Irene, tell her the truth, save her from making yet another bad choice, maybe the worst in a series of many.

She slipped the placard into her purse and exited the bank.

❀

Hearst Castle's service road was even bumpier than the main one. The top of Althea's head ached by the time Reggie stopped the truck.

A relief, to slide out of Beatrice's lap, plant her feet on the packed dirt road.

Overhead the sun had bleached the sky. Althea smoothed her hair. Beatrice took off her glasses and wiped the nose guard with her skirt. Cecil crouched on her shoulder. Althea turned in a circle. "Where're the pens?"

Reggie pointed at a steep incline covered with massive redwoods, twisted coastal oaks, parched brush. "Up this way, the cook said."

"You're kidding." Beatrice put on her glasses. Cecil shifted closer.

Althea looked down at her Mary Janes with their inch-high heels and leather soles. She had saved for a year to buy them. "It's awfully steep."

"Suit yourself." Reggie started walking.

Althea stayed put. Beatrice stood beside her, her arms crossed. Irene took a few steps and looked back at them. Her hair was lighter than the white-hot sky. "You're the ones who wanted to see the tigers. Where's your sense of adventure?"

They watched Reggie climb.

"Wait for me," Irene called and started up, slipping on the rocky soil. When she reached him, he held out his hand to steady her. Her giggle floated down the hill.

"Can you believe her?" Althea said.

Beatrice crossed the road to sit beneath a redwood tree. Cecil nestled near her ear. Althea trudged after her and sat. Tree needles, prickly and dry, crackled beneath her.

"You know he's a show-off," Beatrice said. She offered some redwood needles to Cecil, who picked at them with his curved beak.

Sweat trickled between Althea's breasts, down the insides of her thighs. She imagined Reggie's eyes fixed on Irene, his large hand enveloping her dainty one, the places he would lead her. "She always gets what she wants."

Beatrice stroked Cecil's neck. "If that were true, she'd have a mother who loves her like mine or yours."

"All Mama does is boss me around."

Something rustled behind them. Althea froze. Cecil bristled his crest, swiveled around to investigate. Beatrice grabbed him. The rustling became a rhythmic thump, like a body being dragged through brush.

"Probably a deer," Althea whispered.

"What if it's not?" Beatrice squeezed Cecil. He squawked, pecked her. She gasped and let go. He flew into the tree. The noises stopped.

"Cecil, get down here." Beatrice stood, looked up at the tree, clucked her tongue.

The bird squawked and paced a branch just out of reach. White gook splattered Althea's shoes.

Beatrice glanced down. "Sorry. He's afraid of heights." She clucked again. Cecil's wings flickered; his head bobbed. She grabbed the lowest branches. "Give me a boost."

Althea sighed and laced her fingers together. Beatrice was heavy for such a small person, and quick. She scrambled from branch to branch, murmuring to Cecil, who stared at her and trilled.

The noises started again, closer. Althea froze. Out of the brush hopped a small gray kangaroo. It stopped when it saw her, crouched low, its forepaws dangling inches above the ground. If she reached out, she could stroke its dusty coat. Muscles twitched in its powerful hind legs. She kept still. Above her in the tree, Beatrice and Cecil were silent. Almost casually, as if deciding Althea were part of the landscape, the kangaroo craned its neck and nibbled the dry grass. Its teeth were blunt, yellowish, its tongue long and slender.

A girl's scream split the quiet. The kangaroo darted into the brush. Overhead, a rush of wings. Althea looked up. Cecil clung to Beatrice's sleeve as she scrambled down the redwood. Beatrice's eyes were wide and fearful.

Another scream. Althea ran across the road, up the hill, racing, slipping. Faintly, behind her, Beatrice's rough breaths. In sight, the deserted hillcrest. Then Irene appeared, her head, her shoulders, the length of her slim torso.

"Are you okay?" Althea called.

Closer, she could see Irene's trembling hands, her dirty skirt. Irene stopped walking as they reached her. Dust streaked her arms and legs. Her face looked tight, blunted, like something essential had been erased.

"What happened?" Beatrice gasped out. "Where's Reggie?"

"I fell," she said and wiped her eyes.

Althea stared. The waist of her friend's dress gaped where several buttons had torn. Irene noticed her looking.

"You did that falling?" Althea said.

Irene's red-rimmed eyes were as pale as crystal. "Reggie's still up there. He wanted a closer look at the pens."

Halfway down the hill, Irene stopped and looked at her friends. "Don't tell."

Althea could see from Beatrice's confused expression that she wasn't sure either what they weren't supposed to tell. But it was something shameful, something no girl deserved, even one as spoiled and willful as Irene.

"We won't say anything," Althea answered. "Not ever." She took Irene's hand and, together with Beatrice, helped her the rest of the way down the hill.

The evening after Althea visited the bank, Hank drove down to see Irene. They all gathered at Beatrice and Stuart's house. Pregnant again, Beatrice was under strict instructions to rest. Althea could barely stand saying hello to Hank. In the closet, her purse held the "Bank Clerk" placard. *Fraud!* she longed to yell, then heave the placard at him with everyone watching. For Irene's sake.

"What's wrong?" Hank asked when Althea stiffly hugged him hello while Owen made their drinks in the kitchen. "Cat stole your smile?"

She looked at Beatrice tensed on the couch next to Stuart, Irene clutching a whisky sour.

"Just tired," she said. "Long night with Mama."

Irene exhaled and sipped her drink. Beatrice leaned back against the cushions and smiled at Althea, who turned away. She would tell them once she got them alone. That way Irene could keep her dignity and send Hank packing in private. Then all their lives could go back to normal.

But when finally after dinner the women gathered by themselves in the kitchen, Irene revealed her ring, waving it like a trophy. The diamond was garish, surely over a carat. It couldn't be real. Beatrice admired it from afar, her feet propped on a chair, but Althea stared stonily away while Irene chattered about how Hank wanted children immediately to fill up the new mansion they'd buy in San Jose, how they'd hire someone to run Irene's hardware store, inherited from her grandmother, but they would visit Cambria weekends and summers, after they finished the house near the Castle, so Irene wouldn't miss her friends too much.

Althea smacked the table. "Stop following him blindly, Irene. He's not who you think."

"Althea, what's gotten into you?" Beatrice said.

"She's jealous he's taking me away." Irene looked at Althea. "I can't help it if you came back."

She left the kitchen, her hand with the ring trailing behind, as if too heavy to keep up with her.

Beatrice swung her feet off the chair. "You're being petty," she said to Althea. "Can't you see? She just wants what you have with Owen." Carefully she stood and followed Irene.

Maybe Althea should have chased after them and tried to explain, but they wouldn't have believed her. "First pettiness, now lies," they would have said, shaking their heads.

Through the window over the sink she spied Hank nursing a cigarette on the back porch. He was the liar, not her. She grabbed the placard from her purse in the closet and hurried outside to lean against the railing beside him.

"Quite a ring you gave Irene," she said. The placard felt heavy held behind her back.

He squinted at her through the smoke. "Been in the family for years."

"Maybe. Or maybe it's as fake as your job." She handed him the placard.

He studied it. "Sam told me a pretty lady stopped by. Didn't figure it was you."

Stars pinholed the velvety sky. The heavy scent of jasmine thickened the air. Pretty, he'd called her, as if that would fix things. Beside her, she heard him harrumph. When she looked over, he was smiling.

"If we had accepted your offer," she said, "that would have given you away."

"You wouldn't have. You've never liked me. Besides, what's there to give away? I never said what I did at the bank. Maybe I have family money. Did you ever think of that?"

"You're a fraud."

He slid along the railing until his shoulder touched hers and his breath—slightly smoky and foul—wafted against her cheek. Then the silk of his whisper, so quiet it could have been the wind: "A shame, any of you lovely ladies wasting away in this place." The rankness of his scent, the sharp current of his finger tracing the back of her hand. This was what it was like to be Irene. The thought left her unsteady, unmoored. Unlike herself in any way.

"I'll tell," she said, staring into the yard.

"You only think you will. Girls like you never do."

She stepped away, back into herself. "You'd be surprised what I'd do," she said.

"Althea, you out there?" Owen called behind them, quickly followed by the retort of the screen door slamming. She rubbed her cheek, which still carried the taint of Hank's breath.

Owen walked over, his hands shoved in his pockets. "Beatrice is tired," he said. "We should go."

Althea turned to Hank. "Don't let me surprise you."

"That's certainly worth considering." He straightened his jacket, put the placard in his pocket, gave her a final glance. "I do care about her, you know." Then he patted Owen's shoulder—"She's the ticket, this wife of yours"—and strode into the house.

Owen watched him go, then turned to Althea. "Old puffed-up Hank sure was in a hurry. I assume he behaved himself?" He sounded playful, but his expression was stern.

"He knows better than to get in my way," she said. "Or yours."

He smiled then and pulled a slip of paper from his pocket. "Let's say our goodbyes," he said before handing her the note and walking back inside. "Stuck with me, forever," it said. No pretty, flighty words, just promises he would keep. This man. She folded the note and followed him inside.

Hank broke off with Irene barely a month later. Business was too hectic, he said. It wouldn't be fair for him to marry anyone, especially someone as special as Irene. Irene told them over coffee in Beatrice's living room since Beatrice had already miscarried and couldn't leave the house yet. She looked spent stretched out on the couch underneath a blanket Althea had crocheted for the baby. Irene sobbed on the couch by Beatrice's feet. Althea sat across the room, her fingers threaded in her lap. He wasn't worth his weight in tears, she longed to tell them.

Once Irene stopped crying, she looked at Althea. "I guess you'll say 'I told you so.'"

Beatrice leaned forward, wincing as if even that small motion hurt. "No one's gonna say that. But I will say it's better this happened now, before you married him."

Althea watched her friends. *I made him leave, for Irene's sake*, she should tell them. But that would only make Irene resent her, if not blame her outright. And maybe Althea deserved a little blame, for the seedling of satisfaction planted deep within her belly: now Irene was stuck here, just like Althea. Which was for the best. This was where they belonged, cocooned in the safety of each other's friendship.

She walked over and sat next to Irene so they were all crowded together on the couch, then rubbed Irene's shoulders as her friend began crying again.

"You deserve better," Althea said.

After Beatrice admitted she and Stuart were selling the B and B, Althea spent days upstairs staring at the television. Let Greer retrieve the rolls of quarters from where Owen hid them behind the display cases, rescue laundry from the sale shelf, fetch Owen from wherever he'd gone. At night, she still followed Owen to Irene's, but she stayed in the truck and waited for him to notice her. Sometimes it took hours.

Beatrice and Irene both left message after message. Althea erased them and got a substitute docent to lead her tours. Better to adjust to life without them sooner rather than later. She had never been one to let a Band-Aid linger.

Her only solace was the elephant seal pup. She visited the shelter daily to feed him; by now, he ate only fish. She sang songs, brushed him with a wire brush. He'd slip out of his tank and bay when he saw her, roll on his side to be stroked. Too soon, he was big enough for the vet to approve his return to the beach.

The morning of the release, she rode beside the pup's oversized carrier in the flatbed. That early, the beach was empty except for the seals. Two rangers maneuvered the carrier out of the truck as Althea watched, hugging her coat around her. When the pup emerged onto the sand, Althea knelt to stroke his damp head. He nudged her, then rocked himself away, into the mass of seals by the water's edge. If not for the red tag on his back flipper, she wouldn't have been able to tell him from the other seals lolled together, grunting, snuffling, sighing, splashing. She stood watching while the rangers packed the equipment. Off in the distance, two bulls circled a cow feeding her pups.

"Althea, we need to talk to you."

It was Beatrice, who stood by the fence with Irene and Owen. Weeks had passed since Althea had seen either of her friends. Beatrice opened the gate with her docent's key. Owen held the gate as she walked through and started across the sand toward Althea. When Irene followed, Owen touched her shoulder, like he always did with Althea. Like he thought *she* was Althea.

Althea couldn't help herself. "Irene, you could at least wait until Laguna Woods to steal somebody's husband."

Irene stopped, her face flushed. "Dammit, why're you being so mean lately?"

"So you think you've been replaced?" Owen said, the gate propped against his hand. He sounded more bemused than angry. He sounded like himself.

"I don't know what to think," Althea said and turned away. She heard the gate slam, rubber-soled shoes squeaking in the sand. In her periphery there was motion, maybe the bulls circling the cow, but maybe Irene walking over to try to change her mind. That crazy thought took hold again: payback, for Hank. If only she could balance the scales, embrace Irene and say, *This is who he really was. I never meant to hurt you.* Then, poof, there would be no reason for anyone to leave.

Enough already. The past played no part in what she was about to lose, what she had already lost.

A bull bellowed. Althea kept still.

Behind her, Beatrice said, "Owen told us he's sick. We thought if we all talked to you, you'd see you're not alone."

"There are options, Thea," Owen said, even closer. "Let's figure them out together."

The fury, so close she could touch it, ever since she could remember. It was there, beside her now, like a separate person, someone who would turn and scream at them, *Stop, just stop.* None of them understood, not even Owen. Options weren't appealing anymore. All she wanted was this life, in this place, frozen in time. But illness had a way of progressing stubbornly forward. The tedium, the sameness of the days, his decay continuing to encroach until it engulfed every last memory, even of how to walk or breathe. She would be there until the end, feeding him, wiping sweat from his forehead, from underneath his arms and between his legs, but he would have already forgotten her, though she wanted desperately to be the last to go, to be the one thing he couldn't—no, wouldn't—forget.

How could he let her go, dammit? How could he let it happen?

A gasp ravaged her throat. "How dare you scheme behind my back, Owen Boudreau—"

"For God's sake, we need help, Althea! Let someone help for once!"

His hand was on her arm, spinning her around. The distant bellowing got louder and then there were two bulls raging, surely over a cow, it was the season, her thoughts in slow motion even as the bulls moved closer, tusks flashing, and Owen grabbed her, pulled her to safety, and then a higher bellowing, a flash of darker, softer fur as the pup threw himself at one of the bulls, which turned from its fight, grabbed the pup by the scruff, shook him, tossed him aside.

The pup lay still, gaping puncture wounds bleeding at his nape.

Outside herself Althea heard a scream—"No!"—and she was racing across the beach to the pup, trying to staunch the blood as she sobbed. Someone embraced her from behind, held her close. "Don't, Thea, don't. It'll be okay," she heard whispered in her ear, and for that moment she lost herself in the surety of his voice.

Moving day, six months later. The store had been sold, the condo bought, close to Irene's and Beatrice's. They had found a facility for Owen not far from Laguna Woods. All that remained was to give the apartment above the store one last scrub.

Althea cleaned with Irene and Beatrice while Owen puttered around or watched Main Street from the living room window. Which was fine. There wasn't much left to do. All the furniture was gone, all the years of stuff sorted through and sold, thrown out, or moved to the condo. In the kitchen, Irene tied a kerchief over her hair and attacked the grease built up on the stove hood. Beatrice mopped the bedrooms while Althea scrubbed the grout in the bathroom with a toothbrush dipped in bleach.

When Althea emerged from the bathroom, a little nauseated from the bleach fumes, she heard voices in the kitchen. She walked over, stood in the doorway. Irene was wiping down the counters, chatting about their new homes ("There's that lovely arbor by the Laguna

Woods pool, do you remember seeing it?") while Owen nodded every now and then, as if he were listening. All the while, he opened cabinets and pulled out drawers, running his large palms across the interiors in a final caress. It took every ounce of Althea's energy to keep from stepping between them, holding his hand. Staking her claim. He didn't need reminding yet. He still knew who he was, where his love belonged. Most days, he knew.

They would visit daily, they'd promised, and they would each be busy: craft projects and woodworking for him; knitting classes, cooking classes, beach trips for her. Pleasant enough, but not what she was used to. Not purposeful enough. Not shared with him.

"This place looks spotless," she said.

Irene looked over and smiled. Owen kept opening drawers.

"Almost like new," Irene said. She gathered the cleaning supplies in a bucket, squeezed Althea's hand as she left the kitchen. "Beatrice and I will bring everything down to the car."

Beatrice emerged from a bedroom carrying a dust mop and a garbage bag. Her nose was smudged with grime. "We'll give you two a minute," she said and kissed Althea, waved to Owen, who opened a cabinet door as if he were alone.

Once her friends had clattered down the stairs, Althea touched Owen's arm.

"Hon," she said. "What are you looking for?"

He peered inside another drawer before he turned, his features creased with worry. "Pups been fed?"

The ache of it still hit hard: standing right beside her, he could still be somewhere else.

"Yup," she said. "They're getting big, almost ready to sell."

His fingers plucked at his shirt; a relieved smile smoothed his face, made him appear open and innocent, like he must have as a boy, before she knew him.

One last pass through the apartment, this time with just her hands and eyes tracing every hidden spot that could remain in such an empty space. She felt Owen watching as she ran her palms across baseboards, slid open windows to investigate their sashes, checked closets inch by inch. Ensuring the apartment was immaculate. Really, though, she was searching for a note, some silly reassurance. But she didn't find what she was seeking, what she finally decided didn't exist.

She stood from the last baseboard and covered her eyes, her breathing ragged. When she looked up, he was standing beside the window, plucking at his shirt.

"This place." His voice was thick, rough. "What is it?"

She took his hand. "Irene and Beatrice are waiting," she said. "Time to go."

The door shut behind them. There was no trace of them left, or so she thought. She didn't know, would never know, that the note she had been searching for was wedged behind a kitchen drawer, in the back slats of the cabinetry. It was folded up tight, smudged with dust, as if it had been there forever. "If I had it all to do again," he wrote, "I'd do it all the same, except I would've opened a pet store right here, in the shadow of the Castle. We would've bred some pets ourselves just like we always planned, not blue tips, though, but shepherds, big, smart, brave dogs who listened when we spoke like they were put here to obey. Dogs who would come with me when I wandered off and lead me back to you. Back to home. Anywhere you are is home, Thea. In my bones, I'll always know it, even when my mind forgets."

Acknowledgments

This collection was many years in the making and would not have come to fruition without the support of numerous people:

Lee K. Abbot, Courtney Denney, Rebecca Norton, Erin Kirk New, Steven Wallace, Jason Bennett, Christina Cotter, Beth Snead, and everyone at the University of Georgia Press, who chose this collection as the 2018 Flannery O'Connor Short Fiction Award Winner and have all worked so hard to make it a reality.

My sister and wombmate, Lisanne Sartor, who is my first, last, and best reader and who inspires me with her exceptional creativity and dedication to her craft.

My grandmother, Kay Sartor, who was the original Rose.

My other die-hard readers: Robinne Lee, Debbie Ezer, Aimee Liu, Amy Ludwig, Deborah Cohen, Darryle Pollack, Melissa Johnson, Margaret Grundstein, Danelle Davenport, Dominique Dibbell, Shari Ellis, Laura Brennan, Eileen Funke, Hyun Mi Oh, Swati Pandey, and the rest of the incredibly talented Yale Women LA Writers Group, who sustain me with their superb guidance and insight; Brett Anthony Johnston, who has championed my writing in every way imaginable over the years; Cristina Henriquez and Rebecca Johns, who read this collection in its early phases and cheered me onward; and Mandy Campbell Moore, Loraine Shields, and Rachel Terner Vogel, who patiently and expertly critiqued countless versions of these stories.

Paul Mandelbaum, who has been my mentor, advocate, and friend since I started writing; Charles Jensen, Carla Janas, Nutschell Windsor, Lou Mathews, Judith Simon Prager, Harry Youtt, Linda

Venis, and everyone else at the UCLA Extension Writers' Program who make teaching a joy; and all my students, whose talent and enthusiasm remind me why I love writing.

Sally Shore, who gave voice to my work through her spoken-word series, the New Short Fiction Series, and who is such a generous member of the Los Angeles literary community.

Matthew Limpede, an outstanding editor who published two of these stories and whose faith in this collection encouraged me to keep submitting it; Gretchen Koss and Meg Walker of Tandem Literary, who together perform publicity and marketing miracles; and the other dedicated, tireless editors who have been gracious enough to publish my work in their journals.

The Ragdale Foundation, which gave me the time and space to write with freedom and excitement.

Rayme Silverberg and Novah Kaplan, who are the best photographer and makeup artist anyone could want.

Buster, my big, smart, brave dog who untiringly treks the streets with me while I'm lost in story ideas.

Cheryl Stowell, Nicole Meola, Joe Marek, Leslie Sydnor, Jo Miller, Ashley Gable, John Bernatz, Natacha Sydnor, and Terry Norton-Wright, whose unflagging friendship, strength, and laughter have gotten me through the best and worst times.

My brother, John Sartor, whose humor and determination keep me eager to achieve.

My father, Anthony Sartor, who supports my choices even when he doesn't understand them; and my mother, Maria Sartor, who was my first, most wonderful writing teacher and who taught me that essays are shaped like hourglasses and stories are driven by secrets.

My son, Luke Sartor Ohanesian, whose kindness, quick wit, and huge heart delight me every day.

My husband, Bob Ohanesian, whose quiet, confident love provides me with a steady source of strength.

The Flannery O'Connor Award for Short Fiction

David Walton, *Evening Out*
Leigh Allison Wilson, *From the Bottom Up*
Sandra Thompson, *Close-Ups*
Susan Neville, *The Invention of Flight*
Mary Hood, *How Far She Went*
François Camoin, *Why Men Are Afraid of Women*
Molly Giles, *Rough Translations*
Daniel Curley, *Living with Snakes*
Peter Meinke, *The Piano Tuner*
Tony Ardizzone, *The Evening News*
Salvatore La Puma, *The Boys of Bensonhurst*
Melissa Pritchard, *Spirit Seizures*
Philip F. Deaver, *Silent Retreats*
Gail Galloway Adams, *The Purchase of Order*
Carole L. Glickfeld, *Useful Gifts*
Antonya Nelson, *The Expendables*
Nancy Zafris, *The People I Know*
Debra Monroe, *The Source of Trouble*
Robert H. Abel, *Ghost Traps*
T. M. McNally, *Low Flying Aircraft*
Alfred DePew, *The Melancholy of Departure*
Dennis Hathaway, *The Consequences of Desire*
Rita Ciresi, *Mother Rocket*
Dianne Nelson, *A Brief History of Male Nudes in America*
Christopher McIlroy, *All My Relations*
Alyce Miller, *The Nature of Longing*
Carol Lee Lorenzo, *Nervous Dancer*
C. M. Mayo, *Sky over El Nido*
Wendy Brenner, *Large Animals in Everyday Life*
Paul Rawlins, *No Lie Like Love*
Harvey Grossinger, *The Quarry*
Ha Jin, *Under the Red Flag*
Andy Plattner, *Winter Money*
Frank Soos, *Unified Field Theory*
Mary Clyde, *Survival Rates*
Hester Kaplan, *The Edge of Marriage*
Darrell Spencer, *CAUTION Men in Trees*
Robert Anderson, *Ice Age*
Bill Roorbach, *Big Bend*
Dana Johnson, *Break Any Woman Down*